Jean-Baptiste Louvet de Couvray

The Amours of the Chevalier de Faublas

Vol. 1

Jean-Baptiste Louvet de Couvray

The Amours of the Chevalier de Faublas
Vol. 1

ISBN/EAN: 9783337401665

Printed in Europe, USA, Canada, Australia, Japan

Cover: Foto ©Andreas Hilbeck / pixelio.de

More available books at **www.hansebooks.com**

LOUVET DE COUVRAY

THE AMOURS

OF THE

CHEVALIER DE FAUBLAS

BY

JOHN BAPTISTE LOUVET DE COUVRAY

FOUNDED ON HISTORICAL FACTS. INTERSPERSED
WITH MOST REMARKABLE NARRATIVES

A LITERAL UNEXPURGATED TRANSLATION
FROM THE PARIS EDITION OF 1821

VOLUME I

WITH NUMEROUS BEAUTIFUL ENGRAVINGS
ETCHED BY LOUIS MONZIES
FROM DRAWINGS BY PAUL AVRIL

EDITION STRICTLY LIMITED TO ONE HUNDRED COPIES

LONDON
PRIVATELY PRINTED FOR SOCIÉTÉ DES BIBLIOPHILES
MDCCCXCVIII

PREFACE

BY THE TRANSLATOR.

Tnis Work, on its first appearance in France, was received with the same *éclat* as the novels of the author of
Waverley have since been in this country. Its popu-
larity has continued to this day, and it has been translated
into almost every European language. It affords an excellent picture of French manners, previously to, and at
the period of, the revolution ; and however minutely it
may describe the foibles and vices of our species, it, at the
same time, places in a most elevated point of view all
those virtues which are an honor to our nature. Shak-
speare observes, that " the thread of life is of a mingled
yarn ;" following up this idea, may we not say that society is of a many colored texture, and cannot be described
without being examined on both sides. Such books as
give but the fair side of human nature, are only calculated
to mislead the inexperienced, and cause them to form those
sanguine expectations of frail mortality, which end in mis-
anthropy, in consequence of the repeated mortifications
and disappointments they meet with. Whereas, by the
bad being blended with the good, as it really exists, we
are enabled to form a just estimate of mankind, and by
not expecting too much, are capable of continuing in better
temper with them. The characters in this Romance are,
generally speaking, drawn by the hand of a master, and
some of them are most highly finished. Though the gay
and dissipated libertine and the lively and intriguing Marchioness are delineated with more precision than could be
wished, and though they may dazzle the eyes by the
showy splendor of their coloring, there are other figures
on the canvas, whose superior qualities appeal directly to
our hearts, and whose amiable and heroic virtues strike us

with an indelible impression. Where can we find a more faithful portraiture of youthful innocence and simplicity; of the constancy of female affection and conjugal devotion amidst continued trials and accumulated sufferings; of philosophic fortitude, manly courage, disinterested patriotism, and consummate heroism, than in the Romance of Faublas. The affecting episode of Lodoiska has been dramatized many years since, but the most interesting part of the story will be found to follow the catastrophe which terminates the play.

The present translation was undertaking in consequence of a great demand arising for the work, and the former one being extremely scarce. That published in 1795 was notoriously imperfect and mutilated; it was, therefore, deemed more advisable to make a new and faithful translation, than to be at the pains of correcting the old one. The edition made use of was that printed by Didot, the king's printer, for Ambroise Tardieu, at Paris, in four elegant 8vo volumes, in 1821.

The translator has rendered it as close as the idioms of the two languages will admit, not wishing to alter the style of a work so elegant in the original, although the sententious and interjectional mode of writing, familiar to the French, may not sound quite so natural to an English ear.

G. C.

London, June 5, 1822.

BIOGRAPHICAL

NOTICE OF THE AUTHOR.

———

John Baptiste Louvet de Couvray was born at Paris in the year 1764. His youth was devoted to study, and afforded nothing remarkable. Destined to the profession of the law, but disgusted with an occupation so little conformable to his taste, he gave himself up to literary pursuits.

He published the first part of this romance, under the title of "One Year of the Life of the Chevalier de Faublas," in 1789. A lively and poignant style ; much truth, mingled with a long series of events and stories, told with grace, rendered this production a fashionable book.

It is not that Louvet always paints the society he brings before us with a rigorous exactness; for some of his personages are rather conceived than studied ; but the beings he has created are not unnatural; the passions which he causes to act are ours; and it is pleasant sometimes to forget an afflicting reality, and roam without restraint in the fields of imagination.

The Marquis de Lauraguais assigns an historical origin to Faublas. According to him, this personage was the Abbé de Choisi, who lived under Louis the Fourteenth. Being a priest, and paying his court de Madame Maintenon, in order to obtain some benefice, he dedicated to her a translation he had made of the "Imitation of Jesus Christ." With this motto in the title page, "Concupiscit rex decorum tuum," and which he said could only be rendered with decency as follows: "The charms have excited the concupiscence of the king." This Abbé de Choisi published his memoirs under the name of the Comtesse des Barres, and had played the part of a woman with more than a Marchioness de B***, and more than a Comtesse de Lignolle.

However it may be, Louvet lived a long time in the country near a lady to whom he was passionately attached from his earliest years. A forced marriage separated them in vain; at liberty, after six years of absence, they were united to part no more. Happy, both by temperament and philosophy, Louvet continued his work, of which the first-fruits supplied his wants. Retired from the world, he thought himself sheltered from its storms—but the revolution broke out; with the Bastile fell the yoke which oppressed France. Louvet received the tricolored cockade from the hands of that Lodoiska whose name he has attached to the most pathetic episode of his work. This act of liberty became the cause of a persecution which Louvet experienced from some gentlemen in his neighborhood, and ultimately determined him to go to Paris.

A pamphlet which he published against M. Mounier of the Constituent Assembly, after the affair of 1789, procured him an admission to the Jacobin Club. This club was then open but to patriotism and talent. Launched into a political career, he published "Emilie de Varmont, et les Amours du curé Sevin," a romance, the object of which was to prove the necessity of divorce, and the marriage of priests. He composed, at the same time, three comedies, only one of which was represented; it was intended to ridicule the troops assembled at Coblentz.

Free from ambition, Louvet appeared but seldom in popular assemblies. Persuaded that the natural course of things would bring about the reform they had a right to expect, he remained in the obscure ranks of the revolution, of which he took upon himself all the trouble, entirely regardless of his private interests. As soon as he learnt that a party had conspired against the Constitution which had been sworn to, and that several of the representatives of the people had sold themselves to power, he thought himself obliged, in his turn, to enter the lists.

On the 25th December, 1791, he presented himself at the bar of the legislative assembly, at the head of a deputation from the Section of the Lombards, to obtain a decree against the princes who had emigrated, and a war against the sovereigns who were arming in their favor.

Louvet was very assiduous in the club of which he became a member; he spoke with much force when they discussed the question of the war with Austria. Robespierre opposed him. The reply of Louvet overwhelmed his antagonist, who never forgave him from that time, but continued to bear him the most implacable hatred. The ministers, who were all desirous of war, were pleased to find Louvet so powerful an auxiliary. To testify their gratitude and their esteem, they had it in contemplation to put him at the head of the judicial department. The inimical faction, alarmed at this resolution, employed every resource to prevent its accomplishment. They spared neither menaces nor calumnies, and succeeded in frustrating his appointment. This weakness on the part of government emboldened the adversaries which it thought to calm by an act of condescension, and we know to what a pitch they afterwards carried their audacity.

Connected in a close friendship with the minister Roland, whose house was the rendezvous of all who advocated a prudent liberty, Louvet became the soul of his counsels. This virtuous citizen induced him to conduct "The Sentinel," a journal which he destined to neutralize the fatal doctrines of the demagogues. Louvet, in acquitting himself of this task, displayed such an excess of zeal for liberty, as caused him to lose the ambassadorship to Constantinople, for which Dumouriez, than in full power, destined him. His friends thought to repair this disgrace, by offering him the place of commissary at St. Domingo; but he refused it, that he might not leave his country at a moment when she was a prey to the most dreadful convulsions.

We have not room to follow Louvet through his political career; to do that would require considerable reference to the progress of the French Revolution, and a variety of details, probably, uninteresting to the majority of our readers. From the moment he discovered the violent and ambitious views of Robespierre, he openly denounced him, and opposed him with all his might. He was spontaneously chosen to represent the department of Loiret, which circumstance called down upon him a special proscription from the *Terrorists*.

When Louis XVI. was brought up for judgment, Louvet insisted on an appeal to the people, and said, if it was not made, no power on earth should compel him to vote. Although his opinion was little favorable to the monarch, his heart sought to reconcile the duties of a representative with the rights of humanity. He was convinced, that by investing the nation with the sovereignty, they would do away with the influence of party, and in awakening all the citizens to a sense of their strength and their dignity, they should paralyze the factious.

The appeal to the people being rejected, the punishment then became the question.

"Representatives," said Louvet, after having repeated his opinion, "you are about to pronounce an irreparable "judgment; may the tutelary genius of my country ward "off the evils that are preparing for her! May his all- "powerful hand retrieve you from the abyss into which "some ambitious men have contributed to precipitate you! "May his avenging hand crush the tyrants who have "started up! The dangers of the republic become im- "mense and pressing; but her safety is still in your hands. "Be careful of parting with your power; pay homage to "the rights of those who have sent you; and if, for hav- "ing fulfilled your duties, you should fall by the hands of "assassins, you will, at least, fall worthy of regret and "esteem. Times, men, and circumstances may change, "but principles can never change; nor will I change any "more than principles."

Louvet did not vote for the death of the king.

After being President of the Convention, Member of the Committee of Public Safety, Deputy for La Gironde, one of the Council of Five Hundred, and pursuing a most zealous but consistent political career, up to the year 1797, he found that the heat of political controversy had injured his health; his soul was aggrandized in the school of misfortune, at the expense of his too delicate constitution. He withdrew from active life, and was named Consul for Palermo, but died on the 5th of August, 1797. The celebrated Madame Roland, speaking of our author, says:—

" Louvet is small, delicate, near-sighted, and of a slovenly
" habit, but there is nothing vulgar about him.   Who has
" not remarked the nobleness of his forehead, and the life
" which animates his eyes at the expression of an impor-
" tant truth?   His pretty romances are known to the men
" of letters, and the science of politics is indebted to him
" for labors of a graver nature.   It is impossible to unite
" more wit with less pretensions, and more good nature.
" Courageous as a lion, mild as an infant, he is a sensible
" man, a good citizen, and a vigorous writer.   He could
" make a Catiline tremble at the tribune, and sup with
" Bachaumont."

After having partaken of his dangers and disgraces, his
wife, Lodoiska, who had ever afforded him the sweetest
consolation, could not support the loss of a man she had
loved so much.   She poisoned herself; but her family
compelled her to take an antidote, which, by extending
her life, only prolonged her regrets.

Louvet is generally represented to have been a man of
probity and rigid morals; and of all the members of the
deliberative assemblies the most invariably attached to his
principles.   Neither times nor circumstances had any influence upon him during a revolution so remarkable for
the fickleness and tergiversation of its actors.   Inaccessible
to corruption as to threats, and undeviating in his duties,
he sacrificed his fortune to the interests of the people, and
defended liberty at the peril of his life, and still defended
it, when the victim of anarchy, he paid, by a merciless
proscription, for the honor of so noble a devotion.   "Since
" even in a country which I thought ready to regenerate
" itself," said he when dying, the good people are so indo-
" lent, and the wicked so furious, it is clear that all collec-
" tions of men, improperly called PEOPLE by such fools as
" myself, are nothing but an imbecile herd, who are happy
" in being trampled on by a master."

The feelings of Louvet, in his last moments, seemed
much like those of the virtuous Brutus, when he exclaimed:
" OH, VIRTUE!   I HAVE WORSHIPPED THEE AS A REAL
" GOOD, BUT FIND THOU ART ONLY AN EMPTY NAME!"

*[Extracted from the Memoir prefixed to the
Paris edition, dated Feb. 16, 1821.]*

x

CHEVALIER DE FAUBLAS.

THEY tell me that my ancestors were persons of consideration in their province, having always enjoyed there a handsome fortune, and a distinguished rank. My father, the Baron Faublas, transmitted to me their ancient nobility without disgrace; but my mother died too soon. I was not sixteen years of age, when my sister, still younger than myself by eighteen months, was placed in a convent at Paris. The Baron, who conducted her there, embraced with pleasure that opportunity of shewing the Capital to a son, for whose education he had neglected nothing.

It was in October, 1783, that we entered the Capital, by the suburb of Saint Marceau. I looked for the superb city of which I had read such brilliant descriptions. I saw lofty but ugly cottages; streets long but very narrow; wretches covered with rags, and a crowd of children almost naked; I saw a numerous population and dreadful misery. I demanded of my father, if this was Paris; he replied coldly, that it was not the finest part of it; that next day we should have time to visit another quarter. It was almost night; Adelaide (which was the name of my sister) entered her convent, where she was expected. My father descended with me near the Arsenal, at the house of Monsieur du Portail, his intimate friend, of whom I shall speak more than once in the course of these memoirs.

The next day my father kept his word with me; in a quarter of an hour a swift conveyance conducted us to the square of Louis the Fifteenth. There we got out, and walked: the spectacle which struck my eyes dazzled them with its magnificence. To the right, *La Seine a regret fugitive;* upon the banks extensive mansions; upon the left superb palaces; delightful walks behind me; and in front a noble garden. We advanced, and I saw the dwelling of kings. It is easier to imagine my astonishment than to describe it. My attention was attracted by new objects at every step: I admired the richness of the fashions; the gaiety of the dress and the elegance of the manners of those by whom I was surrounded. All at once I remembered the other quarter of the city, and my astonishment was greatly excited; I could not comprehend how objects so different could be contained within the same circumference; experience had not then taught me that everywhere the palaces concealed cottages; that luxury produced misery; that the great opulence of a single person always produced the extreme poverty of many.

We employed several days in visiting what was most remarkable in Paris. The Baron shewed me a number of monuments celebrated by foreigners, which were almost unknown by those who possessed them. How many *chefs d'œuvres* astonished me at first, for which in a little time I felt but a cold admiration. But what do we know at fifteen years of age about the glory of the arts and the immortality of genius? It requires beauties more animated to warm a youthful heart.

It was at the convent of Adelaide that I was to meet the adorable object in whom my existence centered. The Baron, who loved my sister, went almost every day to see her in the conversation room. All young ladies of good birth find

that in a convent they have good friends; many
fine ladies affirm, that it is difficult to find them
elsewhere. However that may be, my sister,
naturally sensible, had presently chosen hers.
One day she spoke to us of Mademoiselle de
Pontis, and pronounced an eulogium on this
young person, which we thought exaggerated.
My father was curious to see the good friend of
his daughter. I know not what soft presenti-
ment made my heart palpitate, when the Baron
told Adelaide to go and fetch Mademoiselle de
Pontis. My sister ran and brought her—figure
to yourself a Venus of fourteen. I wished to
advance towards her—to speak to her—to salute
her, but I remained with my eyes fixed, my
mouth open, and my hands hanging by my sides.
My father perceived, and was amused at my embarrassment; You will salute the lady, at least,
said he to me. My trouble augmented; I made
a most awkward bow. Mademoiselle, continued
the Baron, I assure you that this young man
has had a dancing master. I was entirely disconcerted. The Baron paid a very flattering
compliment to Sophia; she replied to it mod-
estly, and with a faltering voice which reverber-
ated to my heart. I stared at her with astonish-

My father preceived, and was amused at my embarrassment

Page 1

ment, and I attended most minutely to every
thing she said, but I was still incapable of giving
vent to my feelings. Being about to leave them,
my father embraced his daughter, and made his
reverence to Mademoiselle de Pontis; and I, in
an involuntary transport, made a bow to my
sister, and was going to embrace Sophia. The
old governante, preserving more presence of
mind than myself, took care to tell me of my
mistake; the Baron regarded me with an air of
astonishment, and the face of Sophia was covered with an amiable blush, but a slight smile
nevertheless escaped her rosy lips.

We returned to the house of M. du Portail
and sat down to dinner; I ate like a youth of
fifteen just smitten with love, and when the table
was cleared, pretended a slight indisposition in
order that I might retire to my apartment.
There I freely ruminated on Sophia, and all her
charms. What grace! what beauty! said I: her
charming figure is full of animation, and her
mind, I am sure, must correspond with her person. Her fine black eyes have inspired me I
know not how—it is love, without doubt. Ah!
Sophia, it is with love and for life! Recovered
from this first transport, I remembered to have

seen in several romances, the wonderful effects of an unexpected meeting; the first glance of a beautiful eye had been sufficient to captivate a tender lover, and the fair lady herself, flattered by the powerful impression she had made, became immediately susceptible of a similar sentiment, and irresistibly impelled to follow its bias. I had also read long dissertations wherein profound philosophers had denied the power of sympathy, and called it a chimera. Sophia! I exclaimed, I feel truly that I love you; but have you shared my trouble and my agitations? The manner in which I was presented was not such as to give me much confidence; but her sweet voice, at first so faltering, and which she with so much difficulty recovered; that sweet smile by which she appeared to sanction my mistake, and to console me for my privation!—Hope cheered my heart; it appeared to me very possible that on the subjects of sensibility, philosophers talked nonsense, and the romances had reason on their side.

I had approached, by chance, towards my window; I saw the Baron and M. du Portail walk with hasty steps in the garden. My father spoke with energy, his friend every now and then smiled, and both, at intervals, cast their eyes upon my window; I judged that it was of me they were discoursing, and that my father perhaps had already suspected my new-born passion. This idea made me uneasy, much less, however, than that of the departure of my father, which I believed near at hand. To quit my Sophia without knowing when I should have the happiness of seeing her again! To have more than a hundred leagues between us! I could not think of it without trembling. A thousand painful reflections occupied me during the evening. I made but a poor supper; I was, as yet, ignorant of the pleasures of love, but I already groaned under its most poignant anxieties.

Part of the night passed in the same agitations. I went to sleep in hopes of seeing my Sophia the next day; her image came to embellish my dreams; love, propitious to my vows, deigned to prolong so charming a sleep. It was late when I awoke; I learned with regret that they had suffered me to sleep when I found that father had gone out in the morning, and would not be back before the evening.

While bewailing my misfortune in not being able to visit my sister, M. du Portail entered;

he made me many kind professions of friendship, and asked me if I was satisfied with the Capital; I assured him that I feared nothing so much as quitting it. He told me I should not have that mortification; that my father, anxious to give me a very good education, as the only heir of his house, and that he might watch very closely the happiness of a daughter whom he loved, had resolved to continue at Paris some years: and in order to live there in a manner suitable to a man of his rank, had taken a house. This good news gave me a pleasure which I could not dissimulate; he, however, soon moderated its excess when he informed me that my father had commenced by choosing me a tutor and a faithful servant. At this instant, Monsieur l'Abbé Person was announced.

A very thin and pale little gentleman entered, and his mien fully justified the ill-humour with which his title had inspired me. He advanced with a grave and composed air, and in a low and mild tone began: Monsieur, your figure—satisfied with the words he had uttered, he stopped to consider what he should next say—your figure corresponds with your person. I replied very dryly to this sweet compliment.

Deprived of the happiness of seeing Sophia, I could find no other resource than the pleasure of thinking of her; and M. l'Abbe came to rob me of that consolation. I resolved, therefore, to probe him to the bottom, and from the first day succeeded.

In the evening my father confirmed with his own mouth the arrangements he had proposed; he signified to me at the same time, that I was never to go out but with my tutor: this warned me that I must gain him to my interest. My situation became critical, and my love, irritated by obstacles, seemed to increase with my constraint. I had made a very good progress in my studies, and my tutor was charged with the painful task of making me perfect in them; happily, I had an opportunity, in my first lessons, of perceiving that the pupil knew as much as the instructor. Monsieur l'Abbe, said I to him, you are as capable of teaching as I am curious to learn. Why, then, should we mutually trouble each other? Listen to me, let us leave there the books upon which we can speak at leisure; come and see my sister at her convent, and if Mademoiselle Sophia de Pontis comes to the conversation room, you will see

how pretty she is. The Abbe was inclined to
be angry, but profiting by the advantage I had
over him; I see you do not love exercise, replied
I to him, well, we'll remain here; but this evening I will declare to the Baron the extreme
desire I have to be advanced in my studies,
and your absolute insufficiency to lighten my
labours. If you deny it, I will demand an examination, which my father himself will make
us undergo. The Abbé was overcome by the
strength of my last arguments; he made a
hideous grimace, took his little cane and his
rusty hat, and accompanied me to the convent.

Adelaide came to the conference room accompanied only by her governess whom they
called Manon. This woman was an old domestic of my mother, who had brought her up. I
asked her to leave us, and she did so without
hesitation. The cursed little tutor remained,
and it was impossible to remove him. My sister
complained that we had suffered several days
to pass without seeing her, and I was astonished
to learn that the Baron had neglected her as
well as myself. We concluded that his mind
must have been so much occupied with his new

projects, that he forgot his dear girl. But you, Faublas, what has detained you all this time? Do you slight your sister, and her dear friend? It is ungrateful of you. Mademoiselle de Pontis is gone out; come and see us to-morrow; and above all, take care you give no offence, and Sophia will endeavour to make your peace with her old governante, who has not yet quite pardoned your indiscretions. I told my sister that I must obtain permission of the Abbe, and that he possessed a rage for study without any relaxation. Adelaide, believing that I spoke seriously, addressed the most charming solicitations to my grave tutor, which I followed up by my own entreaties. He sustained this jeering better than I expected; I remarked also, that when I spoke of going home, he observed, that it was all in good time: this complaisance entirely reconciled me to him.

My father expected me at M. Du Portail's, in order to conduct us to a very fine house, which he had taken in the Fauxbourgh St. Germain. I was put, the same evening, in possession of the apartment he had allotted me. I found there Jasmin, the servant of whom they had spoken to me: he was a stout youth, of good appearance, and he pleased me on first sight.

Do you slight your sister and her dear friend? It is ungrateful of you, said Adelaide to me. I repeated this reproach to myself an hundred times, and commented on it in an hundred different ways. Have they then talked about me? Have they expected me? Have I then been wished for? How long the night seemed to me! What a torment it is to hear the hours strike, and not have it in your power to hasten that which will bring us to the much-loved object.

At last the long desired moment arrived, I saw my sister, and I saw Sophia, who appeared to me more beautiful and interesting than when I first saw her. There was, in her simple dress, a something which I cannot express, most attractive and seducing. In this second visit my eyes scrutinized minutely her charms, and more than once our glances met during the charming examination. I admired her long black hair, which contrasted singularly with her fine skin, the whiteness of which dazzled one's sight; her waist so elegant and slender, that I could have embraced it with my ten fingers; the most

enchanting graces spread themselves over her
whole person, her little feet, of which I knew
not the favourable omen, and above all her eyes
—her bright eyes, which seemed to say to me:
" Ah! that we might render the mortal happy
who possesses the power to please us!"

I made Mademoiselle a compliment which
was calculated to flatter her, in as much as it
was easy to perceive that it was not studied.
The conversation was at first general, and
Sophia's governante joined in it; I saw that
they contrived to amuse the old woman, and
that she loved to hear herself talk, therefore I
appeared delighted with her foolish stories. In
the meantime the Abbe chatted with my sister,
and I, in a low and trembling voice, put a hundred questions and paid as many compliments
to my lovely Sophia. The old woman continued
to relate her nonsensical histories, which we no
longer listened to, and she perceived, at last,
that she had been speaking a long time to no
purpose. She rose abruptly, and said, you
made me begin my narrative, sir, and you do
not attend to the conclusion; this is not very
polite. Sophia, on leaving me, consoled me
with a tender look.

We heard the rattling of a carriage; it was that of the Baron, who entered immediately. Adelaide complained of the rarity of his visits; he alleged, in a constrained tone, the embarrassments of a new establishment. He talked with her a few minutes, in a manner as if he had something on his mind, after which he left her hastily, and took me home with him.

We found a brilliant equipage at our door. The porter told my father that *a great black gentleman* had been waiting for him above an hour, and that *a pretty lady* had that moment arrived; my father appeared as much pleased as surprised, he went in with eagerness, and I wished to follow, but he told me to go to my own room. Jasmin, of whom I enquired if he knew " the great black gentleman," and the " pretty lady," answered in the negative.

Curious to penetrate the mystery, I placed myself to watch at one of the windows of my apartment which overlooked the street; I did not wait long without seeing a stout gentleman, dressed in black, go out by himself, and with the appearance of perfect satisfaction. A quarter of an hour after I saw a young lady spring lightly into her carriage. The Baron, much less

nimble, wished to jump as expertly, but fell,
and I thought he had broken his neck. I was
much alarmed, but the burst of laughter which
came from the carriage fully satisfied me. I
was astonished that my father, who was naturally choleric, shewed no signs of ill humour,
but stepped in quietly; he bowed his head to
the porter, saw me at my casement, and appeared rather confused. I heard him order the
servants to tell me he was gone out on business,
and that I need not wait supper for him. I
imparted my curiosity to Jasmin, who appeared
to merit my confidence. He enquired without
affectation of the domestics of the Baron, and
I learnt the same evening that my father fre-
quented public places, and read the newspapers;
that he was gone to take a mistress to the opera:
I concluded that the Baron must be very rich
to charge himself with such a burthen. The reflection did not affect me much. I had hopes of
success with my fair Sophia, and in the spring-
tide of life we know no other wealth.

In a little time I paid my sister very frequent visits; Mademoiselle de Pontis almost
always accompanied her to the conference room.
The old governante was no longer angry, be-

cause I let her finish her histories, and likewise,
because Adelaide took care to make her some
little presents. The Abbe was no longer the
severe tutor, possessed (like many of his profession) with the rage for teaching that of
which he was ignorant; but he became, like
many others also, a little rosy-faced pedant,
with his hair very regularly dressed, minute
in his apparel, lax in his morals, displaying
profound erudition with the women; and with
the men affecting to skim but over the surface.
As mild and complaisant, as he was at first
untractable and obstinate, he appeared to have
no other desire than to anticipate my wishes,
and to facilitate their accomplishment; when
I spoke of going to the convent, I found him
equally eager with myself.

In the meanwhile, my father, devoted to the
noisy pleasures of the Capital, entertained
much company at home. I was caressed by the
fair sex, who gave me enticements which I
could not comprehend. A certain dowager in
particular, tried on me the power of her charms,
gave herself a number of childish airs, and exhausted all her affected conceits: I alone was
ignorant of what it all meant. Elsewhere I saw

no one in the world but Sophia; the love with which she inspired me was pure and innocent, and I knew not, as yet, that there existed a passion of another description.

For more than five months I had seen Sophia almost every day, and we were so accustomed to meet, that we looked upon it as a matter of course, and it seemed as necessary as our daily food. When we are ignorant of our love, or seek to disguise it, we frequently use names or phrases which are familiar and friendly, instead of those still more tender, which would excite suspicion. Sophia called me her young cousin, and I called Sophia my pretty cousin. The tenderness which we felt towards each other was evinced by our most indifferent actions, and expressed by our looks; my lips had not yet hazarded the avowal, and my sister was either blind to it, or she kept well the secret of her fair friend. I followed the first impulses of NATURE, but was far from suspecting the ends she had in view. Content to speak to Sophia, happy to hear her, and to kiss sometimes her pretty hand, I desired no more, or at least I could not have said what I desired. The moment approached, when one of the most charming women in the capital was to dissipate the darkness that environed me, and initiate me into the most delightful mysteries of Venus.

We were in that bustling season of the year when pleasure and folly united hold dominion over the city; Momus had given the signal for the dance, and the days were spent in festivity. The young Count de Rosambert, who had been for three months companion of my exercises, and who was loaded with civilities by my father, reproached me for the retired and tranquil life I led; ought I, at my age, to bury myself alive in the house of my father? to confine my walks to foolish visits to a nunnery to see my sister? Was it not time to quit my childhood which they wished eternally to prolong? and ought I not to hasten my entrance into the world, where with my figure and understanding, I could not fail to be favourably received? Be advised by me, continued he, I will, to-morrow, conduct you to a charming ball, where I go regularly four times a week, and you will there see good company. I hesitated; he is cautious, like a girl, replied the Count: well, do you fear that your chastity will run some hazard? Dress yourself as a woman; in this garb you will be safe. I burst into laughter, without knowing why. Indeed, said he, that will become you best; you have a slender and graceful figure, your cheeks are hardly covered with a light down; you will pass admirably!—and then—mind you, I wish to torment a certain person.—Faublas, dress yourself as a woman, we will amuse ourselves—it will be delightful—you shall see, you shall see!

The idea of this disguise pleased me, and I thought it would be very agreeable to go and see Sophia in the habiliments of her own sex. The next day an expert tailor whom the Count de Rosambert had spoken to, brought me the complete dress of an Amazon, such as is worn by the English ladies when they ride on horseback. An experienced milliner dressed my hair, consistent with my new character, and placed on my virgin head, a little hat of white beaver. I went down to my father; the moment he saw me, he came to me with an air of inquietude; then stopping all at once: Good, said he, laughing, I had at first thought it was Adelaide! I observed to him, that he flattered me very much.—No, I took you for Adelaide, and was endeavouring to guess what motive induced her to quit the convent without my permission, and come here in that strange habit. But as to yourself, be not proud of this trifling advantage; a pretty person is, in a man, one of the lowest merits.

It was my father who in the first place testified a desire to go to the convent, and he conducted me there. Adelaide did not know me until after some minutes examination. The Baron, enchanted with the extreme resemblance there was between my sister and me, loaded us with caresses, and embraced us alternately. Nevertheless Adelaide seemed to repent having come to the conversation room alone: I am sorry, said she, that I have not brought with me my dear friend! How we should delight in her surprise! Permit me, my dear father, to go and fetch her? The Baron consented. In re-entering, Adelaide said to Sophia: my good friend, embrace my sister. Sophia with astonishment eyed me from head to foot, and stood confounded. Embrace Mademoiselle, said the old governante, deceived by the metamorphosis. Mademoiselle, embrace my daughter, said the Baron, who was amused by the scene. Sophia blushed, and trembled as she approached; my heart palpitated. I know not what secret instinct conducted us, I know not with what address we concealed our happiness from the interested witnesses who observed us; they thought that our cheeks alone had met—but my lips had pressed the lips of Sophia!—You, readers, who are susceptible—who have been affected by the lovers of Saint Preux,* judge what bliss we experienced—This was also the first kiss of love.

On our return, we found the Count de Rosambert, who had been waiting for me. The Baron was presently informed of the scheme, and permitted me, more readily than I had expected, to pass the whole night at the ball, where we were conveyed in his own chariot. I am going, said the Count to me, to present you to a young lady that I esteem very much; it is full two months since I have sworn an eternal attachment to her, and more than six weeks that I have proved it to her. This language was quite enigmatical to me, but already I began to blush at my ignorance, and I put on a knowing smile, to make Rosambert think that

* In la Nouvelle Heloise.

I understood him. As I am going to torment
her, continued he; assume an air as if you loved
me very much, you'll see what effect it will
make on her! Above all, let me caution you
against telling her that you are not a girl. We
shall be sure to mortify her.

As soon as we appeared in the assembly, all
eyes were fixed on me; I was vexed to feel that
I blushed, and could not keep my countenance.
Sometimes I thought that a part of my dress
must be out of order, or that my borrowed character had betrayed me; but presently, from the
general attention of the men, and the universal
discontent of the women, I judged that I was
well disguised. One lady threw at me a dis-
dainful look; another examined me with a
pouting air; they agitated their fans, they
whispered among themselves, and smiled mal-
iciously. I saw that I received such a welcome
with which they honour, in a numerous circle, a
rival who is too pretty, when she appears for
the first time.

A very handsome woman entered; it was the
mistress of Rosambert. He presented to her
his relation, who came, said he, from a convent.
The lady (who was called the Marchioness

B***) welcomed me in the most obliging manner; I took a seat by her, and the young folks
formed a semicircle round us. The Count,
much pleased to excite the jealousy of his mistress, affected to give me a marked preference.
—The Marchioness, apparently piqued at his
coquetry, and fully resolved to punish him, in
concealing from him her resentment, redoubled
her politeness towards me: Mademoiselle, have
you a taste for the couvent? said she to me. I
should like it well, madam, if I found there
many persons like yourself. The Marchioness
testified by a smile, how much this compliment
flattered her; she put several other questions to
me, and appeared delighted with my answers.
She loaded me with the caresses which the women lavish on each other; told Rosambert, that
he was happy in having such a relation, and
finally gave me a tender kiss, which I returned
very politely. This was neither what Rosambert wished, nor what he had promised himself.
Hurt at the vivacity of the Marchioness, and
still more at the readiness with which I received
her caresses, he whispered into her ear, and
discovered to her the secret of my disguise. A
very likely tale! cried the Marchioness, after

having regarded me for a few moments: the
Count protested he had told her the truth.—
She looked at me again: what folly! it cannot
be. The Count renewed his protestations.
What an idea! replied the Marchioness and
dropping her voice; do you know what he says?
He insists that you are a young man disguised.
I answered timidly, in a low voice, that he had
said the truth. The Marchioness darted a
tender look at me, gently squeezed my hand,
and pretending to have misunderstood me: I
know it well, said she, sufficiently loud; it has
not the shadow of probability. Then addressing the Count; but sir, to what end are all these
jokes? What! replied he, to this, with astonishment, does mademoiselle pretend—How, if she
pretends! look at her! a child so amiable! so
pretty!—What! said the Count again—Oh!
sir, do pray drop this nonsense, continued the
Marchioness, in a manner peculiarly piquante;
you either take me for a fool, or you are mad
yourself.

I began seriously to think she had not understood me; I said in a low tone: I beg your pardon, madam, I have, perhaps, badly explained
myself; I am not what I appear to be: the

Count has told you the truth. I do not believe you, any more than him, replied she, speaking still lower than myself, and squeezing my hand. —I assure you, madam—Hold your tongue, you are an hypocrite; but you shall not deceive me any more than him; and she embraced me. Rosambert, who had not heard us, remained stupified. The young folks who surrounded us, seemed to wait with as much curiosity as impatience the end and explanation of a dialogue so obscure to them; but the Count restrained by the fear of offending his mistress if he covered himself with ridicule; and also flattering himself, that I should presently put an end to the mistake, bit his lips, and dared not say a word. Happily at this moment, the Marchioness saw her friend the Countess C*** enter the ball-room: I know not what she whispered into her ear, but the Countess immediately attached herself to Rosambert, nor quitted him during the evening.

In the meanwhile the ball had commenced, I joined in a country dance; it happened, by chance, that the Countess and Rosambert were seated behind the place which I occupied. The young lady said to him: No, no, all that is useless, I have taken possession of you for the whole evening, I do not give you up to any one. More jealous than a sultan, I shall not suffer you to speak to any one whatever; you dance not at all, or you dance with me; and if you mean all the obliging things you have said to me, I forbid you to say a word, a single word, to the Marchioness, or your young relation! My young relation? said the Count:—If you knew —I will know nothing—only I wish you to remain here. Suppose, added she, in a softer tone, I have designs upon you; are you going to be cruel? I heard no more of it, for the country dance finished.

The Marchioness had not lost sight of me for a moment; I wished to rest myself, I found a place near her; we began, and re-began! broke off, and began twenty times, a very animated conversation, which was often interrupted by caresses, and in which I saw plainly, that I must leave her in the error which appeared to please her so much.

The Count did not cease to observe us with great inquietude, but the Marchioness would not appear to see him: my intention, said she to me, is not to pass the whole night here, and if you

take my advice, you will be careful of your
health. Come home and have some slight re-
freshment with me; it is past midnight. Monsieur the Marquis will not be long in coming to
join me; we will go and sup, and I will afterwards conduct you to your own house; you will
find the Marquis a very singular man. He has
occasionally fits of tenderness for me—at other
times caprices of jealousy, very ridiculous, and
frequently is inclined to pay me attentions with
which I could willingly dispense. When he
vows fidelity to me, I neither believe it nor care
for it; nevertheless I shall not be sorry to put
him to the proof: he will see you, and find you
charming. You will not begin then with this
pretty tale of your disguise; 'tis an amusing
joke, but we have worn it out; therefore, instead of repeating it before the Marquis de
B****, you will do well, if you have no objection to oblige me a little, to make him some
advances. I demanded of her what advances
she meant. She laughed heartily at the simplicity of my question, and then regarding me
with a tender look: Hear me, said she, it is
clear that you are a woman: therefore, all the
caresses which I have given you this evening,

are only out of friendship: but if you had indeed been a young man disguised, and believing it, I had treated you in the same manner, that would have been called making advances, and very warm ones too. I promised her to make advances to the Marquis.—Very well! smile at his proposals, look at him in a significant manner, but do not let him press your hand as I have done, nor embrace you as I have embraced you; that would be neither proper nor decent.

The Marquis arrived. He still had a young look: he was well made, but of very small stature; his appearance was gay, but the gaiety was of that sort which always causes a laugh at its expense. Here is Mademoiselle du Portail, said the Marchioness (for I had taken that name), she is a young relation of the Count, you will thank me for having introduced her to you; she is kind enough to sup with us. The Marquis found that I had *a very happy phisiognomy,* he lavished on me the most ridiculous eulogiums, and I returned them by the most extravagant compliments. I am very happy, Mademoiselle, said he, in a formal manner, which he thought very fine, that you do me the honour to sup with me; you are very pretty—very pretty, and you may depend on what I say in that respect, for I am skilled in phisiognomy. My dear child, said the Marchioness, you have given me your word, you are too polite to break it; I will disembarrass you of the Marquis as soon as he becomes tiresome: she squeezed my hand, and the Marquis saw it. Oh! that I might press one of those little hands in mine! said he. I cast a scornful glance at him: Let us go, ladies, let us go, cried he, with an air of levity and triumph, and went out to call his servants.

Rosambert, who heard him, came to us not-withstanding the efforts of the Countess to restrain him: Monsieur (said he to me, in a tone of serious irony,) you no doubt find your new dress very convenient, and do not intend to undeceive the Marchioness. I replied in the same tone, but lowering my voice: my dear kinsman, would you so soon destroy your own work? He addressed himself to the Marchioness: I feel myself bound in conscience, madam, to warn you once more, that it is not Mademoiselle du Portail who will have the honour to sup with you, but the Chevalier de Faublas, my very young and very faithful friend. And I, sir, declare to you, that you have reckoned too much on my credulity and my patience. Have the goodness to drop this impertinent badinage, or determine never to see me more.—I have the courage to choose either the one or the other, madam, but I should be sorry to interfere with your pleasures, by my indiscretions, or balk them by my importunities.

The Marquis re-entered at the same moment; he tapped Rosambert on the shoulder, and holding him by the hand, said: What! do you not sup with us? Do you leave your relation with us! Know you that she is pretty! Know you what her phisiognomy promises! He lowered his voice: but between us, I think the little creature is somewhat lively. Oh! yes, very pretty, and very lively, replied the Count, with a sarcastic smile; she resembles many others; and then, as if he had predicted the approaching fate of this good husband; I wish you a good night, said he. What! think you, replied the Marquis, that I keep your relation for? listen then, if she is desirous!—I wish you a good night, repeated the Count, and he went out laughing heartily. The Marchioness contended that Rosambert had become mad; and I considered that he was very impolite. Not at all, said the Marquis, confidently to me, he loves you to distraction; he has observed that I pay my court to you, and he is jealous.

In five minutes we were at the residence of the Marquis. Supper was served up immediately, and I was placed between the Marchioness and her gallant spouse, who never ceased saying to me, what he thought, very pretty things. Too much occupied at first in satisfying an appetite, rather masculine, which dancing had given me, I did not find time to reply to him, except by the language of the eyes. As soon as my hunger was a little abated, I applauded, without exception, all the foolish things that he had been pleased to utter, and his bad *bon mots* produced him a hundred compliments, with which he was enchanted. The Marchioness, who had all along paid me the greatest attention, and whose looks were visibly animated, possessed herself of one of my hands. Curious to see how far the power of my deceitful charms extended, I abandoned the other to the Marquis, who seized it with an inexpressible transport.

The Marchioness, plunged into the most profound reflections, seemed meditating some important project; I observed her blush, tremble by turns, and without saying a word, she gently pressed my right hand, which she held within her own. But my left hand was in a prison less agreeable; the Marquis squeezed it in a manner that made me cry out. Charmed with his good fortune, proud of his happiness, and astonished at the address with which he deceived his wife, even in her own presence, he began alternately to heave deep sighs, and to burst into fits of laughter, which made the ceiling ring; at length, fearing to betray himself, and wishing to stifle this laughter, which the Marchioness might notice, and also, perhaps, thinking thereby to convince me of his passion, he bit my fingers.

The beautiful Marchioness waking from her reverie, said: Mademoiselle du Portail, it is late; you were to have passed the whole night at the ball, and they do not expect you at home before eight or nine o'clock in the morning; stay, therefore, with me. I offer to any one an apartment in my house, but my own room shall be at your service. I ought, added she, in an affectionate tone, to act as your mamma; and I would not that my daughter should have any

The Marquis squeezed it in a manner that made me cry out.

Page 32

other room to sleep in than my own; I will go and make up a little bed for you, near mine. —And why make up a bed, interrupted the Marquis, there is quite room enough for two in your own: when I come to you there, shall I incommode you? I sleep all the night, and so do you. Having said this, he gave me, in an amorous manner, beneath the table, so hard a blow on the knee, that it grazed the skin. I instantly replied to this gallantry in the same manner, and so vigorously, that he uttered a loud cry. The Marchioness rose with an air of alarm. It it nothing, said he, I have only hit my leg against the table. I burst with laughter, the Marchioness could no more restrain herself than me, and her dear spouse, without knowing why, began to laugh still louder than us both.

When our excessive gaiety was a little moderated, the Marchioness renewed her offers. Accept the half of the Marchioness' bed, cried the Marquis, accept it, I beg of you, you will be well there, you will be very comfortable indeed there. I am going for the present, but do pray, in the meantime accept her offer. He left us. Madam, said I to the Marchioness, your invitation is as flattering as it is agreeable, but is it

for Mademoiselle du Portail, or Monsieur de
Faublas that you intend it?—What! the
Count's bad jokes over again, you little rogue!
and do you repeat them! Have I not told you,
that I do not believe you? But, madam—peace,
peace, replied she, putting her hand on my
mouth; the Marquis is coming, let him not
hear such nonsense as this. What a charming
girl! (said she, embracing me tenderly) how
timid and how modest she is! but she is also
very whimsical; come on, you little wag, come:
she held out her hand to me, and we passed into
her chamber.

I hesitated about going to bed. The maids
of the Marchioness wished to lend me their assistance; I trembled and begged them to offer
their services to their mistress, as I could dispense with them. Yes, said the Marchioness,
attentive to all my motions, do not trouble her;
'tis the childishness of the convent; leave her to
herself. I got immediately behind the curtains;
but I found myself much embarrassed when
I was obliged to strip myself of a dress to which
I was so little familiar. I broke the strings,
tore out the pins, pricked myself in one place,
scratched myself in another, and the more I

hurried the less progress I made. A chamber maid passed near me at the very moment when I was pulling off the last petticoat. I trembled lest she should open the curtains; I jumped into bed, astonished at the singular adventure which brought me there, but not as yet suspecting that in sleeping together, we should have any other desire than of chatting with each other, before we went to sleep. The Marchioness was not long in following me; we heard the voice of her husband: these ladies might as well permit me to assist them in going to bed. What! already in bed? He wanted to embrace me; the Marchioness was greatly offended; he closed the curtains himself, and bade us good night.

A profound silence reigned for some moments. Are you asleep already, my sweet child, said the Marchioness in a gentle tone.—Oh! no, I am not asleep. She threw herself into my arms, and pressed me against her bosom. Oh, heaven! cried she, with an astonishment very naturally assumed, if it was assumed, it is a man! ! and then, quickly repulsed me: what! is it possible?—Madam, replied I, trembling, I told you so; You told me so, sir, but was it to be believed? Well, you must not remain in my house—or at least another bed must be prepared for you.—Madam, it is not me, it is the Marquis—But, sir, speak then in a lower tone— you must not remain in my house, you must go away.—Well, madam, I'm going. She then took hold of me by the arm. You are going away! where, and what to do? To awake my maids; to hazard your life in jumping out of the window! to discover, in all probability, to my servants, that I have had a man in bed with me!—Pardon me, madam, be not angry; I am going to recline in the arm chair. Yes, undoubtedly you must—but what a fine resource, (still holding me by the arm) fatigued as you must be! to remain in the cold, and to injure your health! you deserve that I should treat you with this rigour—well, rest there, but promise that you will be prudent. Provided, madam, that you will pardon me.—No, I do not pardon you! but I have still more regard for you, than you have for me. See how cold your hand is already! And out of pity she put it on her ivory bosom. Guided by nature, and by love, this happy hand descended a little; I knew not the stimulus which caused my blood to boil. No woman, said the Marchioness in a milder tone, ever experienced the embarrassment in which you place me. Ah! pardon me then, my dear mamma! Your dear mamma, indeed! you have a great regard for your dear mamma, little libertine that you are! Her arms which had at first repulsed me, gently drew me towards her: presently we were so close to each other, that our lips came in contact, and I was emboldened to print a burning kiss upon hers. Faublas, said she in a voice scarcely audible, is this what you promised me? Her hand strayed; a raging flame circulated in all my veins—Ah! madam! pardon me, I die.—Ah! my dear Faublas—my friend!—I continued motionless. The Marchioness felt for my embarrassment, which could not displease her— She kindly aided my inexperience, and I received, with as much astonishment as pleasure, a charming lesson, which I repeated more than once.

We employed several hours in this agreeable exercise; I began to fall asleep on the bosom of my fair mistress, when I heard the noise of a door which opened gently; somebody entered and advanced on tip-toe; I was without arms,

in a house with which I was unacquainted, and
I could not help experiencing a sensation of
alarm. The Marchioness guessed who it was,
told me in a whisper to take her place, and give
her mine, and I immediately obeyed her.

Scarcely had I changed places, when some
one opened the curtains on the side which I had
just quitted. Who comes to wake me thus,
said the Marchioness? The person hesitated a
few moments, but presently explained himself,
without replying to her. And what a strange
whim is this, sir? continued she, the time too
that you choose sir, is also very improper; without consideration for me, and without respect
for the innocence of this young person, who
perhaps is not asleep, or who may awake! you
are very unreasonable, I beg you will retire.
The Marquis insisted, and endeavoured to appease his wife by some very comic excuses.
No, sir, said she, I will not, it shall not be, I
assure you, you shall not, therefore I beg you
will retire; she jumped out of bed, took him
by the arm and put him out of the door.

My beautiful mistress returned to me laughing, was not that well done; said she, you see
what I have refused on your account. I felt

that I owed her a remuneration, which I offered her with ardour, and she accepted with gratitude: so complaisant is a woman of twenty-five when she loves! and so fertile are the resources which nature gives to a novice of sixteen!

Nevertheless everything has its bounds with us weak mortals; I was not long before I fell into a profound sleep. When I awoke the daylight penetrated the apartment in spite of the curtains: I thought of my father—Alas! my Sophia came into my remembrance! a tear escaped me, and the Marchioness perceived it. Already capable of some dissimulation, I attributed it to my fears on her account and to the painful regret I felt at leaving her; she embraced me tenderly. She appeared to me so lovely! and there was so little time to spare!— The sound sleep had completely invigorated my frame—the intoxication of pleasure dissipated the remorse of love.

We were at length obliged to think of rising. The Marchioness herself served me for a chamber-maid; she was so expert, that the affairs of the toilette had been presently finished, if our own minds had been tranquil. When we thought that nothing more was wanting in the adjustment of my disguise, the Marchioness rung for her women. The Marquis had been up above an hour. He complimented me on my diligence: I am sure, said he to me, you have passed an excellent night; and without giving me time to answer: She appears fatigued, nevertheless; her eyes are hollow! see the effects of dancing, I always tell the Marchioness of it, but she pays no attention to it: come, we must restore the strength of this charming girl, and then we will conduct her home.

Nothing was more calculated to render me more uneasy than this—*we will conduct her.* I told the Marquis that it would be quite sufficient for the Marchioness to take that trouble, but he insisted on going. The Marchioness joined me in persuading him from his purpose. He replied that M. du Portail could not think amiss of his bringing home his daughter since the Marchioness would be with us, and he was anxious to be acquainted with the happy parents of so amiable a child. All our efforts could not prevent his accompanying us.

I began to fear that this adventure, which had so happy a commencement, would terminate badly. I knew no plan better than to give the

Marquis's coachman the correct address of M. du Portail, " at M. du Portail's, near the Arsenal," said I. The Marchioness perceived my embarrassment, and partook of it, no expedient had as yet occurred to me, when we arrived at the door of my pretended father.

He was at home; they told him that the Marquis and Marchioness of B***, had brought home his daughter! My daughter! cried he, with the most lively emotion, my daughter! He ran towards us, without giving him time to say a word, I threw my arms around his neck: yes, said I, you are a widower, and you have a daughter. Speak still lower, replied he, with much vivacity, speak lower; who told you so? My God! do you not understand me? It is I who am your daughter. Pray don't deny me before the Marquis. M. du Portail more tranquil, but not less astonished, seemed to wait for some explanation. Monsieur, said the Marquis to him, Mademoiselle du Portail has passed part of the night at a ball, and the remainder at my house. Are you angry, said the Marquis, who observed his astonishment, that she has passed part of the night with us? You are wrong, for she has slept in my wife's apartment,

and even in her own bed with her, and she could
not be lodged better. Are you angry that I have
accompanied her home? I confess that the
ladies did not wish it; it is my—I am very
sensible, replied M. du Portail, now recovered
from his first surprise, and somewhat better in-
structed by the discourse of the Marquis; I am
very sensible of the kindness you have had for
my daughter; but I ought to declare to you before her (he looked at me, and I trembled) that
I am very much astonished at her going to a
ball disguised in this fashion. How disguised,
sir? said the Marchioness.—Yes, madam, in an
Amazonian habit, which but ill becomes my
daughter? At least, ought she not to have asked
my advice and permission?

Charmed at the ingenious turn my new
father had given the affair, I affected to appear
humbled. Ah! I thought that papa knew it,
said the Marquis; Monsieur you must pardon
this little fault. Mademoiselle your daughter
has a most happy physiognomy; I tell you so,
and I know it; Mademoiselle your daughter—
is a charming girl; she has delighted all the
world, and my wife above all; Oh! believe me,

my wife is enraptured with her. It is true, sir,
said the Marchioness, with an admirable *sang
froid,* that Mademoiselle has inspired me with
the friendship she merits.

I thought myself saved, when my real father,
the Baron de Faublas, who never caused himself
to be announced at the house of his friend, entered suddenly. Ah! ah! said he, on perceiving me—M. du Portail ran to him with open
arms: My dear Faublas, you see my daughter,
whom Monsieur the Marquis and Madame the
Marchioness de B***, have brought me home!
Your daughter! interrupted my father. Yes,
my daughter, but you do not recognize her under this ridiculous habit! Mademoiselle, added
he, with anger, go to your room, that no one
may again surprise you in this indecent garb.

I made, without saying a word, a bow to M.
du Portail, who seemed to pity me, and one to
the Marchioness, who appeared alarmed at the
dilemma we were placed in; for at the name of
my father, she was so agitated, that I feared
she would be taken ill. I retired to an adjoining room and listened. Your daughter! again
repeated the Baron.—Yes! my daughter! who
was advised to go to the ball in the dress which

you have seen, the Marquis will tell you the
rest.   And, indeed, the Marquis did recapitu-
late to the Baron everything which he had told
M. du Portail; that I had slept in his wife's
chamber, and even in her own bed with her.
She is very lucky, said my father, looking at
the Marchioness—very lucky, repeated he, that
so great an imprudence had not had a disagreeable termination.   And what very great imprudence has this dear child committed, replied the
Marchioness, whom I had seen so disconcerted,
but who had so soon recovered her wits?   What!
because she has assumed the habit of an Amazon! Without doubt, interrupted the Marquis, it
is but a trifle! and you, sir, (addressing himself
to my father in an angry tone) permit me to
say, that instead of making reflections upon
this young lady calculated to hurt her feelings,
you had better join us in soliciting her father
to pardon her.   Madam, said M. du Portail to
the Marchioness, I pardon her on your account:
(then addressing himself to the Marquis) but
on condition that she goes there no more in the
habit of an Amazon.   Be it so, replied the
latter, but I hope we shall see her again in her
ordinary dress; it would be a great depriva-

tion if we were not to see the charming girl again. Assuredly, said the Marchioness, rising up, and if Monsieur her father would do us a real favour, he will accompany her. M. du Portail reconducted the Marchioness to her carriage, pouring forth the thanks which he was presumed to owe for her attention to his daughter.

Their departure relieved me from a great burthen. This is a very singular adventure, said M. du Portail on re-entering. Very singular, replied my father; the Marchioness is a very fine woman, and the little wag is very happy.— Know you, replied his friend, that your son had almost penetrated my secret; when they announced my daughter, I thought that my own daughter was come home to me, and some words escaped, which have betrayed me.—Never fear; there is a remedy; Faublas is more reasonable than youths generally are at his age, he wanted but a little practical knowledge, which he has no doubt acquired last night: he has a noble soul and an excellent heart; a secret that we penetrate does not bind us, as you know; but an honest man would think it dishonourable to betray that which a friend has confided to him;

impart yours to my son; no half confidence; you may depend on his discretion.—But for secrets of this importance—he is so young!—So young, my friend! my son, already a youth and ignorant of one of the most sacred duties of a thinking being! A child whom I have educated, must have seen very little of his father if he would do a mean action!—My friend, I must now return. My dear du Portail, believe me, you will never repent it. I hope, moreover, that this confidence, which is become almost necessary, will not be entirely useless. You know that I have made some sacrifices to give my son an education suitable to his birth, and the hopes I have conceived of him; he will remain another year in this Capital to perfect himself in his studies, I think it will be sufficient; afterwards he will travel, and I shall not be displeased if he continues some months in Poland. Baron, interrupted M. du Portail, the contrivance which your friendship has had recourse to, is as ingenious as delicate; I feel all the civility of your proposition, which I confess is very agreeable to me. Then, replied the Baron, you'll do well to give Faublas a letter for the faithful servant you have left in that country;

Bolesas and my son will make new researches.
My dear Lovinski, do not yet despair of your
fortune; if your daughter exists, it is not impossible but she may be restored to you. If
the king of Poland—my father spoke lower,
and took his friend to the other end of the apartment: they conversed there more than half-an-
hour, when both of them having approached the
door behind which I was, I heard the Baron,
who said: I will not require of him the details
of his adventure; probably they are very
pleasant, and I should not hear them with the
gravity I ought. Without doubt he will relate
to you minutely the whole affair, and you can
inform me. From appearances, I think we shall
hear of a very foolish husband. He is not the
only one, my friend, replied M. du Portail. It
is very true, replied the Baron, but we must say
nothing about it. I heard them coming towards
my door, and I went and threw myself on an
arm chair. The Baron said to me, on entering:
my carriage is below, let it take you home; go
and rest yourself, and I forbid you to go out in
that dress again. My friend, said M. du Portail, who followed me to the door, one of these
days we will dine together by ourselves; you

know a part of my secret, I will tell you the rest; but above all things be discreet; remember also that I have rendered you a service. I assured him that I should never forget it, and that he might rely upon me. As soon as I arrived at home, I went to bed and slept profoundly.

It was very late when I awoke: the Abbe accompanied me to the convent; with what soft emotion did I again behold my Sophia! her modest countenance—her ingenuous simplicity —the timid yet tender welcome which she gave me—the air of embarrassment caused by the remembrance of the last night's kiss, all combined to inspire me with love—a love the most pure and respectful.

Nevertheless, the idea of the Marchioness' charms followed me even to the conversation room of the convent; but what precious advantages her young rival had over her! It is true that the pleasures of the last night had made a lively impression on my heated imagination; but how much did I prefer to that, the delightful moment when I found on the lips of Sophia an immortal soul! the Marchioness reigned in my astonished senses, but my heart adored Sophia.

The next day I remembered that the Marchioness expected me to visit her; I recollected also that the Baron had said: *I forbid you to go out in that dress.* Besides, how was I to go to the Marchioness, without being at least accompanied by a *femme de chambre?* I could not think of the Count, it was not likely he would conduct me there; and as to the Marquis, would he not think it odd for a young lady to come out entirely alone?

Impatient once more to behold my fair mistress, but restrained by the fear of displeasing my father, I knew not which way to resolve myself. Jasmin came to tell me that a middle-aged woman, sent by Mademoiselle Justine, wished to speak with me.—I know not who this Justine is; but let her enter: Mademoiselle Justine has charged me to present her compliments to you, said the woman to me, and to give you this packet, and this letter. Before opening the packet, I took the letter, of which the address was simply, to *Mademoiselle du Portail.* I opened it with eagerness, and read:

"Send me some news of yourself, my dear child; have you passed a good night; you had need of repose; I fear that the fatigues of the ball, and the disagreeable scene which took place in the presence of your father, may have injured your health. I am grieved to think you incurred displeasure on my account; believe me, that during that interview, I suffered as much as yourself. The Marquis talks of going to the ball again this evening; but I do not feel disposed to go, and I think you'll have no more desire than myself. Nevertheless, as a mother ought to have some complaisance for her daughter, and particularly when she has one as amiable as yourself, we will go there if you wish it. I have not forgot that your Amazonian dress is forbidden you, and I thought that you might not have another ball dress, as it is not a necessary article in a convent, therefore I have sent you one of mine, we are very nearly of the same stature, and I think it will fit you well.

" Justine has told me that you are in want of a *femme de chambre;* she who brings you this letter is prudent, *intelligent and adroit!* you can take her into your service, and place your *entire confidence* in her, I will answer for her.

" I do not invite you to dinner with me, I know that M. du Portail seldom dines without

his daughter; but if you love your dear mamma
as much as she loves you, you will come in the
evening as soon as you can. The Marquis does
not dine at home; come in good time, my dear
child, I shall be alone all the evening, and you
can keep me company. Believe that no one
loves you so well as your dear mamma.

"The Marchioness de B***.

"P. S.—I have not the patience to write all
the foolish things which the Marquis bade me
tell you on his part. You can scold him well
when you see him; he wished this morning to
send in his own name to M. du Portail's. I had
great trouble in persuading him that it was not
proper, and that it was more becoming for me
to write."

I was enchanted with this letter. Monsieur,
said the intelligent woman who brought it to
me, Justine is the *femme de chambre* of Madame the Marchioness de B**, and if Mademoiselle wishes it, I can be her's today and to-
morrow. In short, Monsieur or Mademoiselle
may equally confide in me; when Mademoiselle
Justine and Madame Dutour engage in an intrigue, they never spoil it, that is why I am
chosen. Very well, said I, Madame Dutour, I

see you know your business; you shall accompany me to the Marchioness. I offered my duenna a double Louis d'Or, which she accepted. It is not but they have already well paid me, said she: but Monsieur ought to know that persons of my profession always receive from both parties.

As soon as the Baron had dined, he set out for the opera, according to his custom. My milliner was sent for; a plume of feathers was placed on my head instead of the little hat. Madame Dutour dressed me completely in the charming ball dress, sent by the Marchioness, and which became me wonderfully; my resemblance to Adelaide was now more striking. I took a fan, and a large nosegay, and flew to the rendezvous the Marchioness had assigned me.

I found her in her boudoir, negligently reclining upon an ottoman; an elegant dishabille, instead of concealing, showed her charms to advantage. She rose as soon as she saw me. How charming you look in this dress, Mademoiselle du Portail! how well this gown becomes you! and as soon as the door was shut: Oh! how happy am I to see you, my dear Faublas, how your punctuality flatters me! my heart told me you would find the means of coming in spite of your two fathers. I only replied by the most tender embraces; and compelling her to take the position from which she rose to receive me, *I proved to her that her lessons were not forgotten;* when we heard a noise in the adjoining room. Dreading to be surprised in a situation by no means equivocal, I rose precipitately, and, thanks to my convenient garments, I had only to change my posture, for my disorder to be repaired. The Marchioness, without appearing embarrassed, merely put that in order which was most necessary; this was only the affair of a moment. The door opened; it was the Marquis. I knew well, sir, said she to him, that no one but yourself, could come in to me without being announced, but I thought at least that you would knock at this door before opening it; this dear child had some secret griefs to impart to her dear mamma; a moment sooner you would have surprised her!—it is not usual to enter thus abruptly where there are ladies! Good, replied the Marquis, I surprise her—oh, no! I have not surprised her, there cannot be much mischief done if that is all; however, I am sure the dear girl will pardon me; she is

more indulgent than you. But we must agree
that her father was right in wishing her to lay
aside that Amazonian habit; she is so much
more lovely in her present attire.

He resumed with me, that ridiculous strain
of gallantry which had already so much amused
us; he found that I was perfectly recovered,
that my eyes were brilliant, my countenance
very animated, and even that there was something extraordinary, and which augured well in
my *phisiognomy*. After this he said: fair
ladies, do you go to the ball this evening? The
Marchioness answered in the negative. You are
jesting with me, certainly. I am come home
purposely to conduct you there. I assure you
that I shall not go. And why not? You told
me this morning—I said that I might go there
out of complaisance to Mademoiselle du Portail;
but she does not care to go; she is afraid of
again meeting there the Count de Rosambert,
who conducted himself very improperly the last
time; I interrupted the Marchioness: certainly
his behaviour to me was very impolite, therefore in future his company will give me as
much uneasiness, as it formerly afforded me
pleasure. You are right, said the Marquis, the

Count is one of those coxcombs who think all the women are in love with them; it is proper that these gentlemen should sometimes be taught that there are those in the world who know how to treat them,—I perceived his drift, and to justify his remark, I darted at him, by stealth, a glance of the eye, which was very expressive—and who treat them with the contempt they deserve, added he, immediately, raising his voice, and rising on tip-toe to give himself an affected swing, which he accomplished in a very unfortunate manner. He struck his head with great violence against the wainscot, and experienced a very heavy fall on the floor, which gave him a large bruise on the forehead. Ashamed of his misfortune, but wishing to dissemble, he appeared insensible to the pain which he felt. Charming girl, said he to me with great *sang froid,* but making every now and then some ugly grimaces which betrayed him, you have reason to avoid the Count; but be not afraid of meeting him this evening, it is a masqued ball, the Marchioness has luckily two dominos, she will lend you one, and take the other herself; we will go to the ball, you shall come back and sup with us; and if you were not too badly accommodated the night before last—oh! yes, that will be delightful, cried I with more vivacity than prudence; we will go to the ball. What! with my dominos, which are so well known to the Count, interrupted the Marchioness, more thoughtful than myself.— Yes, madam, with your dominos! we must treat this child with a sight of a masqued ball, she has never seen such a thing; the Count will not recognize you, he may not perhaps be there. The Marchioness appeared dubious, I could see she was embarrassed between the desire to keep me another night with her, and the fear of going there again in the presence of the Marquis, to be subject to the sarcasms of the Count. As for myself, said the accommodating husband, in a mysterious tone, I will conduct you there, but I have business, and cannot stop, I shall leave you there, and come and look for you at midnight. This last remark of the Marquis, more than all his entreaties, determined the Marchioness upon going; she still declined it for a while, but in a tone which gave me to understand that I must press her, and that she was about to consent.

In the meanwhile, the contusion which the

Marquis had received, became more apparent,
and the bump seemed to increase while one
looked at it. I demanded of him, with an air
of astonishment, what he had on his forehead.
It is nothing, said he to me, with a forced
laugh; when we are married, we are exposed to
such accidents. I remembered the torture he
had made me undergo when my hand was within his—and resolving to avenge myself, I drew
a piece of money out of my pocket, placed it on
his forehead, and then struck it with all my
force, as if to beat down the bump. The
patient pressed his sides with his closed fists,
ground his teeth together, groaned grievously,
and made the most horrible contortions. She
has strength in her wrist, said he, in great pain.
I redoubled my efforts: he at last uttered a terrible cry, and escaping from me with violence,
would have tumbled heels over head if I had
not caught him. Oh! the little devil has almost
split my skull!—The little wag has done it on
purpose, said the Marchioness, who with difficulty restrained herself from laughing.—Do
you think she did it on purpose?—Well! I'll
embrace her to punish her.—To punish me?—
be it so: I presented my cheek with a good

grace, and he thought himself the happiest of men: if I had been willing to listen to him, I should have continued, at the same price, to put his courage to the proof.

Let us have done with this nonsense, said the Marchioness, pretending to be a little angry, and let us think of this ball, since we must go there.—Oh! madam is out of temper! replied the Marquis: let us be prudent, said he to me, in a low tone, there is a little jealousy. He looked at us both with an air of satisfaction; you love each other very much, continued he, but if you should quarrel about me one of these days— that would be very singular! Do we go to the ball, or do we not? interrupted the Marchioness. She immediately began to prepare herself; they brought her the dominos, but she did not wish to use them; she sent for two others, in which we were gaily muffled up. You know mine, said the Marquis; I shall put it on when I come to look for you: I am not afraid to be recognised, not I! He conducted us to the ball, and promised to join us at twelve o'clock precisely.

As soon as we appeared at the door of the assembly-room, we were surrounded by a crowd of masques; they examined us minutely, and

made us dance; my eyes were at first greatly
delighted with the novelty of the spectacle—the
elegant dresses—the rich ornaments—the singular and grotesque costumes—even the ugliness
of their droll metamorphoses—the odd repre-
sentation of all the faces with paint and paste-
board—the mixture of colours—the buzz of a
hundred confused voices—the multitude of objects—their perpetual motion, which unceasingly varied and animated the picture, all combined to arrest my attention, which was soon
fatigued. Some new masques having entered,
the country dance was interrupted, and the
Marchioness, profiting by the circumstance,
mingled with the crowd: I followed her in silence, curious to examine in detail this many-
coloured scene. I was not long in observing
that some of the actors were busily occupied in
doing nothing, and talked prodigiously without
saying any thing. They seek you with eagerness, they regard you with curiosity, join you
with familiarity, and quit you without knowing
why: the next moment they meet you again
with a sneer; one deafens you by boring your
ear with his squeaking voice; another, in a
nasal tone, stammers a hundred dull things,

which he scarcely comprehends himself: this
one, lisps a gross *bon mot,* which he accompanies with ridiculous gestures; that, puts a
stupid question, which is answered by an attempt at wit still more foolish. I saw, nevertheless, some persons cruelly tormented, who certainly would have paid very dear for the opportunity of escaping from malicious tricks and
spiteful looks. I saw others very much wearied,
whose principal object appeared to be in pass-
ing the night at the ball in any manner they
could; and who no doubt remained there with
the slender consolation of saying, the next day,
how much they were amused the night before.
Is this, then, a masqued ball? said I to the Marchioness. I am not astonished that good people
are here abused by scoundrels; and persons of
wit perplexed by fools. I should certainly not
remain here if I was not with you. Hold your
tongue, replied she to me, we are followed, and
perhaps recognised—do you not see the masque
which is treading in our steps? I fear much that
it is the Count; let us go out of the crowd, and
do not be alarmed.

It was indeed M. de Rosambert: we had no
trouble in recognising him, for he did not even

disguise his voice, but merely dropped it sufficiently low to be heard only by the Marchioness and myself.—How does Madame the Marchioness and her charming friend? demanded he of us with an affected interest. I dared not reply. The Marchioness, feeling that it would be useless to attempt to make him believe that he was mistaken, preferred entering into a polite conversation, which she might, perhaps, by her address, have terminated happily, if the Count had been less informed of our affairs. —Ah! it is you, M. de Rosambert!—You have recognised me!—I am astonished at that!—I thought you had sworn never to see me, or speak to me again. It is true that I have promised it, madam, and I know how much that assurance which I gave you, has given you satisfaction. I do not understand you, and you misunderstand me; if I did not wish to see you, what obliges me to speak to you? Why am I come here in order to meet you?—In order to meet me, madam! flattering as such a profession is, I might, perhaps, have had the weakness to deem it sincere, if this dear child who is here— Sir, replied the Marchioness, have you not brought the Countess? The Countess is very amiable! What say you?—I say, madam, that she is, moreover, very officious! The Marchioness interrupted him again—the Countess is very amiable! You ought to have brought her. —Yes, madam! and you apparently would again have confided to her the polite employment which she so generously accepted, and executed with so much complaisance.—What! would you insinuate that I employed her to occupy you the whole evening, to engage you in a disagreeable quarrel with myself, to repeat to me a hundred times an uncivil pleasantry, to push me to such extremities, that I was at last obliged to speak to you in very harsh terms, which you have not failed to take in the most literal acceptation, and of which I should have repented, if you had come the next day; as I hoped to beg your pardon. My pardon! you would have granted me, madam. Oh, how generous you are!—but be tranquil, I will not abuse so much goodness; I fear that I embarrass you too much, and also that I give pain to my young relation, who listens to us so attentively, and who has such good reasons for remaining silent. What, sir! replied I immediately, what can I say to you?—Nothing—nothing but what

I know, or what I can guess.—I acknowledge
Monsieur de Rosambert, that you know something which Madame does not know—But,
added I, in a lower voice, have a little discretion; the Marchioness was not willing to believe
you the day before yesterday; what does it cost
you to leave her but for one day more in an error
which still continues agreeable? Very well,
cried he, it is an admirable turn!—You, such a
novice before yesterday, to day so artful!—You
must certainly have received some good lessons!
—What say you, then? replied the Marchioness,
a little mortified.—I say, madam, my young
relation is advanced greatly in four and twenty
hours; but I am not astonished, we know how
soon girls become enlightened. You do us the
favour at last then, to acknowledge, that Mademoiselle is of her own sex! I shall not think
proper to deny it any more, madam, since I
perceive how painful it would be to you to be
undeceived. To lose a fair friend, and to find in
her place but a young suitor! the misfortune
would be too severe.—What you say is very
reasonable, replied the Marchioness, with an impatience very badly disguised: but the tone in
which you say it is so singular!—Explain your-

self, sir; is this child, whom you have introduced to me as your relation, (speaking low) Mademoiselle du Portail, or Monsieur de Faublas?—you compel me to ask you a very extraordinary question, but you must tell me seriously which is the truth.—Tell you the truth, madam!—I could have hazarded such a thing the day before yesterday; but to day it is for me to ask you that question.—Me, replied she, without being disconcerted, I have no kind of doubt about it: her air, her looks, her conduct, her discourse, all proclaim to me that she is Mademoiselle du Portail; and, besides, I have proofs which I did not look for.—Proofs!—Yes, sir, proofs; she supped with me the night before last.—I know it well, madam; and she was still with you at ten o'clock the next morning.—At ten in the morning?—be it so; but after that we conducted her home.—To her house in the Fauxbourg Saint Germain!—No, near the Arsenal; and Monsieur her father—Her father, the Baron de Faublas?—No such thing! but M. du Portail. M. du Portail returned many thanks to the Marquis and myself for taking his daughter home!—The Marquis and you, Madam! What! the Marquis accompany you to the house of M. du Portail?—What is there so astonishing in that?—And M. du Portail thanked the Marquis?—Yes, sir.

Here the Count burst into a fit of laughter. Oh! the good husband! cried he aloud—what a charming adventure!—oh, what a polite husband! He was preparing to quit us. I thought that it would be for the interest of the Marchioness and myself if we could moderate his excessive gaiety. Monsieur, said I to him, lowering my voice, could I not have a more serious explanation with you? He regarded me with a smile. A serious explanation between us this evening, my dear friend?—(he lifted my masque up a little)—you are too pretty: I leave you TO LOVE and TO PLEASE: moreover, it is fit I should profit to-day of my advantages; the explanation will do for to-morrow, if you desire it. For to-morrow, sir, at what hour, and in what place? The hour I cannot fix with you; that will depend upon circumstances. Do you not go to sup with the Marchioness? —To-morrow, it will, perhaps, be noon when the very accommodating Marquis will reconduct you to the very complaisant M. du Portail's; you will probably be fatigued, I will not take an improper advantage of you, it is necessary that you have time to rest; I shall pass near your house in the evening; I shall not take my leave of you, I shall have the pleasure of seeing you again by-and-by, before the hour of departure from hence. He bowed to us, and left the room.

The Marchioness was much pleased at his absence. He has given us some home-thrusts, said she to me; but we could not have defended ourselves better. I observed to her, that the Count endeavoured to lower his voice whenever he launched at us any very pointed remark; and that his intention being only to torment us severely, he seemed unwilling to compromise the matter until it reached a certain point.—I do not trust to that, said she; he knows that you have passed the night with me, and he is piqued at it. The return that he announced to you is no good omen; he is, without doubt, preparing a stronger attack for us: let us go without waiting for him, or the Marquis either.

We were preparing ourselves to go out, when two masques stopped us. One of the two said to the Marchioness—I know you, beautiful masque. Good evening to you, Monsieur de Faublas, said the other to me. I did not reply. Good evening, Monsieur de Faublas, repeated he. I felt that I must summon up my strength, and answer with boldness.—You have not the art of divination, beautiful masque; you deceive yourself as to my name and my sex.—One or the other must be very doubtful.—You are mad, beautiful masque.—Not at all; some baptize you Faublas, and contend that you are a fine boy, and others call you du Portail, and swear that you are a very pretty girl.—Du Portail or Faublas, replied I, much confounded, what matters it? We will explain, beautiful masque. If you are a pretty damsel, it is of consequence to me; if you are a fine young man, it is of importance to that fair lady (pointing to the Marchioness). I remained stupified. He resumed: Answer me, Mademoiselle du Portail; speak, then, Monsieur de Faublas; decide to give me one of the names.—Ah! if I only considered my personal interests and appearances, you are Mademoiselle du Portail; but if I believe the chronicles of scandal, you are M. de Faublas.

The Marchioness did not lose a word of this dialogue, but already too hard pressed by the unknown who had attacked her, she could render me no assistance. I know not but my embarrassment might have betrayed me, but there arose in the assembly-room a great tumult; they all crowded towards the door, and surrounded a masque who was just entering; some pointed with their fingers, others broke out into long peals of laughter, and altogether cried out: *It is Monsieur the Marquis de B***, who has a bump on his forehead!* As soon as the two demons who were persecuting us had heard these joyous exclamations, they quitted us to swell the number of laughers. At length, behold the party! said my fair mistress to me, a little astonished: but, among these reiterated cries, do you not hear the name of the Marquis?—I'll wager that it is some new trick that they are playing my poor husband!

In the meanwhile, the rumour continued increasing; we approached, we heard a confusion of voices, who said, Good evening to you, Monsieur the Marquis de B***; what have you on your forehead, monsieur? How long have you had this bump? And presently, in the transports of their turbulent gaiety, all the masques cried, *It is the Marquis de B***, who has a bump on his forehead!* By dint of elbowing our

neighbours, we were enabled to join the masque
who was so much ridiculed: it was neither the
yellow domino of the Marquis, nor his short
stature, but it was, notwithstanding, the Marquis himself! We perceived that some one had
stuck between his shoulders a slip of paper, upon
which was written, in very legible characters,
these words, which he had already heard so often
repeated: *It is the Marquis de B***, who has
a bump on his forehead!* He instantly recognised us. I cannot comprehend what all this
means, said he to us, in a mortified tone; let us
go. Still pursued by the shouts of derision, and
pressed to suffocation in the crowd, he had as
much difficulty in regaining the door, as he had
in penetrating into the middle of the room.

We followed him closely. Zounds: cried the
Marquis, so confounded that he had not power
to take his seat in the carriage, I cannot comprehend all this; I never was so well disguised,
and yet every one recognised me. The Marchioness asked him what was his design. I was
desirous, replied he, of affording you an agreeable surprise; as soon as I saw you in the ball-
room, I returned home and imparted my project to Justine, your *femme de chambre*, and

to that of this charming girl, for I found them both together. I took a new domino, and shoes with very high heels, which elevated me a great deal, so that no one might recognise me. Justine presided at my toilette. (While he was speaking, the Marchioness adroitly removed the perfidious label from his back, and put it into her pocket.) Ask Justine: she will tell you that I was never so well disguised, for she told me so an hundred times, but nevertheless, all the world discovered me!

The Marchioness and myself easily guessed that our *femmes de chambre* had served us faithfully. But, replied the Marquis, after a moment's reflection, how could they see that I had a bump on my forehead? Have you spoken of my accident?—To no one, I assure you.—That is very singular; my face was covered with a masque, and they saw my bump! I was disguised better than usual, yet every one recognized me! The Marquis did not cease to testify his astonishment by exclamations such as these; while the Marchioness and I congratulated ourselves on the address of our women, who had saved us in so comic a manner from the disagreeable consequences to which we should have been exposed, by the disguise of her husband, and the vengeance of my rival.

What was our astonishment when, on arriving at the hotel of the Marquis, we found the Count de Rosambert had been waiting for us some minutes. He approached in an easy and familiar manner:—I was sure, ladies, that you would not remain long at the ball: this masqued ball is a very dull thing! those whom we do not know are tiresome to us, and those we do know torment us! Oh! replied the Marquis, I had not time to get tired, not I! You see how I am disguised!—Very well, indeed!—Well! as soon as I entered, everybody knew me.—How, everybody?—Yes, yes, everybody; they immediately surrounded me:—*Ah! good evening to you, monsieur, how came that bump on your forehead?* and they squeezed me! they pushed me! they laughed at me! made faces at me! and made such a noise, that I thought I should never have recovered my hearing. I'll be hung if ever I go there again! But how could they have known that I had this bump on my forehead!—Zounds! it might be seen for a league! said the Count.—But my masque!—That matters nothing! Look at me, I also was recognized.—

Good! replied the Marquis, a little consoled,—
Yes, continued the Count, my adventure is very
droll; I met there a very pretty lady, who esteemed me very much, last week!—I understand you, I understand you, said the Marquis.
—This week she has shifted me off in a very
curious manner!——

Imagine that I was at the ball with one of
my friends, who was very prettily disguised.—
The Marchioness, being alarmed, interrupted
him: Monsieur the Count sups with us this evening, without doubt? He answered in the most
polite and flattering manner: If it will not embarrass you too much, madam.—What! interrupted the Marquis, are you going to stand upon
ceremony with us? endeavour rather to make
your peace with your young relative, who requires it of you.—Me, sir, not at all! I have
always thought that the Count de Rosambert
was a man of honour, and I believe him too gallant a man to take advantage of circumstances.
—We must abuse nothing, said the Count to
me, but we must make use of everything.—
What are these circumstances? cried the Marquis. What means she by circumstances?
What circumstances are these? Rosambert, you

will tell me that: but go on with your story.—
Most willingly.—Gentlemen, again interrupted
the Marchioness, they have already told you
that supper was served.—Yes, yes, let us to go
to supper, replied the Marquis; you can relate
to us your misfortune while we are at table.
The Marchioness then approached her husband,
and in a low voice, said, Do you think it proper,
sir, that one should relate an affair of gallantry
before this child?—Well, well, replied he to
her, at her age they are not so ignorant; and
then addressing himself to the Count: Rosambert, you will go on with your adventure, but
you must gloss everything over in such a manner that this child——You understand me?

The Marchioness arranged us in such order
that the Count was placed between me and
her, so that I found myself between the Count
and the Marquis. My beautiful mistress gave
me a particular look, which warned me to pay
every attention to our critical situation; not to
speak without reflection, and to act with the
greatest circumspection.

The Marquis ate a great deal, and talked
still more; I replied but by monosyllables to the
kind things he said to me. The Count, en-

couraged by the eulogiums of the Marquis, began to lavish on me, in a tone of raillery, the
most fulsome and overstrained compliments;
asserting that no one in the world was more
amiable than his young relation, and demanded
of the Marchioness, what she thought of her; at
the same time protesting that she alone, up
to this moment, knew precisely how much
Mademoiselle du Portail merited to be beloved.
The Marchioness, equally adroit and prompt, replied quickly and with great aptitude, always
measuring the defence to the attack, she eluded
without affectation, or defended without asper-
ity: determined to manœuvre an enemy she
could not hope to vanquish, to pointed questions
she opposed equivocal answers; she parried
strong allegations by mitigated negations, and re-
butted sarcasms more bitter than embarrassing,
by recriminations more subtle than spiteful: extremely interested to penetrate the designs of
the Count, with whom vengeance was so easy,
she examined him often with a piercing eye;
then endeavouring to bend him by interesting
him, she overwhelmed him with politeness and
attention. Pretending to have a bad headache,
she uttered her sweet accents in a faint and

languishing manner, and by supplicating looks solicited his mercy, but could not obtain it.

As soon as the servants had placed the dessert on the table and retired, the Count commenced a still warmer attack, which threw both the Marchioness and myself into the most dreadful anxiety.

The COUNT. I was telling you, monsieur, that last week a young lady honoured me with a very particular attention.

THE MARCHIONESS. [Aside.] What a coxcomb! [Aloud.] Again in good fortune! It is your old subject.

The COUNT. No, madam, a sudden infidelity, with circumstances very novel, which will amuse you.

THE MARCHIONESS. Not at all, sir, I assure you.

The MARQUIS. Good! the women always say that the relation of an affair of gallantry tires them. Rosambert, tell us yours.

The COUNT. This lady was at the ball;— I forget the night. [To the Marchioness.] Madam, assist me, you were there also.

The MARCHIONESS. [In a lively manner.] The night, sir! of what consequence is the night? Besides, do you think that I noticed——

The Marquis. Go on, go on: the night signifies nothing.

The Count. Well, then, I went to the ball with one of my friends, who was disguised so admirably that no one knew him.

The Marquis. That no one knew him! He was very clever! What habit had he then?

The Marchioness. [With gaiety.] He went in character, most probably.

The Count. Dressed in character! no, but [looking at the Marchioness,] nevertheless, it shall be so, if you wish it; dressed in character! no one recognised him; no one, except the lady in question, who guessed that it was a very fine youth.

> [Here the Marchioness rung for a servant, whom she detained some time under different pretences; the Marquis became impatient, sent him away, and the Count resumed.]

The lady, charmed with her discovery—— but I will say no more, because the Marquis knows her.

The Marquis [laughing.] That may be: I know a great many; but that's no matter, go on.

The Marchioness. Monsieur, they gave us a new play last night.

The Count. Yes, madam, but permit me to finish my tale.

The Marchioness. No; I wish to know what you think of the piece.

The Count. Permit me, madam.

The Marquis. Yes, madam, let him then tell us.

The Count. To be short, you shall know that my young friend pleased the lady very much; that my presence became embarrassing to her; and the means which she devised to get rid of me——

The Marchioness. This adventure of yours is nothing but a romance.

The Count. A romance, madam! Ah, I can presently, if I am forced, convince the most incredulous. The means which she conceived was to detach me by a young Countess, her intimate friend, a very skilful and obliging woman, who took possession in such a manner as——

The Marquis. Ah! Did she play her part well, then?

The Count. Not amiss, not amiss; but not so well as the husband, who arrived——

The Marquis. Ah! a husband in the case! So much the better: I am fond of an adventure where a husband figures; at least, such as I know many of! Well, the husband arrived. What is the matter with you, madam?

The Marchioness. A most shocking headache! I am in torture. [To the Count.] Monsieur, have the goodness to defer the recital of this adventure until another day.

The Marquis. Oh no; go on, go on; it will cure her headache.

The Count. Yes, in two words; I have done.

Mademoiselle du Portail. [To the Marquis, in a very low voice.] M. de Rosambert is very fond of tattling, and tells falsehoods, sometimes, with a good grace.

The Marquis. I know it well, I know it well; but this story is droll: there is a husband in it; I'll wager that they entrap him like a fool.

The Count. [Without listening to the Marchioness, who wished to speak with him.] The husband arrived, and what is most astonishing, that on seeing the slender figure, agreeable person, and fresh complexion of this young man, who was so well disguised, he took him for a woman.

The MARQUIS. Good! Oh! that was excellent. I could not have been taken in like that,
not I; I am too well skilled in physiognomy.

MADEMOISELLE DU PORTAIL. But it is not
credible.

The MARCHIONESS. Impossible! M. de
Rosambert has been inventing tales for us;
which he had better finish, for I feel myself
very unwell.

The COUNT. He thought himself so happy,
that he lavished compliments, a variety of attentions, and even went so far as to take his
hand, and pressed it gently. [To the Marquis.]
For instance, much after the manner as you
do at present to my cousin.

The MARQUIS. [Astonished, immediately
quitted my hand, which, in truth, he had been
pressing.] He has done it on purpose, said he
to me; I think that he would the Marchioness
should perceive our understanding. He is jealous! He is mischievous! And a liar, replied
I; he lies like a counsellor.

    [The Count, always deaf to the entreaties
        which the Marchioness had had time to
        renew, resumed:]

Whilst the good husband, on the one side, exhausted all the commonplaces of antiquated gallantry, and fondly pressed the cherished hand—the lady, not less sensible, but more happy——

The MARCHIONESS. Oh, Monsieur! what sort of women have you then known; You represent this to us under such colours! Might she not have been deceived by appearances, as well as her husband?

The COUNT. That was possible; but I believe it was not the case. But of that you shall judge for yourself, if you hear me to the end.

The MARCHIONESS. If it is absolutely necessary that you should finish this story, I beg at least you will have some regard [looking towards Mademoiselle du Portail] for certain persons who listen to you.

The MARQUIS. Madam is right; gloss it over a little, on account of this child.

The COUNT. Yes, yes. The lady, much captivated——

The MARCHIONESS. Do, pray, sir, abridge the details, which are not—decent.

MADEMOISELLE DU PORTAIL. [In a very abrupt tone.] It is midnight, sir.

The COUNT. [Harshly.] I know it well,

Mademoiselle; and if the conversation tires you, I will say but one word—to finish it.

The Marquis. [To Mademoiselle du Portail.] He is much piqued against you. The kindness you show to me!—He is jealous as a tiger.

The Marchioness. Monsieur, *a propos*, while I think of it, have you obtained of the minister——

The Count. Yes, madam, I have obtained every thing I wished; but let me see—

The Marquis. Ah! ah! what is it, then, that you solicited?

The Count. A little pension of ten thousand livres for the young Viscomte de G***, my kinsman; it is now some days past—but to return to my adventure.

The Marquis. Yes, yes, let us return to it.

The Marchioness. I suppose the Viscount must be very well pleased with you?

The Count. The lady was very much affected——

The Marchioness. Monsieur, why do you not answer my question.

The Count. Yes, madam, he is very well pleased—the lady was very much affected——

The Marchioness. And his dear uncle, the commander?

The Count. He is very well pleased also, madam; but you interest yourself very much.

The Marchioness. Yes, everything which regards my friends touches me sensibly, and this affair torments me on your account; if you had spoken to me of it sooner I could have served you.

The Count. Madam, I am very sensible— but permit me—

The Marchioness. Has the Viscount, in point of fact, rendered any service to the state?

The Count. [Laughing.] Yes, madam, without him, the Duke de B*** would not have had an heir; the family would have been extinct.

The Marchioness. But if they recompense so munificently all those who serve the state in this manner, I am no longer astonished at the embarrassment of the royal treasury.

The Count. Very true, madam; but nevertheless permit me—

The Marchioness. Well, it's no matter; if ever the like occasion should occur, employ me, or we shall quarrel seriously.

The Count. Madam, I return you thanks: permit me at last to finish the recital of my adventure.

The Marchioness. Oh! if you apply to any one else, I shall not pardon you, I assure you.

The Marquis. Come enough of that; let him finish his story.

The Count. The lady, quite enraptured, lavished on the young Adonis—

The Marchioness. Oh! what a headache I have!

The Count. Lavished on the young Adonis—

The Marchioness. [Taking the Marquis aside, and speaking to him in a low voice.] Monsieur, I repeat it, it is not decent to relate before this child.

The Marquis. Never mind; she knows more than you are aware of; the little wag is crafty! I'm skilful in physiognomy.

The Count. I shall never be able to finish my narrative, they interrupt me so at every moment; I am going home, to-morrow morning I will send you the details in writing.

The Marchioness. A good joke, certainly.

The Count. [To the Marquis.] No, I'll send it you, upon my honour; and I will put the initial letters to each name—at least, unless they'll let me finish it this evening.

The Marquis. Well, go on, then, finish it.

The Marchioness. Well, make haste, then, and finish it; but reflect—

The Count. The lady, quite enraptured, lavished on the young Adonis the most delicate and flattering confidence, the kindest offers, and the most tender embraces; in fact, one ought to behold so delightful a scene to form a proper idea of it: it cannot be described, but one might act it—here, let us perform it.

The Marquis. You are in jest.

The Marchioness. What folly.

Mademoiselle du Portail. What an idea!

The Count. Let us act it; Madame shall be the lady in question; I will be the poor discarded lover. Ah! but we shall want a Countess!—[To the Marchioness.]—But Madame is very clever, she can easily fill two characters at the same time.

The Marchioness. [Endeavouring to restrain her anger.] Monsieur!—

The Count. I beg your pardon, madam; it is only a supposition.

The Marquis. Certainly; you cannot be angry at that.

The Marchioness. [In a faint voice, and with tears in her eyes.] The question is not about the parts you offer me, but it is very cruel, when I have been complaining, for this hour past, of being very ill, that you do not deign to pay me the least attention. [To the Count, in agitation.] Could one, sir, without offence, observe to you that it is late, and I have need of repose!

The Count. [A little affected.] I am grieved to importune you so, madam.

The Marchioness. You do not intrude upon me, sir; but I repeat it to you, that I am ill—very ill.

The Marquis. Well! but what are we to do now? Where does Mademoiselle du Portail sleep?

The Marchioness. [In a lively manner.] Indeed, sir, it would seem as if we had but one apartment in the house.

Alarmed at the turn which the conversation was likely to take, I approached the Count. Charming girl, said he to me, in a very low voice, leave it to me; nothing you can say to me will have any effect, because I am curious to know the whole, and shall have it presently.

The MARQUIS. There are apartments, madam; but will not this child be afraid to be alone?

The COUNT. [With great vivacity.] No more so than the last time.

The MARQUIS. [Abruptly, and pointing towards the Marchioness.] But the last time she slept with Madame.

The COUNT. Ah!

The MARCHIONESS. [With much embarrassment, and stammering.] She slept in my chamber—and I——

The MARQUIS. She slept in your own bed with you; I know it well, because I closed the curtains myself; do you not remember it?

> [The Marchioness, confounded, made no
> reply; the Marquis continued, affecting
> to speak low.

Do you not remember my coming in the night?

> [The Marchioness held her hand to her
> forehead, cried out, and fainted.]

I could not discover if the fainting was very natural, but I know that as soon as the Marquis had quitted us, to fetch some waters, which he

said were a sovereign remedy in such cases, the
Marchioness recovered her senses, cheered up
immediately, and addressing herself to the
Count: Monsieur, said she to him, have you
then sworn to ruin me? No, madam, I wished
to inform myself of certain matters that I was
ignorant of, to prove to you that I am not to be
tricked with impunity, and to make you acknowledge that I am capable of avenging myself.—Of avenging yourself? cried she, and for
what?—I know, nevertheless, continued he, how
to govern my resentment, and do not carry my
vengeance too far. Now, madam, you may be
tranquil, but upon one condition. I feel, added
he, looking at us in a malignant manner, that I
have afflicted you both; you promised yourselves a happy night—happy as the night before
the last; but you, sir—you have had too little
skill to interest me in the success of your gallant
projects; and you, madam, expect, without
doubt, that as a complaisant minister to your
pleasures, I——Me, sir! cried she, I expect
nothing from you; but I believe, also, that I
have nothing to fear: and whatever has been my
conduct, from whence do you derive, I should
like you to know, the right you claim to investi-

gate it?—Rosambert only replied to this question by a sarcastic smile: As a complaisant
minister to your pleasures, I can see as a husband.—Dare you to use that epithet?—I can
see M. de Faublas clasped in your arms, even
in my presence.—M. de Faublas in my arms!
—Or Mademoiselle du Portail in your bed, is it
not the same thing! Ah! but, madam, I believe we are agreed upon that score. The time
is precious, let us not lose it in disputing any
longer about words: let us be composed. Let
this charming girl give me the honour of accompanying her, that I may conduct her presently to her father: on this condition I hold my
tongue.

The Marquis entered, with a bottle in his
hand. I am very sensible of your care, said the
Marchioness to him, but you see that I am
better; I wish I was quite well, that I might
keep Mademoiselle du Portail.—What! cried
the Marquis.—I am always incommoded. It
is impossible for this dear child to pass the
night with me.—Hey dey! madam, is there not,
as you said just now, more than one chamber in
the house?—Yes, sir, but you have made an
objection to which I agree—this child would be

afraid.   Besides, to leave her all alone! I
could not suffer it.—She shall not be alone,
madam; her *femme de chambre* is here.—Her
femme de chambre!—her *femme de chambre!*
Well, sir, since we must tell you everything,
M. du Portail does not wish that his daughter
should sleep here to-night.—Who told you so,
madam?—Monsieur the Count has just announced to me that M. du Portail begged him
to come here, and bring home his daughter.
Wherefore did you not tell us that before? But,
replied Rosambert, laughing, it was because I
would not interfere with your mirth during
supper.—M. du Portail send for his daughter!
replied the Marquis. Does he think she is not
safe here? And why, moreover, did he charge
you with such a commission? He owes us a
visit of acknowledgment; when he comes himself!—I shall see him. I would know his
reasons—I shall see him.

I made a profound reverence to the Marchioness; she rose, and came to embrace me. M.
de Rosambert threw himself between us: madam, you are fatigued; do not disturb yourself;
and taking her gently by the hand, he forced her
to sit down; after which he took me by the arm,

with an air of gallantry, and the Marquis saw, with a lively regret, Mademoiselle du Portail and Madame Dutour go away in the carriage of the Count.

At the turning of the first street, M. de Rosambert ordered his coachman to stop. I know that face, said he, on looking at my pretended *femme de chambre;* I do not think the service of this good woman will be required at the house of the Baron de Faublas, therefore we will dispense with her accompanying us so far. La Dutour got out without saying a single word, and we continued our route. I remarked to the Count that we were now at liberty; that he had taken too much advantage of the awkward circumstances in which I was placed, and that he could not excuse himself from giving me immediate satisfaction.—I see no one this evening but Mademoiselle du Portail, replied he to me; to-morrow, if the Chevalier de Faublas has anything to say to me, he will find me at home. We will breakfast together, and I will tell my friend what I think of his conduct; and if he is reasonable, I hope to convince him, without much trouble, that he ought to be satisfied with mine.

In the meanwhile we arrived at the door of my father's mansion; it was the Abbé Person himself who opened it to me; he informed me that the Baron had expected my return with more anxiety than anger, and that despairing at last to see me this evening, he retired to bed, after having told Jasmin about twenty times, to go as soon as it was light, and seek me at the ball, or at the house of the Marquis de B***.

I went to my chamber, where, calling to mind the various events of this bustling day, I was astonished at being able to pass it without once thinking of my Sophia; and to make amends for this long forgetfulness, I repeated to myself, a hundred times, her much loved name.

I confess also, that that of the Marchioness came sometimes upon my lips; I acknowledge that, at first, it seemed hard to be reduced to vent such useless sighs in my solitary bed; but I determined to offer to my adored Sophia the sacrifice of my pleasures, involuntary, or at least unsought for, as they had been, and went to sleep almost reconciled with the celibacy to which the Count's vengeance had condemned me.

As soon as it was morning I made my respects to the Baron. He said to me, in a very mild manner, Faublas, you are no longer a child; I shall give you a reasonable liberty; I hope that you will not abuse it, and I trust you will never pass your night otherwise than in this house; remember that I am your father, and that if my son loves me, he will be careful not to displease me.

I hastened to the house of M. de Rosambert, who was already waiting for me. The moment he saw me, he came to me laughing, and without giving me time to say a single word, he threw his arm round my neck: let me embrace you, my dear Faublas! Your adventure was delightful! the more I think of it, the more it amuses me.—I interrupted him bluntly. I am not come to receive your compliments.—The Count begged me, in a serious tone, to sit down: You may, said he, wish them to me again. I see you in the same disposition. Come on, then, my young friend, you are mad. What! an ungrateful beauty favours you, and discards me; it is I who am sacrificed; it is to you that I am immolated; and yet you are angry about it. I punished but by a momentary uneasiness the deceitful gallantry of the skillful couple who play

upon me; and it is by the blood of his friend
that M. de Faublas pretends to avenge the petty
tribulations of Mademoiselle du Portail: I swear
to you, it shall not be. My dear de Faublas,
I have over you the advantage of six years' experience; I know very well that at sixteen we
know but one's mistress and one's sword; but at
twenty-two a man of the world fights no more
for a woman.

I evinced some symptoms of astonishment,
which he observed. Do you believe there is
such a thing as true love? added he, immediately; it is one of the illusions of youth, and I
warn you against it. For my part, I have seen
throughout nothing but gallantry. What else
is there in your adventure? Great success, and
nothing more; and out of a comic tale we should
make a tragedy! We should cut each other's
throats for a fine lady, who quits me to day, and
tomorrow will discard you. Chevalier, keep
your courage for a more important occasion;
you cannot hereafter suspect mine. It is too
true that the fatal concourse of circumstances
compels us sometimes to shed the blood of a
friend; may honour, inflexible honour, never
reduce you to this horrible extremity! My

dear Faublas, I was about your age when the
Marchioness de Rosambert, whose son I am,
completed her thirty-fifth year; she was still as
comely as if she had been only twenty-five;
and when among strangers, she was taken
for my eldest sister. With all the agreeable-
ness of youth, she had preserved its propensities; she loved crowded assemblies and the
bustle of public places. One night, when I had
conducted her to the ball of the opera, she was
publicly insulted. I heard the cries of the
Marchioness, and ran to her assistance; she was
about to take off her masque; already the insolent unknown had apologized for his mistake,
and mingled with the crowd. I followed him,
and obliged him to unmasque; I recognised in
him the young Saint Clair,—Saint Clair, the
companion of my youth! and of all friends the
most dear, "I knew not that it was the Marchioness de Rosambert!" This was all he said
to me: it was enough, no doubt. But, alas! a
general murmur gave us to understand that it
was not sufficient: honour would have blood; we
fought—Saint Clair fell—I sunk insensible
near my dying friend. For more than six weeks
a dreadful fever raged in my veins, and disor-

dered my reason. In my frightful delirium, I saw nothing but Saint Clair; his wound bleeding before my eyes; the convulsions of death agitated his trembling limbs; yet he, nevertheless, regarded me with a tender look, and, in a faint voice, he bade me a most affectionate farewell. In his last moments he seemed sensible of no other grief than what he felt at quitting the barbarian who sacrificed him. This frightful phantom of the imagination pursued me for a long time; for a long time my life was despaired of; at length, nature, seconded by the efforts of art, brought about my cure; but I recovered my reason, without losing my remorse. Time, which reconciles everything, dried up my tears; but never, never, will the remembrance of that frightful combat be effaced from my mind. Chevalier, it is always with regret that I am obliged to fight, even with a stranger; judge, then, if I would go rashly to oppose my life in order to threaten yours. Ah! if ever inflexible honour compels us to it, my dear Faublas, I swear to you that your victory will neither be difficult nor glorious; I have too often experienced that in such cases, he who dies is not the most unhappy.

Rosambert stretched his arms toward me; I embraced him with all my heart, and his seriousness was soon dissipated. Let us breakfast, said he to me; and resuming his former gaiety: You came to pick a quarrel with me, you ungrateful rogue, at the very time that you owe me a thousand thanks.—I owe you?—Without doubt: was it not I who introduced you to the Marchioness? It is true I did not foresee the mischievous trick that was to be played upon me: I had calculated upon an infidelity, but never guessed that it was to happen so speedily, and under such singular circumstances! (He burst into a fit of laughter.) Oh! but the more I think on it, the more I ought to congratulate you. Your adventure was most delightful! How charming it is to be introduced to the world through such a beautiful door! The Marchioness is young, handsome, witty, of consideration in the city, well received at court, and intriguing as the devil: her interest and her influence are very extensive, and she is zealous in serving her friends.—I assured the Count that I should never employ such means in seeking my fortune.—Then you are wrong, replied he; how many persons of real merit are, notwithstanding, advanced by such means alone! But let us drop this subject: do you not give me any details of this joyous night? You must have been completely happy; you must have been bathed in extacy, and lapped in Paradise!

I complied with his request. Ah! the crafty Marchioness! exclaimed the Count, after having heard me. Ah! the subtle dame! how admirably she manœuvred for her own pleasure! And her honest spouse, the dear Marquis, the most kind, credulous, and complaisant, of all the accommodating husbands with which France abounds. Indeed, it makes me believe that certain men have been created to serve for the amusement of their friends. But his wife! his wife!—Is very amiable.—I know it well; I knew it even before you; and we should have killed each other on her account. Ah! I agree, Rosambert, that we should have done wrong—very wrong; and then such a freak would have been a very dangerous example.—How?—Listen, Faublas: in the small circle of each of the societies which compose what is called the fashionable world, there are a number of intrigues which interfere, and a variety of interests which jar, the one with the other: such as the husband of this lady, who is the lover of that: one is discarded that another may be embraced to-day, and the last, perhaps, will be sacrificed to-morrow.

The men are enterprising, and they attack unceasingly; the women are weak, and they always yield. It results from this, that celibacy is a very agreeable state, and that the yoke of matrimony appears less insupportable; the young are amused, subjects are produced for the state, and all the world are satisfied. Now if jealousy was at this day to spread among us its deadly poison; if the husbands whose heads we embellish were to arm themselves to repair the honour of their frail ribs; if the lovers they discard killed each other in disputing about an inconstant heart, you would see a general desolation; the city and the court would become a vast field of slaughter. How many wives, who are considered virtuous, would presently become widows! how many fine children, reputed legitimate, would have to mourn the loss of their fathers! how many charming bastards would then be left destitute! the present generation would pass away after having produced, but without having brought up its offspring!—What a picture you draw, Rosambert; you paint gallantry, but love, tender and respectful love!—Exists no more; it was tiresome to the women; the women have destroyed it.—You estimate the women but lightly, then?—True; I love them as they wish to be loved.—Ah! replied I, with the greatest vivacity, I pardon your blasphemies, you know not my Sophia! He demanded an explanation of these last words; but I refused him with that discretion which, particularly in the beginning, accompanies a sincere affection.

In the meantime we took a breakfast substantial enough for a dinner; the champagne was not spared, and we know that Bacchus is the father of gaiety. It appeared to me that the Count valued the women very little, loved them very much, and was fond of talking about them. Full of the system which he had detailed, he supported it by a recital of scandalous anecdotes concerning the gallantry of the day. Rosambert embarrassed me without persuading me; to every example which he gave me, I uniformly replied that an exception, far from destroying the rule, served but to prove it. But you know not, said he, with some warmth, you do not know to what a pitch the greater part of

this sex, so much honoured, carry every day,
their forgetfulness of that natural timidity, that
innate modesty, which you suppose them to possess. He rose with great vivacity, and laughing
with all his might. Zounds! I'll convince you.
You have not engaged yourself to-day? Come
with me, come; I will in a moment present you
to a fine lady; we shall find her among several
others: they are all pretty; you shall have an
opportunity of estimating the whole of them, or
as many as you like.

We were both elevated with wine; we took a
decent hackney chariot, and were driven to a
house of respectable apearance; the air of free-
dom, however, which was remarkable in the
mistress of it, the familiarity with which the
Count treated her, and the no less familiar welcome with which she honoured me, made me suspect that I was to be introduced to a party of
Cyprians. I was presently convinced of it,
when the good lady, to whom the Count appeared very well known, and who wished, as she
said politely, to initiate me, had shewn me all
the curiosities of her house.

Rosambert took the pains to explain everything to me himself; behold there, said he, the

bath, where they scour and perfume the sturdy and athletic recruits, which both the city and the country daily furnish to this active procuress. In this closet, you see several flasks of a very astringent liquor, the great merit of which is to repair every species of breach made in what virgins call their virtue. Thousands of young ladies, of the first respectability, use it with discretion, and have the satisfaction, on their wedding night, to offer to the happy mortal who marries them a new virginity. On another side is " L'Essence a l'usage des Monstres," which produces effects entirely opposite to the other; and, therefore, it is never wanted! Alas! the age of miniatures is gone! and I would wager that, in all Paris, you would not find a single little woman who stood in need of this remedy: on the contrary, if that which you see in those very large bottles possessed the virtues they pretend, it would have a prodigious consumption; you would see the Doctor Guibert de Preval beset with a crowd of lawyer's clerks, some lawyers, numerous great lords, many of the military, and almost all the Abbés; it is the " Infallible Specific."

You know, Faublas, what the closet of a dressing-room is; this has nothing remarkable, let us go further. This is the ball-room; but they do not dance here, they only disguise. Look at this door, you would take it for a closet; it is only a passage of communication; it comes from a house, the entrance of which is in another street. If a lady of quality has certain delicate and secret wants, which she is anxious to satisfy, she enters by that door, disguised as a waiting-woman, exposes her charms for attraction, and receives the vigorous embraces of some robust countryman, dressed up, perhaps, like a bishop; or of a fat bishop, so naturally metamorphosed, that one would take him for a rustic. Thus they render each other a mutual service! and, as they are entirely unknown, they are under no obligation.

Presently we will enter the infirmary—but let not the name alarm you. Open, if you like, these licentious pamphlets; examine the obscene prints; they were placed here to warm the imagination of those old debauchees whom Death has already struck in the most sensible part; and it is here, likewise, that, with little *fasces* of perfumed broom, they endeavour to " rouse the Venus loitering in their veins."

You think, perhaps, that a like method would be too violent for the fair sex, but some of them resort to it, and others avail themselves of these pastiles, which are so stimulating that no sooner has a woman eaten one, than she is infected with what they call *la rage d'amour*. These are, however, seldom employed except against some pretty country girl, who is cold by temperament, and resolutely virtuous. Our ladies of fashion and education never evince sufficient resistance to require our attacking them with such manœuvres.

Come here, look at this; among the curious plants in the king's garden, have you never observed this? It is what many poor girls call their comforter; you cannot conceive how many devotees Madame has furnished with it.

This last apartment is called the hall of Vulcan: there is nothing remarkable in it but that infernal arm-chair. The wretched fair one who sits down on it, finds herself immediately thrown on her back; her arms are spread open; and in fact she is fixed, by means of springs, in such a position, as to be violated without her being capable of making the least resistance. You shudder, Faublas! and for this time you have reason. I am young, ardent, and a libertine not over scrupulous; but, indeed, I think I could never resolve to rifle a poor girl, by force, in this machine.

The Count added: If we had come sooner, they would have furnished us with two young lasses from the city; but, for want of better, let us see the seraglio. It was thus he called the saloon, wherein we found a great many nymphs assembled, who all passed before us as candidates for the honour of the handkerchief. Rosambert chose the prettiest, and I had the singular whim to select the most ugly amongst them.

While we are waiting, said the Count, for the dinner which I have ordered, we can each of us have a dish of chat with our girls; at table, we will form a party for general conversation. Naturally curious, I thought I would examine minutely the nymph I had chosen; it appeared to me important to ascertain whether there was any difference between a handsome Marchioness and an ugly courtezan. The investigation amused me at first, merely by the objects of comparison which she offered me; I was insensibly inflamed, and began mechanically to think of pushing the examination as far as it could go. The nymph, perceiving how I was disposed, left me no time for reflection, but invited me to the attack, and prepared herself vigorously to sustain it; but all at once, without my having had occasion to explain to her my pacific intentions, the experienced heroine perceived that there would not have been between us even the slightest skirmish, she rose up with great *sang froid,* and looking at me earnestly: So much the better, said she, " it would have been a pity!" —It is impossible to conceive how I was struck by the idea, so forcibly conveyed in these words —" It would have been a pity!" I enquired not what had become of Rosambert, but fled from this infamous house, swearing never to enter it again.

The Count called on me the next morning by ten o'clock: he came to know what panic terror had seized me, and assured me, that my adventure was spread throughout the house, and had afforded them very great diversion.—What! Rosambert, that girl said to me, " It would have been a pity!" And you call my alarm a panic of terror!—Oh, that is different! The girl has a little misrepresented the adventure: she took care not to tell us, that " it would have been a pity!" which changes her story entirely. Well! Faublas, do you esteem this woman for having coldly suffered you to escape a danger into which she had invited you to run?—You ask me a very droll question, Rosambert; what deduction could you draw from my answer against her sex in general?—You quibble, my friend; you are incorrigible. Well! esteem them—esteem them, since you are resolved to do it: as for me, I must go to bed.—How! go to bed?—From whence come you then? From where would you have me come? In this world we must amuse ourselves with every thing. I met with the Commander de G***, the little Chevalier de M**, and the Abbé de R**; we spent all the evening, and all the night, in revelry—in Bacchanalian orgies! Oh! it was delightful!— but I must go to bed.

I was scarcely dressed, when my father came up to me, and informed me, that M. du Portail expected me to dinner. You will pass the whole evening together, added he, and as I shall sup in that quarter, I will call and bring you home.

I hastened to get out, as I longed to see my pretty cousin. She came to the conversation room with my sister. You are lucky, said Adelaide to me in a very lively manner, to go to balls, to pass whole nights at them, and to get acquainted with a very fine lady!—And who has told you all that?—The Abbé, who keeps no secret from us. Sophia held down her eyes and was silent; but my sister continued: Tell us, then, who this lady is; and a masqued ball! that must be very grand!—Very tiresome, I assure you; and as to the lady, she is pretty, certainly; but much less so than—oh! much less so than my charming cousin. Sophia, still silent, still looking on the ground, appeared to be entirely occupied with some trinket on the string of her watch; but the deep crimson blush with which her countenance was suffused, betrayed her. I perceived that our conversation touched her in proportion as she affected to be least interested in it. Something vexes you, my pretty cousin?—Why do you not reply, Mademoiselle? said the old Governante.—No, sir; but it is that——I did not sleep well last night.—Yes, said the old woman, that is true; she has not slept for these three or four nights past; it is a very bad habit, very bad, and will soon kill you. I knew a young lady—Mademoiselle Storch—you did not know her, you are too young; it is five-and-forty years since it happened—Mademoiselle Storch—

The old woman had thus commenced her story, and if I did not wish to be deprived of the happiness of seeing my pretty cousin, I must of course listen to her long narration. Sophia spared me this mortification, by giving a still greater. She rose; the Governante demanded, with some warmth, what was the matter with her; she replied that she was very unwell; her voice faltered. This is the way you always serve me, replied the old woman; one never has time to speak to a person. Monsieur the Chevalier, come to-morrow, you will find it interesting, and that there is good reason for saying young people ought to sleep.—Permit me, brother, to follow my dear friend.—Yes, my dear Adelaide, yes; take good care of her.—At length, Sophia lifted her eyes to salute me; and gave me a look so full of anguish, that it penetrated to my heart, and awakened my remorse.

It was time for me to visit M. du Portail. After having repeated my thanks to him, I related all my adventures, not forgetting the breakfast with Rosambert; but did not tell him where our gaiety conducted us afterwards. I am glad, said he, that M. de Rosambert, who, from the details you have given me, appears to be a fop, in every sense of the word, has, at least, just ideas regarding real honour. Keep in mind, my young friend, that of all the laws of your country, that which forbids duels is the most respectable. In this age of literature and philosophy, the ferocity of mankind is greatly softened down. How many lives have been spared to the nation, and how many families have been saved from the most poignant distress, by the happy revolution which has taken place on this subject in the minds of men! As to the women, it appears, indeed, that the Count does not esteem them; if it is only through the example of so many young men, like himself, who affect for them the most profound contempt, which, in reality, they have not, I pity him; but I pity him still more, if he has only known such women as were unworthy of esteem.

Faublas, trust to my experience, which is much greater than that of the Count, who thinks, at the age of twenty-two, that he has seen a great deal. Rely on my judgment, which is deeper, and my observation, which has been more extensive. If we do meet in the world some women without shame, we meet with more young men without principle. Be cautious of listening to the stale declamation of these fops. There are women existing, whose modest graces can inspire the most pure and tender love, whose susceptible hearts are formed for tenderness, who command our homage by the amiableness of their manners, and our respect by the mildness of their virtues. We meet, less rarely than they have told you, with affectionate and disinterested females, with prudent wives, and excellent mothers of families. There are some who would shed their blood for their husbands and their children. I have known some who united to the mildest virtues of their sex the most masculine virtues of our own; who have given to men worthy of them, examples of generous devotion, of heroic courage, and of patience, which was proof against everything.

Your Marchioness is not a heroine, added he with a smile, she is very young, and very imprudent. My friend, endeavour to be more reasonable than her, and put an end to this dangerous connection; for, however credulous the husband may be, some unforeseen event must necessarily bring everything to light; promise me never to visit Madame de B*** any more.

I hesitated: M. du Portail pressed me; but, while making his eulogium on woman, he had recalled the charming Sophia to my mind. I at length promised that it should be as he wished. Now, said he, I have some important secrets to reveal to you; when you shall have heard me, you will feel that you must repay the great confidence I place in you by an inviolable secrecy.

My history affords a frightful example of the vicissitudes of fortune. It is generally very convenient, but sometimes very dangerous, to have an ancient name to sustain, and great wealth to preserve. The only heir of an illustrious family, the origin of which it is now impossible to trace, I ought to be occupying the principal offices of the state in the country which produced me, instead of being condemned to languish in a foreign nation, and in idle obscurity. The name of Lovinski is honourably inscribed in the annals of Poland, and that name is about to perish with me! I know that an austere philosophy rejects vain titles and corrupting riches; perhaps I could console me if I had lost nothing else; but my young friend, I mourn a wife whom I adored, I seek a daughter whom I dearly love, and I shall never behold my native country again! what fortitude can be hardened against misfortunes like these?

My father, Lovinski, still more distinguished by his virtues than his rank, enjoyed at court that consideration which always follows the favour of the Prince, and which personal merit sometimes obtains. He gave to the education of my two sisters the attention of a most tender father; he occupied himself, above all, concerning mine, with the zeal of an old gentleman jealous of the honour of his house, of which I was the only hope, and with the activity of a good citizen, who desired nothing more than to leave to the state a successor worthy of himself.

I pursued my studies at Varsovia; whilst there the young M. de P*** distinguished himself amongst us by the most amiable qualities; to a very agreeable person he joined a highly cultivated understanding; he possessed an address rarely to be met with among our young warriors; and his modesty was such that he seemed uniformly desirous of concealing his own merit, and of exalting the humbler talents of his rivals, who were almost always vanquished; the urbanity of his manners, and the gentleness of his character, attracted attention, commanded esteem, and rendered him dear to the brilliant assemblage of youth who partook of our labours and our pleasures. To say that it was the resemblance of characters and sympathy of minds which began my connection with M. de P***, would be arrogating too much to myself; let it be as it will, we became presently the most inseparable friends. How happy, but how quickly fled, is that age, when we are ignorant either of the ambition which sacrifices everything to the ideas of fortune and of glory which possesses it, or of love, whose power supreme, absorbs and concentrates all our faculties upon a single object! that age of innocent pleasure, and implicit confidence, when the heart, still inexperienced, pursues freely the growing impulses of sensibility, and devotes itself, without reserve, to the object of its disinterested affections! Then, my dear Faublas, then, friendship is not a vain and empty name. Being the confidant of all the secrets of M. de

P***, I undertook nothing of which I did not previously inform him; his counsels regulated my conduct, mine determined his resolutions; and by this agreeable reciprocity our youth had no pleasures which were not participated, no pains which were not alleviated.

With what grief I saw the fatal moment arrive when M. de P***, obliged, by his father's orders, to leave Varsovia, bade me the most tender farewell. We promised each other that we would preserve throughout life the same lively attachment, which had been the happiness of our youth; I swore rashly, that the passions of another age should not alter it.

Oh! what a void the absence of my friend left in my heart! At first, it seemed as if nothing could recompense me for the loss of him; the tenderness of a father, the caresses of my sisters, affected me but slightly. I thought that there remained no other means of dispelling my ennui, than by occupying my leisure with some useful labour. I learned the French language, which was already spread throughout Europe. I read with delight some famous works, eternal monuments of genius, and wondered how, in an idiom so unfavourable for poetry, so many great poets

had been able to distinguish themselves, and so
many great writers had, with justice, obtained
immortality. I applied myself seriously to the
study of geometry; I adopted, moreover, that
noble trade which makes a hero at the expense of
a hundred thousand victims, and which men,
less humane than valiant, have called the grand
art of war.

Several years were employed in these studies,
as difficult as profound. At last, they occupied
my whole mind. M. de P***, who wrote to
me often, but rarely received answers, and those
were short: our correspondence languished in
this manner until love put an end to it, by making me forget friendship.

My father had been for a long time very
closely connected with the Count Pulauski. Remarkable for his rigid morals, and the inflexi-
bility of his truly republican virtues: Pulauski,
at once a great captain and brave soldier, had
signalized, in more than one engagement, his
heroic courage, and his ardent patriotism. Ad-
dicted to reading the ancients, he had derived
from their history lessons of noble disinterested-
ness, of unchangeable constancy, and absolute
devotion. Like the heroes, to whom idolatrous

Rome, out of gratitude, erected altars, Pulauski
had sacrificed all his wealth to the prosperity
of his country; he had shed his blood in her defence; he had even immolated his only daughter,
his dear Lodoiska.

Lodoiska! oh, how beautiful she was! Oh,
how I loved her! Her cherished name is always
on my lips; her adored image is still fresh upon
my heart. From the moment I had seen her, I
saw no one but her; I abandoned my studies,
entirely forgot my friendship, and consecrated
all my time to Lodoiska. My father and hers
could not be long ignorant of our amour: they
never spoke to me of it.—Did they not then approve it?—This idea appeared to me so well
founded, that I gave myself up, without solicitude, to the pleasing fascination of hope and
love. I concerted measures, in order to see
Lodoiska almost every day, either at her own
house or that of my sisters, by whom she was
loved very much. In this delightful occupation,
two years passed away.

At length, Pulauski took me aside one day,
and said to me: Thy father and I have formed
great hopes regarding thee, which thy conduct
hitherto justifies; I have observed thee, for a

long time, employing thy youth in labours as honourable as useful. To-day—(he saw I was about to interrupt him, and he prevented me)— What art thou going to say to me? Dost thou think to inform me of anything I do not know? Thinkest thou that it was necessary for me to be every day witness of thy transports, to convince me how much my Lodoiska deserves to be beloved? It is because I know, as well as thou dost, the worth of my child, that thou wilt not obtain her but by meriting her.

Young man, know that weaknesses, being legitimate, is not a sufficient excuse for them; that a good citizen ought to turn everything to the advantage of his country; that love, even love, will be like all the vile passions, but despicable and dangerous if it does not present to generous hearts a more powerful stimulus to tread in the paths of honour.

Now attend to me: Our monarch is drawing towards his end; his health, each day more tottering, has awakened the ambition of our neighbours; they are preparing, without doubt, to sow divisions amongst us; they calculate, by biasing our votes, to give us a king of their choice. Foreign troops have dared to show themselves on the frontiers of Poland: already, two thousand gentlemen have assembled to check their audacious insolence; go and join these brave youths; go, and above all, at the end of the campaign, come back covered with the blood of our enemies, and present to Pulauski a kinsman worthy of himself.

I did not hesitate a moment; my father approved my resolutions, but it was with regret he consented to my precipitate departure. He held me for a long time clasped to his breast; his countenance was marked by the most anxious solicitude; he bade me farewell in the most painful manner; his looks evinced the anguish of his heart, and our tears mingled on his venerable face.

Pulauski, who was present at this affecting scene, reproached us stoically with what he called a weakness. Dry thy tears, said he to me, or keep them for Lodoiska; it belongs but to weak lovers to shed them at parting for only six months. He even informed his daughter, in my presence, of my departure, and the motives which determined it. Lodoiska turned pale, sighed, looked at her father with a blush, and assured me in a trembling voice, that her prayers would hasten my return, and that her happiness was in my hands. Encouraged in this manner, what dangers could I fear? I set out; but in the course of this campaign, nothing passed deserving of notice. The enemy, as careful as ourselves in avoiding an action, which might plunge the two nations into open war, contented themselves with fatiguing us by frequent marches. We confined ourselves to following and observing them; they did the same by us, whenever the country was sufficiently open to afford them easy access. At the approach of bad weather, they prepared themselves to retire homeward for winter quarters; and our little army, composed almost entirely of gentlemen, separated.

I returned to Warsaw, full of joy and impatience. I thought that Love and Hymen were about to present me with Lodoiska. Alas! I had no longer a father! I learnt, on entering the capital, that the night before my father died of an apoplexy. Thus I had not even the melancholy satisfaction of receiving the last sighs of the tenderst of fathers; I could only recline upon his tomb, which I watered with my tears.

It is not, said Pulauski, very little touched by

my grief, it is not by useless tears that they
honour the memory of a father like thine.
Poland regrets in him an heroic citizen, who
would have been of important service in the
critical circumstances to which I am about to
draw your attention. Exhausted by a long illness, our monarch has not many days to live,
and on the choice of his successor depends the
happiness or the misery of our citizens. Of
all the rights which the death of your father
transmits to you, the most valuable, without
doubt, is that of assisting at the states, where
you will go as a representative; it is there that
your father should revive in you; it is there that
you must prove a courage much more difficult
than that of braving death in the field of battle.
The valour of a soldier is but a common virtue;
but those are not ordinary men who preserve a
tranquil firmness on the most trying occasions;
and by displaying a penetrating activity, discover the projects of the powerful who cabal,
frustrate secret intrigues, and set at defiance the
most daring factions; who, always firm, incor-
ruptible and just, never give their votes but to
those they deem the most worthy of them; who
study nothing so much as the welfare of their

country; whom neither gold nor promises can seduce, entreaties bend, or menaces intimidate. Those are the virtues which distinguished thy father; this is the truly precious inheritance which you should eagerly possess. The day when our states assemble for the election of a king, is an epoch when several of our fellow-citizens, more occupied with their personal interests, than jealous for the safety of their country; and the insidious designs of powerful neighbours, whose wicked policy destroys our strength, by dividing us, manifest their pretensions. If I do not deceive myself, the fatal moment approaches, which will fix forever the destinies of my tottering country; her enemies conspire her ruin; they have planned, in secret, a revolution, which they shall never carry into execution whilst my arm can lift a sword. May God, the protector of my country, spare it from evil war! But that extremity, however dreadful, may, perhaps, be necessary. I flatter myself, however, there will be but one violent crisis; after which, this state, being regenerated, will resume its ancient splendour. Thou shouldst second my efforts, Lovinski; the trifling interests of love ought to be waived before interests more sacred: I cannot give thee my daughter in times of mourning, when the country is in danger; but I promise thee that the first days of peace shall be marked by thy marriage with Lodoiska.

Pulauski did not speak in vain; I was sensible of the very important duties it was incumbent on me to perform; but these weighty cares which I took upon myself did not afford my grief sufficient alleviation: I own it without blushing: the sorrow of my sisters, their affectionate friendship, the embraces, more reserved, but not less sweet, of my fair mistress, made a more lively impression upon my heart than the patriotic counsels of Pulauski. I beheld Lodoiska sensibly affected at the irreparable loss I had sustained, and equally afflicted as myself by the cruel events which deferred our union: my griefs, being thus participated, were considerably lightened.

In the meanwhile the king died, and the Diet was convoked. On the very day that it was about to open, and at the moment I was going there, a person whom I knew not, presented himself in my palace, and demanded to speak to me, without witnesses. As soon as my servants had retired, he entered with precipitation, threw himself in my arms, and embraced me with tenderness. It was M. de P***: the ten years which had passed since our separation, had not so much changed, but that I recognised him. I testified the joy and surprise which his unexpected return gave me. You will be much more astonished, said he, when you know the cause. I have this instant arrived, and am going to the assembly of the states. Is it too presumptuous of thy friend to reckon on thy vote? On my vote! And for whom? For myself, my friend. He observed my astonishment. Yes, for me, continued he, with vivacity; there is no time to tell you of the happy revolution which has taken place in my fortune, and prompts me to indulge such lofty hopes; let it suffice you for the present to know, that my ambition is justified by the greater number of votes, and that it is in vain for my two feeble rivals to dispute the crown to which I pretend. Lovinski, continued he, embracing me again, if you were not my friend, if I esteemed you less, I might perhaps dazzle you by great promises; I might, perhaps, point out the great favour that attends you, the honourable distinctions which are reserved for you, and

the noble and extensive career which is open to
you; but I have no need to seduce you, I shall
only persuade you. I see it with grief, and
you know it as well as I do, that for several
years Poland has been so weak, that she has only
been indebted for her safety, to the understanding of three powers which surround her, and
that the desire of enriching themselves with our
plunder, might unite, in a moment, our divided
enemies. Let us prevent, if we can, so unfortunate an occurrence, of which the dismemberment
of our provinces would be the infallible result.
There is no doubt but, in happier times, our
ancestors maintained the liberty of elections;
we must at present yield to the necessity which
presses upon us. Russia will, as a matter of
course, protect the king who shall be of her own
making; in receiving that which she has chosen,
you prevent that triple alliance which would
render our fall inevitable; and you are sure of
a powerful ally, which we can oppose with success to the two enemies that remain. These,
then are the reasons which have determined me.
I abandon some of our rights, to preserve others
that are more precious. I would not mount a
tottering throne, but to strengthen it by a sound

policy; I do not, in fact, alter the constitution of this state but to save it altogether.

We went to the Diet; I voted for M. de P***, and he obtained the greatest number of suffrages; but Pulauski, Zaremba, and some others, declared for the Prince C***: nothing could be decided in the tumult of this first assembly.

When the assembly broke up, M. de P*** came to me again, and invited me to follow him to the palace, which some secret emissaries had prepared for him in the capital. We shut ourselves up for several hours: we renewed our protestations of eternal friendship; I informed him of my connection with Pulauski, and my love for Lodoiska. He returned my confidence by a confidence still greater; he told me the events which had paved the way to his approaching greatness; he explained to me his most secret designs, and I quitted him, convinced that he was less occupied by the desire of elevating himself than of restoring to Poland her ancient prosperity.

Under these impressions, I flew to my future father-in-law, whom I was anxious to bring over to the party of my friend. Pulauski was walking, with hasty strides, the apartment of his daughter, who appeared as much agitated as himself. Behold him, said he to Lodoiska, as soon as he saw me enter: Behold this man that I esteemed, and you loved! he has sacrificed us both to a blind friendship.—I was going to reply, but he continued: You have been bound, from infancy, to M. de P***; a powerful faction bears him towards the throne; you know it—you know his designs; this morning, at the Diet, you voted for him; you have deceived me; but think not to deceive me with impunity.—I begged of him to hear me; he preserved a stern silence. I informed him that M. de P***, whom I had so long neglected, had surprised me by his unforeseen return. Lodoiska appeared delighted on hearing my justification.—You cannot deceive me like a credulous woman, said Pulauski, but it's no matter, go on.—I gave him an account of the short conversation I had with M. de P*** before I went to the assembly of the states.—And these are your projects, cried he: M. de P*** sees no other remedy for the misfortunes of his fellow citizens than their slavery! He proposed it, and Lodoiska approved it! and they despise me sufficiently to tempt me to enter into this infamous plot! Do you think I could see the Russians commanding in our provinces, while it was pretended we were governed by a Pole? The Russians, repeated he, regenerate my country!—(he came towards me with the greatest impetuosity)—Perfidious wretch! thou hast deceived me, thou hast betrayed thy country! get out of this palace instantly, lest I tear thee in pieces.

I acknowledge to you, Faublas, that an affront, so cruel, and so little merited, made me forget myself in the first transport of my passion. I put my hand upon my sword; quicker than lightning, Pulauski drew his. His daughter, his distracted daughter, threw herself upon me: Lovinski, what are you about?

The sweet accents of her much-loved voice recalled my scattered senses, but I felt that in a moment he might snatch Lodoiska from me for ever. She had quitted me, to throw herself in the arms of her father; the cruel man perceived the poignancy of my anguish, and was pleased to augment it. Go, traitor, said he, you see her for the last time.

I returned home in despair; the odious epithets which Pulauski had lavished on me presented themselves continually to my mind. The interests of Poland and those of M. de P*** appeared to me so strictly allied, that I could not conceive how I could betray my fellow citizens in serving my friend. Nevertheless, I must either abandon that, or renounce Lodoiska. How must I resolve? Which part must I take? I passed the whole night in this cruel uncertainty; and, in the morning, I went to Pulauski without knowing how I should determine.

One domestic alone remained in the place, who informed me that his master, after having taken leave of his friends, went away early in the evening before with Lodoiska. You may judge of my grief at this news. I demanded of the domestic where Pulauski was gone.—I am entirely ignorant, said he: all I can tell you is, that last night, you had scarcely left here, when we heard a great noise in the apartment of his daughter. Still frightened at the dreadful scene which was likely to have taken place between you, I ventured to approach and listen; Ladoiska wept; her father was loading her with insults; he even cursed her—and I heard him say to her: Who would love a traitor, could be one also. Ungrateful wretch! I am going to put you into a place of security, where you shall be hereafter free from seduction.

Could I be any longer ignorant of my misfortunes? I called Boleslas, one of the most faithful of my domestics; I ordered him to place around the palace of Pulauski some vigilant spies, who might render me an account of everything that passed there; to follow Pulauski every where, if he entered the capital before me; and not despairing to meet with him again in the neighbouring districts, I set off myself in the pursuit.

I went over all the estates of Pulauski; I enquired for Lodoiska of all the travellers I met—but it was useless. After having spent eight days in this painful search, I determined upon returning to Warsaw. I was not greatly astonished at beholding a Russian army encamped almost under its walls, on the borders of the Vistula.

It was night when I entered the capital; the palaces of the great were illuminated; an immense populace filled the streets, and I heard the acclamations of mirth; I saw wine running from fountains in the public squares; every thing announced to me that Poland had a king.

Boleslas had expected me with impatience. Pulauski, said he, returned alone the second day; he has never left his house but to go to the Diet, where, in spite of his efforts, the ascendancy of Russian interest manifested itself more and more every day. In the last assembly, held this morning, M. de P*** obtained almost all the votes, and was elected; Pulauski pronounced the fatal *veto;* at that instant, twenty sabres were drawn. The fierce Palatine de ***, whom Pulauski had so little pleased in the preceding assembly, was the first who drew and aimed a terrible stroke at his head. Zaremba, and some others, flew to the defence of their friend, but all their efforts could not have saved him, if M. de P*** himself had not sprung amongst them, crying out that he would immolate, with his own hand, the first that dared approach. The assailants retired. In the meanwhile, Pulauski lost both his blood and his strength! he fainted, and was carried away. Zaremba went out, swearing to avenge him. The numerous partizans of M. de P***, remaining masters of the deliberations, immediately proclaimed him king. Pulauski, when taken to his palace, soon recovered his senses. The surgeons, called in to examine his wound, declared that it was not mortal: then, although he experienced very great pain, and though several of his friends opposed themselves to his design, he made them place him in his carriage. It was almost noon when he set out from Warsaw, accompanied by Mazeppa and some other discontents. Your spies have followed him, and will, no doubt, in a few days, inform you of the place of his retreat.

It was scarcely possible for them to announce to me more disagreeable intelligence. My friend was on the throne, but my reconciliation with Pulauski appeared hereafter impossible; and, seemingly, I had lost Lodoiska for ever. I knew her father sufficiently to make me fear he had taken very violent resolutions; I was terrified at the present aspect of things; I dared not reflect upon the future, and my grief oppressed me to such a degree, that I did not even go to congratulate the new king.

One of my people, whom Boleslas had dispitched in pursuit of Pulauski, came back the fourth day; he had followed him even to fifteen leagues from the capital; there, Zaremba, always seeing an unknown at some distance from the post-chaise, had conceived suspicions. A little further on, four of his people, hid behind some ruins, surprised my courier and conducted him to Pulauski. A pistol was presented at him, and he was compelled to acknowledge to whom he belonged. I will send you to Lovinski, said Pulauski to him, and tell him from me, that he shall not escape my just vengeance. At these words, they bound the eyes of my courier; he could not tell where they had conducted him, and shut him up: but at the expiration of three days they came to fetch him, and having again taken the precaution of binding his eyes, after riding for several hours, the carriage stopped, and they made him descend. He had scarcely set his foot to the ground when his guard left him at swift pace: he detached the bonds from his eyes, and found himself precisely in the same place where they had first arrested him.

This news gave me much uneasiness; the menaces of Pulauski frightened me much less on my own account than that of Lodoiska, who remained in his power; he might, in his wrath, go to the last extremities with her. I resolved to expose myself to everything, in order to discover the retreat of the father, and the prison of his daughter. The next day, I informed my sisters of my design, and quitted the capital,

Boleslas alone accompanied me, and I treated him as a brother. We went all over Poland: I then saw that the events justified too much the fears of Pulauski. Under pretence of making people take the oath of fidelity to the new king, the Russians spread themselves in our provinces, committed a thousand exactions in our towns, and laid waste the fields. After having lost three months in vain researches, despairing of finding Lodoiska, most sensibly touched by the misfortunes of my country, lamenting at the same time both her fate and my own, I was about to return to Warsaw, to inform the new king what excesses the foreigners had committed in his states, when a rencontre, which threatened to be very unlucky for me, compelled me to take another direction.

The Turks had declared war against Russia, and the Tartars of Budsiac and of Crimea, made frequent incursions in Volhymie, where I then found myself. Four of these brigands attacked us coming out of a wood near Ostropol. I had very imprudently neglected to charge my pistols, but I availed myself of my sabre, with so much dexterity and success, that presently two of them fell, grievously wounded. Boleslas

occupied the third; the fourth combatted me
with great vigour; he gave me a slight wound in
my thigh, and received at the same time a terrible blow, which threw him from his horse.
Boleslas saw himself at this moment disembar-
rassed of his enemy, who, at the noise of the fall
of his comrade, took flight.

The one whom I had last overthrown, said to
me, in bad Polish:—a man so brave as you
ought to be generous. I beg my life of you.
Friend, instead of finishing me, assist me; trust
me, help me, and bind up my wounds. He
demanded quarter in a tone so noble and so singular, that I did not hesitate. I descended from
my horse: Boleslas and myself relieved him and
bound up his wounds. You do well, brave man,
said the Tartar; you do well. As he spoke, there
arose around us a cloud of dust; more than
three hundred Tartars appeared in sight. Fear
nothing, said he, whom I had spared; I am
the chief of this troop. And, indeed, by a sign
he stopped the soldiers, who were ready to mas-
sacre me. He said to them, in their language,
some words which I did not understand; they
opened their ranks to let myself and Boleslas
pass. Brave man, said the captain again to me,

had I not reason to tell you that you did well?
Thou hast spared my life—I save thine: it is
sometimes good to spare an enemy, and even a
robber. Hear me, my friend: in attacking thee,
I was following my trade: thou hast done thy
duty in well thrashing me; I pardon thee: let
us embrace. He added: the day begins to close;
I would not advise thee to travel in these cantons; those men are each going to their post, and
I cannot answer for them. Thou seest that
castle on the height to the right; it belongs to
a certain Count Dourlinski, who owes us a great
deal, because he is very rich; go and request of
him an asylum; tell him thou hast wounded Titsikan, that Titsikan pursued thee; he knows mo
by name: I have already made him pass some
disagreeable journeys. You may reckon on his
house being respected while you are there; but
be sure you do not leave it under three days, nor
remain in it more than eight. Adieu!

It was with real pleasure that we took our
leave of Titsikan and his company. The advice
of a Tartar was an order. I said to Boleslas:
Let us gain immediately the castle which he has
shown us; I know this Dourlinski very well by
name. Pulauski has sometimes spoken to me of

him: he may not be ignorant where Pulauski has retired; it is not impossible but with a little address we may obtain some knowledge of him. I will say, at all hazards, that it is Pulauski who has sent us; his recommendation will be worth more than that of Titsikan: thou, Boleslas, forget not that I am thy brother, and do not discover me.

We arrived at the moat of the castle; the people of Dourlinski demanded of us who we were. I replied, that we came to speak with their master on the part of Pulauski; that robbers had attacked us, and we were pursued. The drawbridge was raised, and we entered: they told us that, for the present, we could not speak with Dourlinski, but that the next day, at ten o'clock, he could give us audience. They demanded our arms of us, and we gave them up without hesitation. Boleslas examined my wound; the flesh was scarcely entered. They lost no time in serving us with a frugal repast in the kitchen. We were afterwards conducted into a humble chamber, where a couple of indifferent beds were prepared for us; they left us without a light, and fastened us in.

I could not shut my eyes all night: Titsikan

had given me but a slight wound, but that in my heart was so deep! At daybreak, I was impatient of my prison; I wished to open the shutters, but they were locked. I shook them vigorously, and the bolts flew; I perceived a very beautiful park; the window was low; I jumped from it, and found myself in the gardens of Dourlinski. After I had walked there some minutes, I sat down on a stone bench, placed at the foot of a tower, the ancient architecture of which engaged my attention for some time. I remained absorbed in profound reflection, when a tile fell at my feet: I thought it had slipped from the roof of this old building; and to avoid a similar accident, I placed myself at the other end of the bench. Some moments after a second tile fell by my side; the circumstance appeared to me surprising. I rose with inquietude, and examined the tower attentively. I perceived, about twenty-five or thirty feet high, a narrow opening; I gathered up the tiles which were thrown at me; upon the first I deciphered, traced with some chalk,—" Lovinski, is it then you! Do you live!" And on the second, as follows: " Deliver me! Save Lodoiska!"

You cannot, my dear Faublas, figure to yourself the various feelings which agitated me at one time; my astonishment, my joy, my grief, my embarrassment, cannot be expressed. I examined the prison of Lodoiska; I sought how I could take her from it. She sent me yet another tile: I read,—"At midnight bring some paper, pens and ink; to-morrow, after sunrise, come and seek a letter. Go away."

I returned to my chamber; I called Boleslas, who assisted me in entering by the window, and we fastened the shutters as well as we could. I informed my faithful servant of the unhoped for meeting, which put an end to my searches, but redoubled my anxiety. How was this tower to be penetrated? How extricate Lodoiska from her prison? How was she to be snatched from under the eyes of Dourlinski, from the midst of his people, in a fortified castle! Even supposing that so many obstacles were not insurmountable, could I attempt an enterprise so difficult, in the short time that Titsikan had given me? Titsikan had recommended me to remain but three days with Dourlinski, and at all events, not to stop longer than eight. To go out of this castle before the third day, or after the eighth, was it not to expose ourselves to the attacks of Tartars? To release my dear Lodoiska from prison to deliver her to robbers, was to be for ever separated from her by slavery or death! It was horrible to think of. But why was she in such a frightful prison? The letter which she has promised me will instruct me, without doubt. It was necessary to procure some paper: I charged Boleslas with their care, and prepared myself to sustain the delicate part of an emissary of Pulauski.

It was broad day when they came to set us at liberty; they informed us that Dourlinski was now at leisure, and desired to see us. We presented ourselves with assurance: we beheld a man about sixty years of age, whose address was blunt, and whose manners were repulsive. He asked us who we were. My brother and myself, said I, belong to Seigneur Pulauski; my master has charged me with a secret commission to you; my brother has accompanied me for another purpose; I ought to be alone when I explain myself; I ought to speak but to yourself. Well! replied Dourlinski, let thy brother go; and do you also go away, said he to his servants; but as for you, (pointing to him who was his

confidant,) you will do well to remain; you can
say everything before him. Pulauski has sent
me—I see well that he has sent you—To inquire
of you—What?—(I took courage.) To inquire
of you news regarding his daughter.—Pulauski
said so?—Yes, my master told me Lodoiska was
here. I perceived that Dourlinski turned pale;
he looked at his confidant, and fixed his eyes on
me a long time in silence.—You astonish me,
replied he, at last; to confide in you a secret of
this importance, your master must be very imprudent.—Not more so than yourself, seigneur;
have not you a confidant?—The great would be
much to be pitied, if they could not put confidence in someone.—Pulauski has charged me
to tell you that Lovinski has already run over
great part of Poland, and will, no doubt, visit
your cantons.—If he dares come here, replied
he, immediately, with the greatest vivacity, I
keep for him a lodging which he will occupy a
long time. Do you know this Lovinski?—I
have seen him often at my master's in Warsaw.
—They say he's a fine man?—He is well made,
and near about my height.—His countenance?
—Is engaging: it is a—He is an insolent fellow,
interrupted he, with anger; if ever he falls into

my hands——My lord, they say he is brave.
He! I'll wager that he knows nothing but the
seduction of girls. Let him fall into my hands!
—I was about to reply, when he added, in a
more calm tone: It is a long time since Pulauski has written to me: where is he at present?
—My lord, I have positive orders not to answer
that question, all that I must tell you is, that he
has many reasons for concealing his retreat, and
not writing, which he will shortly come and explain to you himself.

Dourlinski appeared very much astonished;
I thought I even perceived some signs of alarm;
he looked at his confidant, who seems as much
embarrassed as himself: You say that Pulauski
will come shortly?—Yes, my lord, in a fort-
night, or better.—He looked at his confidant,
and then affecting as much *sang froid* as he had
evinced embarrassment: Return to thy master,
I am sorry that I have nothing but bad news
for him; tell him that Lodoiska is no longer
here.—I was astonished in my turn: What! my
lord, Lodoiska——Is no longer here, I tell thee.
—To oblige Pulauski, whom I esteem, I undertook with repugnance, to keep his daughter in
my castle. No one but him and myself (point-

ing to the confidant) knew that she was here. About a month since, we went, as usual, to take her daily refreshments, and there was no one in her apartment—I am ignorant how she accomplished it, but I know well that she has escaped, and I have not heard of her since: she is, without doubt, gone to join Lovinski, at Warsaw, if the Tartars seized her not on the road.

My astonishment became extreme; how was what I had seen in the garden, to be reconciled with what Dourlinski told me? There was some mystery in it which I was impatient to unravel, nevertheless I was cautious of appearing the least doubtful: My lord, this is very sad news for my master.—Undoubtedly it is, but I cannot help it.—My lord, I have a favour to ask of you.—What is it?—The Tartars are infesting the environs of your castle; they have attacked us, we have escaped them by a miracle; will you permit my brother and myself to rest here for two days?—Only two days; I consent.—Where have they lodged? demanded he of his confidant.—On the ground floor, in a common chamber——Which looks into my gardens! interrupted Dourlinski, with anxiety.—The shutters fasten with a lock, replied the other. No matter, we must put them elsewhere.—I trembled at these words. The confidant replied: that is impossible,—but—(he said the rest in a whisper,—Very well, replied the master, and let it be done immediately; and addressing himself to me: Thy brother and thou wilt go the day after tomorrow; before setting out, thou wilt speak to me; I will give thee a letter for Pulauski.

I went to join Boleslas in the kitchen, where he was taking his breakfast; he gave me a little bottle, full of ink, several pens, and some sheets of paper, which he had procured without trouble. I burnt with desire to write to Lodoiska, but I was embarrassed to find a convenient place where the curious might not disturb me. They had already informed Boleslas that we were not to enter the chamber where we slept, until bedtime. I thought of a stratagem which succeeded admirably. The servants of Dourlinski were drinking with my pretended brother, and invited me politely to join them. I drank freely, cup after cup, several glasses of a very bad wine; presently, my limbs tottered; I told the merry throng a hundred stories, as droll as they were unreasonable; in a word, I acted drunkenness so well, that Boleslas himself was deceived by it. He trembled, lest in a moment when I appeared disposed to tell everything, my secret should escape me.— Gentlemen, said he to the astonished topers, my brother is not very strong in the head to-day; perhaps it is the effects of his wound; we must not suffer him either to talk or drink any more; I fear it would do him harm, and if you would oblige me, you will help me to carry him to his bed.—To his bed? No, that cannot be, replied one of them; but I will cheerfully lend you my chamber.—They carried me up into a garret, of which the only furniture consisted of a bed, a chair, and a table. They shut me up in this place; it was everything that I wished. The moment I was left alone, I wrote to Lodoiska a letter of several sheets. I began by justifying myself fully from the crimes which Pulauski had imputed to me, and then related to her everything which had happened to me from the period of our separation unto that when I arrived at Dourlinski's; I detailed the conversation I had with him, and finished by assuring her of the most tender and respectful love; I pledged myself, that as soon as she had given me the necessary explanations, I would risk everything to deliver her from such horrible slavery.

As soon as my letter was finished, I gave myself up to reflections which greatly perplexed me. Was it, indeed, Lodoiska who had thrown me the tiles in the garden? Could Pulauski have the injustice to punish his daughter for a love he had approved? Had he the inhumanity to plunge her in this frightful dungeon? And even if the hatred which he had sworn towards me had blinded him to this pitch, how was it that Dourlinski could resolve thus to aid his vengeance? But, on the other side, I had worn, the better to disguise myself, the most humble garb; the fatigues of a long journey, and my own cares, had greatly changed me—who, then, but a lover, could have recognized Lovinski in the garden of Dourlinski? Had I not, moreover, seen the name of Lodoiska traced upon the tile? And had not even Dourlinski himself confessed that she had been a prisoner under him? He added, it is true, that she had escaped; but was that credible? And wherefore the hatred that Dourlinski had avowed towards me, without knowing me? Why that air of in-

quietude when they told him the servants of
Pulauski had occupied a chamber that looked
into the garden? Why, above all, that air of
alarm when I announced to him the approaching visit of my pretended master? The whole
of this was calculated to give me the most poignant anxiety. I could form nothing but the most
frightful conjectures, which I could not explain. I continued, for a couple of hours, pro-
posing to myself questions which I was very
much embarrassed to solve, when at length
Boleslas came to see if his brother had recovered
his reason. I had no trouble in convincing him
that my intoxication was feigned; we went
down into the kitchen, where we passed the rest
of the day. What an evening, my dear Faublas!
none in my life appeared so long; not even those
which followed it.

At last they conducted us to our chamber,
where they fastened us in, as on the night before, without leaving us a light: we had still to
wait two hours before it struck twelve. At the
first stroke of the clock, we gently opened the
shutters of the window: I prepared myself to
jump into the garden: my embarrassment was
equal to my despair when I found myself re-

strained by bars. There, said I to Boleslas, see what it was that the cursed confidant of Dourlinski whispered into his ear: this is what his odious master approved, when he replied: *It is well; let it be done immediately.* See what they have executed during the day: it was on this account we were forbidden to come here.—My lord, they have worked outside, said Boleslas, for they have not perceived that the shutter has been forced.—Ah! whether they have seen it or not, cried I, with violence, what matter? This fatal grating overturns all my hopes; it confirms the slavery of Lodoiska, and insures my death!

Yes, without doubt, it insures your death, said some one to me, on opening my door. Dourlinski, preceded by armed men, and followed by others who carried torches, entered with his sabre in his hand. Traitor! said he to me, glancing at me a look sufficiently expressive of his fury, I have overheard all: I'll know what thou art; thou shalt tell me thy name; thy pretended brother shall tell it. Tremble! I am of all the enemies of Lovinski, the most implacable! Let them be searched, said he to his people. They seized me; I was without arms; I made a vain resistance: they took from me my papers, and the letter I had prepared for Lodoiska. Dourlinski betrayed, while reading it, a thousand signs of impatience; he could ill conceal it. Lovinski, said he, suppressing his rage, I merit already thy hatred; presently I shall merit it more. In the meantime thou shalt remain with thy worthy confidant in this chamber, which thou lovest. At these words, he went out, double-locked the door, placed a sentinel without, and another opposite the window in the garden.

You will imagine the overwhelming situation Boleslas and myself were placed in. My misfortunes had reached their height; those of Lodoiska affected me more intensely. Unfortunate creature! What must be her anxiety! She expected Lovinski, and Lovinski abandoned her! But no; Lodoiska knows me too well; she will never suspect me of so base a perfidy. Lodoiska will judge of her lover by herself! She will feel that Lovinski participated her fate, since he did not relieve her! Alas! the certainty of my fate will aggravate her own.

Such were my painful reflections in the first moments: they left me time enough to make many others, not less gloomy. The next day, they gave us, through the bars, our allowance of provisions. From the quality of the food which they furnished us, Boleslas judged that they did not intend to render our prison very agreeable. Boleslas, less wretched than myself, supported his lot more courageously; he offered me my portion of the slender repast he was about to make. I would not eat; he pressed me, but in vain; my existence had become an insupportable burthen. Oh! live, said he to me, bursting into tears: live, if not for Boleslas, let it be for Lodoiska!—These words made a more lively impression upon me; they re-animated my courage, and cheered my heart with hope: I embraced my faithful servant. O! my friend! cried I, with transport: Oh! my true friend! I have sacrificed thee, and my own cares touch me more than thine! Yes, Boleslas, I will live for Lodoiska, I will live for thee: would heaven this moment restore my fortune and my rank, thou shouldst see that thy master was not ungrateful. We embraced again: Ah! my dear Faublas! if you knew how misfortune links us together! how delightful it is, when one is suffering, to hear another unfortunate being address to us a word of consolation!

We had groaned twelve days in this prison, when they came to conduct me to Dourlinski. Boleslas wished to follow me, but was repulsed in a brutal manner; they nevertheless permitted me to speak to him for a moment. I drew from my hand a ring, which I had worn from the age of ten years. I said to Boleslas, this ring was given me by M. de P***, when we studied together at Warsaw: take it, my friend, and keep it for my sake. If Dourlinski consummates his treason by causing me to be assassinated, and thou art permitted to leave this castle, go to thy king, show him this jewel, remind him of our long friendship, and relate to him my misfortunes; he will recompense thee, Boleslas, he will send succor to Lodoiska. Adieu, my friend.

They conducted me to the apartment of Dourlinski. As soon as the door was opened, I perceived a female, fainting on an arm-chair; I approached; it was Lodoiska. Oh, God! how changed I found her! But what beauty she still possessed! Barbarian! said I to Dourlinski. At the voice of her lover, Lodoiska recovered her senses.—Ah, my dear Lovinski! knowest thou what the wretch proposes? Knowest thou

at what price he offers me thy liberty?—Yes,
replied the furious Dourlinski; yes, I will;
thou seest it is in my power: if within three
days I obtain nothing, he shall die.—I would
have thrown myself on my knees to Lodoiska,
but my guards prevented me. I see thee again;
all my tortures are forgotten. Lodoiska, death
has nothing in it to terrify me. Thou coward,
remember that Pulauski will revenge his daughter, and that the king will revenge his friend.—
Take him away! cried Dourlinski.—Ah! said
Lodoiska, my love has sacrificed you!—I would
have replied, but they dragged me out, and reconducted me to my prison. Boleslas received
me with inexpressible transports of joy: he
confessed that he thought me lost. I related
to him how my death had been deferred. The
scene of which I had been witness confirmed
all my suspicions; it was clear that Pulauski
knew not the unworthy treatment his daughter
was experiencing; it was clear that Dourlinski,
amorous and jealous, would satisfy his passion
at any price he could.

In the meantime, of the three days which
Dourlinski had given Lodoiska to make up her
mind, two had already passed; we were in the

middle of the night which preceded the third day; I could not sleep, I was pacing up and down my chamber; all at once I heard a cry, " to arms! "—the most frightful howling arose from every quarter without the castle; it made a great bustle in the interior; the sentinel placed before our window quitted his post; Boleslas and myself distinguished the voice of Dourlinski; he called—he rallied his people; we heard distinctly, the clash of arms, the cries of the wounded, and the groans of the dying. The noise, at first very great, seemed to diminish; presently it began again; it continued and redoubled; they cried " victory! "— numbers ran in and shut the doors after them with violence; the night became less dark; the trees in the garden began to assume a yellow and reddish tint; we flew to the window: the castle of Dourlinski was wrapped in flames; they spread on every side of the chamber we were in; and, to complete the horror, the most piercing shrieks came from the tower where I knew Lodoiska was confined.—

Here M. du Portail was interrupted by the Marquis de B***, who having found no servant in the ante-chamber, entered without being announced. He started two paces on seeing me, Ah! ah! said he, saluting M. du Portail, have you a son also?—Then addressing himself to me: Monsieur is apparently the brother?—Of my sister, yes, sir.—Ah! you have a very amiable sister; she is a charming girl!—You are as polite as you are indulgent, interrupted M. du Portail.—Indulgent! oh, I am not always so; for example, I am come to reproach you, sir.—Me? have I had the misfortune?—Yes, you played us a cruel trick the day before yesterday.—How, sir!—You charged that little Rosambert to take Mademoiselle du Portail from us; the Marchioness had made sure that her dear daughter would pass the night with her.—I fear, sir, that my daughter has caused you a great deal of trouble.—None; none, sir: Mademoiselle du Portail is very agreeable; my wife is passionately fond of her, as I have told you before; indeed, added he, tittering, I believe the Marchioness loves that child more than she loves myself. I am, notwithstanding, her husband! If you had come yourself to fetch her ——Pardon me, sir, I was unwell; I am still very——I know that I owe Madame de B*** many thanks——It is not for that——

During this dialogue, I was not much at my ease. The Marquis observed me with an attention which made me very uncomfortable. Do you know, said he at last, that you resemble your sister very much?—You flatter me, sir.—But it is very striking; I know it well; all my friends agree that I am a skilful physiognomist at the first sight: I have never seen you before, and I recognise you immediately.— M. du Portail could not help laughing with me at the simplicity of the Marquis.—Monsieur, said he to him, it is as you have very justly remarked; my son and my daughter are very much alike, we must agree that there is a family resmblance.—Yes, replied the Marquis, continuing to look at me, this young man is well, very well—but his sister is still better, much better.—[He took me by the arm.]—She is a little taller, has a more serious air; although she is a little wag, her manner is somewhat grave, but there is a something in your features more bold; you have less grace in your action, and in all the motions of your body something more vigorous and robust. Do not be angry; all this is very natural; it would not do for a boy to be made like a girl!—[Phlegmatic as M. du

Portail was, he could not keep his countenance at these last remarks; the Marquis saw us laugh, and began to laugh heartily himself.] Oh! replied he, I have told you that I am a great physiognomist; but I have not the pleasure to see the dear sister.—M. du Portail hastened to reply: No, sir, she is gone to take her leave.—To take her leave!—Yes, sir, she sets out to morrow for her convent.—For her convent in Paris?—No, at Soissons.—To Soissons to morrow morning? That dear child to leave us?—It is for the best, sir.—And is actually taking farewell?—Yes, sir.—And, without doubt, she will come and bid farewell to her mamma?—Most assuredly, sir; she ought even to be at your house at this moment.—Ah! how sorry I am! The Marchioness was still unwell this morning; she wished to go out this evening; I represented to her that the air was sharp, and would give her cold; but the women will have their way—she is gone out: Well, so much the worse for her, she will not see her dear girl, and I shall see her, for she certainly will not be long before she comes home.—She has several visits to make, said I to the Marquis.—Yes, added M. du Portail, we only expect her to supper.—

You eat suppers then? you are right; it is all the mania now, not to eat of an evening; for my part, I love not to die of hunger, because it is the fashion: I'll stop and sup with you. You'll say, perhaps, that I make free, but 't is my way; I wish people to do the same with me: When you know me better, you will find that I am a good devil.

There was no means of receding from what we had said. M. du Portail instantly took the necessary measures. I am very happy, sir, that you will be free with us. You will excuse my son quitting us for an hour or two, as he has some urgent business.—Monsieur must not hinder himself on my account.—Let him leave us by all means, that he may see us again the sooner, for your son is very amiable, sir.—You'll excuse me also a few minutes as I have something to say to him.—Do the same, sir, as if I was not here.—I bowed to the Marquis, he rose precipitately, took me by the hand, and said to M. du Portail: Stop, sir, you may say what you will, but this young man is as like his sister as two drops of water. I am skilled in countenance; I will sustain it before the Abbé Pernetti.*—Yes, sir, said M. du Portail, he has a family likeness.

Having said this, he went with me into another apartment.—Zounds! said he to me, what a singular man this Marquis is; he does not constrain himself with those he loves.—It is very true, my dear father, that the Marquis comes, without ceremony, to make free with us —but, as for myself, I have no right to complain, for I was happy when at his house.— As to yourself, you say true; but let us drop this pleasantry, and see how we are to get out of the scrape we are in. If I only looked to him it would be soon settled; but, my friend, you have to manage matters properly, on account of his wife. Hear me; go home, make your servant take another dress, and come here to announce that Mademoiselle du Portail sups with Madame de ***, the first name that comes into your head.—Well! what next? the Marquis will sup with you, and wait tranquilly the return of your daughter: this is what he will do; he has told you so himself.—What, then, is to be done?—

* M. l'Abbe Pernetti wrote a work on Physiognomy, entitled "The Knowledge of the Moral Man by the Physical Man."

Why, my dear father, I can play the girl so well, I will go and change myself, and your daughter shall in reality come and sup with you. It shall be your son, on the contrary, who is detained, and cannot come. It is now six o'clock; I need not be home until ten: I shall have plenty of time.—With all my heart. But you must agree, nevertheless, that Lovinski will have to play rather a singular part. You have embarked me in a curious adventure; but it is too late to find fault: go and effect it as soon as possible.

I ran home. Jasmin told me my father was gone out, and that a pretty girl had been waiting for me above an hour. A pretty girl, Jasmin? I flew to my apartment. Ah! Justine, is it thee! Jasmin was right when he told me it was a pretty girl: I embraced her.—Keep that for my mistress, said she, pretending to be sullen. For thy mistress, Justine? Thou art as good as her.—Who told you so?—I think so; it rests with thee to make me certain of it. I embraced her again, and she suffered me to do so, still repeating,—Keep that for my mistress. My God! how well you look in your own dress, added she; and will you ever quit it again, to disguise yourself as a woman?—To-night, for the last time, Justine: after that I shall always be a man,—at thy service, sweet girl.—At my service?—Oh, no; at the service of Madame —At hers and thine at the same time, Justine. Hey dey, so you must have two at a time!—I feel, my dear, that it is not too much. I embraced Justine, and my hands strayed upon her snowy hills, which she scarcely defended.—How impudent he is, said Justine. What has become of the modesty of Mademoiselle du Portail?— Ah, Justine, thou knowest not how one night has changed me!—That night also made an alteration in my mistress; the next day she was pale and fatigued. My God! when I saw her, I was not at a loss in guessing that Mademoiselle du Portail was a very nice young man.

I was going to embrace her again. For this time, she prevented it by recoiling a few paces: my bed was behind her; she fell on her back; and by an accident which might, perhaps, be expected, I lost my equilibrium at the same moment.

Some minutes after, Justine, who was in no haste to repair her disorder, asked, with a smile, what I thought of the little piece of waggery she

had played the Marquis.—What about, my
dear?—The placard stuck on his back. What
say you of the trick?—Charming, delightful;
almost as good as that which we are now playing
the Marchioness.—I am glad you mentioned
her, I had forgot my commission. My mistress expects you.—She expects me? I'll go
directly.—There, he's going: and where are you
going?—I do not know.—See how bluntly he
leaves me!—Justine, it is——You know——I
know you are a careless libertine.—Stop, Justine, let us be friends; a Louis d'or and a kiss.
—I take, said she, the one very willingly, and
give you the other with all my heart. Oh, what
a charming young man! handsome, lively and
generous! Oh, I am sure you will rise in the
world! But let us go; follow me at a little distance, and take no notice. You will see me go
into a shop; close by is a great gate, which you
will find partly open; enter it quickly. A
porter will demand of you who you are; you
will answer, *Love*. You will go up to the first
floor. Upon a little white door you will read
the word, *Paphos*. Open it with this key, and
you'll not be there long without a companion.

Before going out, I called Jasmin, and ordered him to change his dress, and go on the part of M. de Saint-Luc, to announce to M. du Portail that his son would not come home to supper.

Justine was impatient: I followed her. She went into a milliner's shop. I brushed hastily through the gate. *Love,* said I to the porter, and in an instant I was at *Paphos.* I opened it, and entered. The place appeared to be worthy of the god they adored there. A few wax candles were burning. It was hung with the most luxurious and fascinating pictures; the furniture was as elegant as convenient: I observed above all, at the back of a gilt alcove, lined with looking-glass, a spring bed, the clothes of which, being black satin, were calculated to afford an agreeable contrast to a fine white skin: I then recollected I had promised M. du Portail never again to see the Marchioness, but it may easily be guessed that my recollection came too late.

A door, which I had not observed, opened all at once. The Marchioness entered. To fly into her arms—to give her twenty kisses—to carry her to the alcove—to place her on the springing couch—and to plunge with her into a delightful extacy, was the affair of a moment. The Marchioness recovered her senses at the same time with myself. I asked her how she did. What say you? replied she, with an astonished air.—I repeated: My dear little mamma, how do you do?—She burst into a fit of laughter: I thought I had misunderstood you; the *how do you do* is excellent; but if I was unwell, it would have been a very queer time to ask me such a question. Do you think that this exercise would agree with a sick person? My dear Faublas, added she, embracing me tenderly, you are very lively.—My dear little mamma, it is because I now know several things of which I was ignorant three days since.—Are you afraid that you'll forget them?—Oh, no!—Oh, no! repeated she, counterfeiting my voice; I believe it indeed, Mr. Libertine. She embraced me again. Promise that you will never remember those things but with me.—I promise it, my dear mamma.—You swear to be faithful?—I swear it.—Always?—Yes, always.—But you delayed a long while in coming to me.—I was not at home; I dined with M. du Portail.—With M. du Portail! Did he speak to you of me?— Yes.—You have not told him anything?—No, mamma. She continued, in a very serious tone: You told him that I was, like the Marquis, deceived by appearances?—Yes, mamma.—And that I am still so? continued she, with a trembling voice, and at the same time giving me a most tender kiss.—Yes, mamma.—Charming child! cried she, I must then adore you! If you will not be ungrateful I shall.—I valued this reply more than all the caresses; but a degree of uneasiness still remaining: So you assured M. du Portail that I think you—a girl? added the Marchioness, blushing.—Yes.—You know, then, how to lie?—Have I lied?—I think the rogue is mocking his mamma!

I pretended that I wished to go, but she detained me. Beg my pardon directly, sir. I begged it as a man would do who was sure of obtaining it; the badinage pleased her, and the peace was signed.

You are no longer angry, said I, to the Marchioness.—Good! replied she, laughing; does the anger of a lover last long about such matters?—My dear mamma, I am spending some delightful moments with you; do you know to whom I am obliged for them?—It is very singular that you should think you are indebted for them to anyone but myself.—It is singular, I agree; but it is so.—Explain yourself, my friend.—I was ignorant of the happiness you intended me; I should still have been with M. du Portail, if your dear husband had not paid us a visit.—To M. du Portail?—And to me, madam. He has seen you at M. du Portail's?

Here I related to my beautiful mistress everything that had passed in the Marquis's visit to M. du Portail. She had great difficulty to restrain herself from laughing. The poor Marquis, said she, was born under an unfortunate star. It seems as if he went to seek for ridicule! A wife is very unhappy, my dear Faublas; from the moment she loves anyone, her husband is no more than a fool.—My dear mamma has not much to complain of: it seems, in this case, that the misfortune is on the husband. —Ah! but, replied she, assuming a serious air, one always feels the humiliations that a husband receives.—They feel them sometimes I admit; but do they never profit by them?— Faublas, you are cutting at yourself. But tell me; must you sup with the Marquis? You have no gown: and then, do you reckon to quit me so soon?—As late as possible, my dear mamma.—But you can dress yourself here. At these words, she rung for Justine: Go, said she, and get one of my gowns; we want to dress Mademoiselle. I shut the door upon Justine, who gave me a box on the ear; the Marchioness did not perceive it, and I returned near her.

My dear mamma, are you quite sure your *femme de chambre* will not talk?—Yes, my friend; I give her, to hold her tongue, a great deal more money than any will give her for tattling. I could not receive you at home; I must either renounce the pleasure of seeing you, or decide upon doing what is imprudent. My dear Faublas, I have not hesitated; it is not the first folly thou hast made me commit.— She took my hand, which she kissed, and then covered her eyes with it.—My dear mamma, will you not look at me any more?—Ah! at all times, and in all places, cried she, or it had been better I had never seen thee.

My hand, which lately concealed her eyes, was now pressing against her heart; her heart palpitated; her long eye-lashes were filled with tears; and her charming lips, approaching mine, demanded a kiss: she received a thousand!— a devouring flame burnt throughout me; I felt

that it was participated, and I wished to allay it ;
but my mistress, entirely absorbed and intoxicated by an overflow of tender sensations tasted
the inexpressible sweets of those pleasures which
come from the soul, and she refused enjoyments
less ravishing, although delightful.

Never to see thee more, replied she, would be
to exist no more, and I have only existed since—
An imprudence, added she quickly, rolling her
eyes on all the objects which surrounded us:
Ah! have I committed but one? How many
must I yet risk, if I judge by those which, in
so short a time, thou hast obliged me to commit!
—My dear mamma, permit me to ask a question, which is perhaps very indiscreet, but you
excite my most anxious curiosity; at whose
house, then, are we now?—This question awoke
the Marchioness from the ecstacy she was in:
At whose house are we?——at—at one of my
friends.—This friend loves—Madame de B***,
entirely recovered, hastened to interrupt me:
Yes, Faublas, she loves; you have said right;
she loves——It is love that has made this charming place; it is for her lover.—And for yours,
my dear mamma.—Yes, my good friend, she
was very willing to lend me this boudoir for the

evening.—That door, by which you entered—
Goes into her apartments.—One more question,
mamma.—Well?—How do you do?—[She
looked at me with an air of surprise, and
laughed.]—Yes, continued I, joking apart: you
were ill the day before yesterday: M. de Rosambert——Do not speak to me of him: M. de
Rosambert is an unworthy man, capable of
playing me a thousand dirty tricks, and of telling you a thousand stories. If he found you
disposed to believe him, he would confidently
assert that he had known all the women in the
world. Still, if he were nothing but a coxcomb,
I could pardon him; but his odious proceedings
towards me, even if I had merited them, would
be inexcusable.—It is true that he greatly tormented us the day before yesterday:—I did not
close my eyes all night! Let us drop that nevertheless. When I see thee, my dear friend, I
think no more of what I have suffered for thee.
How well you look in your male attire! How
handsome! how charming you are! but what a
pity, added she, rising with an air of gaiety,
that they must be laid aside. Come on, make
way for Mademoiselle du Portail. At these
words she undid, with a single stroke of her

hand, all the buttons of my waistcoat. I re-
venged myself on her neck-handkerchief, which
I had already considerably deranged, and which
I now took entirely away. She continued the
attack, and I was pleased with her vengeance;
we took off all without replacing anything. I
showed to the half-naked Marchioness the alcove, and once more she let me conduct her
there.

Some one gently knocked at the door. We
must do her justice, for this once she has executed her commission promptly. Though not
very decently covered, I was going, unthink-
ingly, to open the door to the *femme de chambre;* the Marchioness pulled a string, some
curtains closed around us, and the door opened.
—Madam, here is everything that's necessary,
shall I help you to dress?—No, Justine, I can
do that; but thou shalt dress my head: I will
ring for thee. Justine went out; we amused
ourselves some time in contemplating the laugh-
able and multiplied pictures which were presented by the glass which surrounded us. Come,
said the Marchioness, embracing me, I must
dress my daughter: I would have marked the
moment of my retreat by a final victory. No,

my good friend, added she, we must not abuse anything.

The duties of my toilette commenced. While the Marchioness was seriously occupied, I amused myself in a very different manner. We shall soon finish you, said my beautiful mistress; come on, recollect that you must be prudent now you are a girl. I was muffled up with stays and petticoats. My dear mamma, Justine must now dress my head; after which she can finish me. I was going to ring. How thoughtless he is! Do you not see the condition in which you have put me? I must dress also. I offered my services to the Marchioness; I did everything wrong. It requires more time to repair you than to pull you in pieces, my dear mamma.—Oh, yes, I see it will. What a fine *femme de chambre* I have; she is still more curious than unskilful.

At last we rung for Justine. We must dress this child's head.—Yes, madam. But must I not arrange your hair also? Why so? Is my head out of order?—Yes, madam, it seems so. The Marchioness opened a closet, where they thrust my male garments. To-morrow morning, said she, a discreet agent will carry them home

for you.   In another, but deeper closet, there
was a toilette table which they drew towards me,
and Justine began to exercise her little active
fingers.

The Marchioness, placing herself near me,
said: Mademoiselle du Portail, permit me to
make my court to you.—Yes, yes, interrupted
Justine; in expectation that M. de Faublas will
still make his to you.—What says that hair-
brained girl? replied the Marchioness.   She
says that I love you well.—Does she say true,
Faublas?—Do you doubt it, mamma? and I
kissed her hand.   That apparently displeased
Justine.   The devil's in the hair, said she, giving a vigorous stroke of the comb, how it is
entangled!—Ha!   Justine, you hurt me!—
Never mind, sir; think of your own business:
madam speaks to you.—Justine, I am saying
nothing; I am looking at Mademoiselle du Portail; thou makest her very pretty!—It is that
she may please Madame the more.—I think, at
the bottom, it amuses yourself.   Mademoiselle
du Portail, does it displease thee?—Madam, I
prefer M. de Faublas.—She is candid, at least.
—Very candid, madam; inquire of himself.—
Me, Justine?   I know nothing about it.—You

"*Here Justine tickled me gently in the neck in turning a curl.*"
Page 171.

tell stories, sir.—How tell stories?—Yes, sir, you must know that when I must do anything for you, I am always ready. When madam sends me to you, I go with alacrity. But, interrupted the Marchioness, you do not come back.—Madam, it was not my fault to-day, he made me wait. (Here Justine tickled me gently in the neck, in turning a curl.)—It is because he is not in a hurry when he comes to see me.—Ah! my dear mamma, I am never happy but when I am near you. I embraced the Marchioness, who affected to prevent it. Justine found this badinage too long; she pinched me rudely, the pain forced me to cry out. Take care what you do, said the Marchioness to Justine, with a little anger. But, madam, he cannot hold himself still for a moment.

We had a few moments' silence. My fair mistress had one of my hands within her own: the waggish Abigail occupied the other, by making me hold an end of ribbon, which she was plaiting in my hair; and seizing the moment, she dabbed a little pomatum on my face. Justine! said I.—Justine! said the Marchioness.—Madam, I employ but one hand, could he not defend himself with the other? And then, pretending that the puff had slipped from her hand, she threw some of the powder in my eyes.—Justine, you are very foolish! I will send you no more to his house!—Good! very good! Madam, is it because he is dangerous? I have no fear of him.—But, Justine, it is because you do not know how mischievous he is.—Oh, yes, I do, Madam.—Thou knowest it?—Yes, madam, Madam remembers the night that this sweet miss slept at our house!—Well?—I offered to undress her; madam would not let me.—Certainly; she appeared so modest and timid! Who might not have been deceived? I know not how I could pardon her.—It is because madam is so good? Madam, I said, then, that you did not wish it. Mademoiselle du Portail undressed herself behind the curtains. I passed, by chance, near her, at the moment when, having pulled off her last petticoat, she leaped into bed. —And what then?

To conclude, this droll young lady jumped so quick, and so singularly, that——Well! finish, then, said I to Justine.—Ah! but I dare not.—Finish, then, said the Marchioness, hiding her face with her fan.—She jumped so singularly, and with so little precaution, that I perceived

——What! Justine, interrupted the Marchioness, in a tone almost serious, did you perceive?—That it was a young man, madam.—What! and you did not tell me of it?—Good madam, how could I? your women were in the apartment! the Marquis about to enter! that would have made a fine confusion! and perhaps, Madame knew of it.—At these last words, the Marchioness turned pale. You are mocking me, miss; know, that if I choose to forget myself, I would not have other people forget their manners! The tone in which these words were pronounced made poor Justine tremble; she excused herself as well as she could. Madam, I was only joking.—I believe it, miss; if you had spoken seriously, I would discharge you this evening.—Justine began to cry. I tried to appease the Marchioness.—You must agree, said she, that she has been impertinent. How! dare to suppose; dare tell me to my face, before you, that I knew—She took me by the hand, and squeezed it gently.—My dear Faublas, my good friend, you know all that came to pass; you know if my weakness is excusable! your disguise deceived all the world. I saw a young lady at the ball, whose beauty and wit made me attached to her; she supped with me; she slept with me; every one has retired, the amiable girl is in my bed, at my side;—I find that he is a charming young man!—So far, chance, or rather love, did everything! After that, I have, without doubt, been very weak; but what woman, in my place, could have resisted; The next day I applauded the accident, which caused my happiness, and ensured it. Faublas, you know the Marquis; they married me against my consent; they sacrificed me; what woman would they excuse if they judge me with rigour?—I observed that the Marchioness was ready to cry, and I endeavoured to console her by a most tender kiss; I was going to speak: A moment, said she to me, a moment, my friend. The next day I confided to Justine my astonishing adventure; I told the whole—everything! Faublas. She has the secret of my life—my dearest secret! She appeared to pity me, and to love me; but her appearance was deceitful, for she has abused my confidence; she supposes what is horrible; she tells me to my face——

Justine burst into tears; she fell upon her knees before her mistress, and begged her pardon twenty times. I joined my entreaty to hers,

for I was sensibly affected. The Marchioness
was softened: Go, said she; I pardon you, Justine; yes, I pardon you.—Justine kissed her
mistress' hand, and begged her pardon. It is
sufficient, said the Marchioness to her, it is
sufficient, I am easy, I am satisfied; rise, Justine, and remember, that if your mistress has
weaknesses, they are not to be magnified into
vices; that, instead of making her out more
culpable than she is, you ought to excuse or
pity her; and, finally, that you render yourself
unworthy of her goodness when you are wanting in fidelity and respect. Come, added she
with much sweetness, leave off crying; get up, I
tell you that I pardon you; finish this head-
dress, and drop the subject.

Justine went on with her work, leering at me
in great confusion. The Marchioness looked at
me in a very languishing manner. We all
three kept silence, and the business of my toilette proceeded the quicker, as I had two *femmes
de chambre* instead of one. It was nine o'clock,
and time for us to separate: we took a parting
kiss. Go, you little rogue, said the Marchioness, and amuse my husband; to-morrow,
you can tell me what occurs. I went down; a

hackney-coach was at the door. As I got in, two young men passed; they looked very hard at me, and cracked some jokes, which were more gross than gallant. I was surprised at it: could the house from which I came be of a suspicious character? it belonged to one of the Marchioness' friends. My appearance was not that of a courtesan; why, then, did these *gents* cast their jeers at me? Perhaps it appeared strange to them, that a young woman of respectable appearance, and without a servant, should go alone in a hackney-coach at nine o'clock at night.

As the vehicle advanced, my reflections took another turn, and changed their object. I was alone; I thought of my Sophia. I had made her but a short visit in the forenoon, and during the evening I gave myself but a moment to think of her; but, if the reader would excuse me, let him think of the sweet enticements which were thrown in my way by the handsome and voluptuous *femme de chambre;* that Justine possessed very fascinating and luxurious charms; and, above all, let him remember that Faublas was scarcely sixteen when he commenced his noviciate.

I arrived at M. du Portail's. The Marquis made the most profound respects, and asked me if I had seen his wife. To say no, was to tell a lie; I must, nevertheless, resolve to do it. No, sir; said I.—I knew it well, I was sure of it. M. du Portail interrupted: You made us wait a long time for you, my dear; we are going to sit down to supper,—Without my brother?—He has sent word that he sups in the city.—What! on the eve of my departure?—Mademoiselle, you never told me you had a brother, said the Marquis.—I thought, monsieur, that I had informed the Marchioness of it.—She never mentioned it to me.—Indeed!—I give you my word and honour that she has never told me of it.—I believe you, sir.—Your father thought that I played the connoisseur without being one.—How?—How, mademoiselle! you will hardly believe what has taken place! When I arrived here, I recognised your brother whom I had never seen.—Ha! ha!—Ask your father.—It is very true, sir, that you recognised him; but Madame the Marchioness —She has never told me of it, I swear to you. —Indeed!—I give you my word and honour of it.—It was M. de Rosambert, then?—Neither has he told me of it.—I think, nevertheless, I have heard you say something to that effect.—Not a word of it, I protest.—(The Marquis was almost angry.)—It is I, then, who am mistaken! In that case you must be a very great physiognomist.—Oh, that is true! replied he in ecstacy; no one is so well skilled in physiognomy as I am.

M. du Portail was amused with this conversation, and fearing it would conclude too soon, We must agree also, said he to the Marquis, that there is a great family likeness.—I agree to it, replied he, I agree to it; but it is precisely this likeness we must catch, that we must distinguish in the features; it is that which constitutes real judges! Between father, mother, brothers, and sisters, there is always a family resemblance.—Always! cried I, always! do you believe?—If I believe! but I am sure of it.—Sometimes it is enveloped in the deportment, in the manners, in the looks: enveloped, I tell you, and concealed in such a manner as 'tis not easy to perceive it. Well, then! an expert man seeks for it—analyses it—do you conceive me!—In short, if, after having seen me, but not having seen my father, you had, by chance, met him in the midst of twenty persons——Him! amongst a thousand I should have known him.

M. du Portail and myself burst into laughter. The Marquis rose, left the table, went to M. du Portail, took his head with one hand, and with a finger of the other traced the face of my pretended father, saying, Do not laugh, sir, do not laugh. Here, mademoiselle, do you not see this line which rises here, passes along there, and comes back here? Does it come back? No, it does not come back; it stops there. Well! see—(he came towards me).—Sir, said I, I do not like to be touched.—(He stopped, and pointed with his finger, but without putting it on my face.)—Well! mademoiselle, behold this same line, there, here, and again there. There, do you not see it!—How, sir, how can I see it! —You laugh! you must not laugh; it is serious. You see it well, do you not, sir?—Very well.— Besides that, there is in the *tout ensemble,* in the configuration of the body, certain shadows— of resemblance; certain secret affinities—occult ——Occult! replied I, occult!—Yes, yes, occult! You do not know, perhaps, what is meant by occult? That is not astonishing for a girl! I say, then, monsieur, that there are certain secret resemblances——No, it was not resemblances I said——it was another word—more—better——By our Lady! I know not where I was, they have interrupted me so.—You said, sir, secret affinities.—Ah! yes, affinities! affinities! and I will explain it to you, sir, who are reasonable.—How! sir, do you mean to insult me!—No, my sweet girl, you cannot know everything your father knows.—Ah! in that sense——Yes, in that sense, my sweet lady; but let me beg that I may explain it to you, monsieur?—Monsieur, the fathers and mothers, in the procreation of individuals, make beings who resemble—who have secret affinities to the beings who have generated them, because the mother, on her side, and the father on his———Hush! hush! interrupted M. du Portail.—Oh! she does not comprehend that, said the Marquis; she is too young. It is, nevertheless, clear, and you can understand me. Those things, sir, are physical, and they have been philosophically proved by—by great physicians who understand such matters.

Why, then, speak so low? said I to the Marquis.—I have done, mademoiselle, I have done;

your father understands it.—You are well
skilled in physiognomy, monsieur, but are you
not also a judge of stuffs? What do you say to
this gown? It is very pretty; very pretty. I
think the Marchioness has one like it. Yes,
exactly like it.—Of the same stuff, and the same
color?—Of the same stuff I cannot say, but as
to the color, it is precisely the same. It is very
pretty; it becomes you very much. He then
began to pay many compliments in his peculiar
manner, and M. du Portail, who had guessed to
whom the gown belonged, regarded me with a
look of displeasure, and seemed to reproach me
for having so soon forgot the promise I had
made him.

We were rising from the table when my real
father, M. de Faublas, who had promised to
fetch me, arrived. His astonishment was very
great at finding his son a second time disguised,
and in company with the Marquis de B***.
Again! said he, looking at me with much severity; and you, M. du Portail, you have the
goodness——Ah! good evening to you, my
friend; do you not recognise monsieur the Marquis de B***? He has done me the honour to
sup with me, in order to take farewell of my

daughter, who sets off to-morrow.—Who goes to-morrow? replied the Baron, coldly saluting the Marquis.—Yes, my friend, she returns to her convent; did you not know it? Indeed, my friend, I tell you she goes to-morrow.—Yes, sir, interrupted the Marquis, she is going; I am very sorry for it, and my wife will be much grieved about it.—And I, replied my father, am very glad of it; it is time it was finished, added he, looking at me. M. du Portail, fearing he might get into a passion, drew him on one side. Who, then, is that man? said the Marquis to me: did I not see him here the other day?—Certainly.—I knew him at first sight; when once I have seen a countenance, I know it again. But this man displeases me; he always looks angry. Is he a relation of yours?—Not at all.—Oh! I could have wagered he was not of the family! There is not in your countenances the slightest resemblance; yours is always gay, his ever gloomy; at least, but a Platonic smile; no, *sartonic*—is it *sartonic* or sard—— In short—you understand me. I would say, that if he did not look sideways at you, he would laugh in your face.—Never mind that, he is a philosopher.—A philosopher! replied the Marquis, with an air of alarm; I am no longer astonished. A philosopher! Ah! I must go. M. du Portail and the Baron were conversing together, and turned their backs towards us. The Marquis bade adieu to M. du Portail. Do not disturb yourself, said he to the Baron, who was turning round to salute him; do not disturb yourself, sir; I do not like philosophers, not I, and am very happy you do not belong to this family. A philosopher! a philosopher! repeated he, and flew out of the room.

When he was gone, my father and M. du Portail began to chat in a low tone. I went to sleep by the fireside. I had a delightful dream; the image of my lovely Sophia was presented to my dormant senses. Faublas! cried my father, let us go.—To see my pretty cousin? said I, in my stupor.—His pretty cousin! See, he has been sleeping as he sat there.—M. du Portail smiled. He said, go home, my friend, go and sleep, I think you have need of it; we will see each other again: I owe you some reproaches, and the continuation of my story: we will meet again.

When I got home, I asked for the Abbé Person. He was gone to bed. I did the same, and did right. Never did any one sleep sounder under the fraternal harangues of our free masons; at the public lectures of the modern museum; under the precious pleadings of D***, of C***, of D'L***, and of many other great orators represented in the famous picture.

When I rose, I rang for Jasmin, to inform him that they would bring home my clothes, which I had left the night before with a friend in the city. Afterwards, I bade him call M. Person. I asked him after Adelaide and Mademoiselle du Points.—You saw them yesterday, replied he.—And you also, M. Person, you have seen them, and even told them that I had made an acquaintance at the ball.—Well, sir, and what evil was there in that?—And what necessity, sir? Tell my sister your own secrets, if you please; but for mine, I beg you will respect them.—Indeed, sir, you speak in a very high tone. For some days past you are quite altered. I shall complain to your father, sir.— And I, sir, to my sister; (I saw him turn pale.) Believe me, let us be friends; my father desires me to go out with you.—Well, finish dressing yourself, and let us go to the convent.

We were going, when Rosambert arrived. As

soon as he knew where we were going, he begged
me to let him accompany us. For these four
months past, said he, you have promised to introduce me to your amiable sister.—I am going
to keep my word, Rosambert, and you will see
a girl whom you will be compelled to esteem.—I
am well convinced, my friend, that Mademoiselle de Faublas is, in this case, an exception; but I retort upon you the formidable argu-
ment with which you have armed yourself
against me: an exception does not destroy the
rule, but proves it.—Just as you please. I
warn you that you are going to see a lass of
fourteen years and a half, innocent and ingenuous, even to simplicity; nevertheless, she is as
tall as one can be at her age, and she wants
neither understanding nor education.

No one could be more unhappy than I was:
my sister came to the conference room; my
Sophia did not come. After the first salutations
and a few moments general conversation, I could
no longer dissemble my uneasiness. Where,
Adelaide, is my pretty cousin?—Oh, my dear
brother, her illness must be very serious, for she
confines herself all day. I no longer recognise
her: formerly, she was as thoughtless, gay and

lively as myself; now I behold her gloomy, thoughtful and unhappy. We find her, it is true, nearly as mild and affectionate when we go to her, but she rarely comes to us. During our hours of recreation, she used to play and run in the gardens with our companions; at present, she seeks some retired corner, and walks by herself. Oh! she is ill; she is ill, indeed: she eats little, sleeps less, and never smiles; and I, whom she loved so much, am now shunned, as if she feared me! Yes, indeed, I have remarked it; she flies from everybody, but avoids me above all. Yesterday, I saw her enter a little shaded walk at the bottom of the garden; I approached her unperceived, and found her wiping her eyes: My dear friend, what is the matter with you? She gave me such a look; such a look as I never saw any one have before. At last, she replied,—Adelaide, dost thou not guess? Ah! how happy thou art! But I am to be pitied. And then she blushed, she sighed and wept. I tried to comfort her. The more I spoke to her, the more she grieved. I embraced her; she held me a long time, and appeared tranquil: all at once, she put her hand on my eyes, and said, Adelaide, hide thy face! Oh!

hide it! It is too much; it makes me ill. Leave
me; go in a moment; leave me alone: and she
began to weep again. Perceiving that her illness increased, I said: Sophia!

At the name of Sophia, Rosambert whispered
into my ear: Sophia is the pretty cousin; it is
this Sophia that I have blasphemed. Ah, pardon me. My sister continued:

I said to her: Wait a moment, Sophia; I will
go and fetch thy governante. She then recovered herself, dried her eyes, and begged me to
say nothing. I was obliged to promise her that I
would not. But still it was very unreasonable
of her, to be ill, and not wish her governante
to know it!—Why did she not come here with
you to-day, my dear Adelaide?—It is because
she is so distracted, so absorbed! She loved you
almost as much as me, formerly.—And now?—
I think she loves you no more. Just now I told
her that you were here.—My young cousin!
cried she, with an air of satisfaction; she was
coming; but she stopped. No, I will not go,
said she; I will not, I cannot! tell him from me,
that——She appeared as if thinking what to
say, and I waited her explanation. Do you not
know what to say to him? To which she added,

with a little anger: What they say in similar cases, the customary compliments! and she quitted me abruptly.

I was intoxicated with pleasure to hear my ingenuous sister describe, with the innocence of a child, the tender agitations and sweet anxieties of Sophia. Rosambert seemed struck with astonishment, and lent an attentive ear; and the little Abbé, looking at us all three, appeared at the same time both restless and delighted.

You think then, Adelaide, that Sophia loves me no more?—I am almost sure of it, brother. Everything which relates to you puts her out of temper, and I am sometimes the victim of her ill humour.—How?—Yes, the other day, monsieur the Abbé Person informed us that you had passed the whole night at a ball with Madame the Marchioness de B***. Well! when he was gone, as soon as we were alone, Sophia said to me, in a very serious tone: Your brother did not sleep at home. That is not right—*Your* brother!—In general she said thee, thou, and thy. *Your* brother! If you have done anything wrong, Faublas, why should she be angry with me? *Your* brother! The

next day, I believe you had been to a masked
ball. The Abbé came to tell us, for he tells
us everything. As soon as we are alone, Sophia
said: Your brother amuses himself at the ball,
whilst we pass our weary hours here.—Not at
all, replied I; one is never tired in the company of a dear friend.—Ah! yes, added she:
ah! yes, with one's dear friend; that is true.
Nevertheless, Faublas, behold her singularity:
a moment after, she repeats, in a melancholy
manner: He amuses himself at the ball, while
we weary ourselves here!—We weary ourselves!
And even if it was true, it was not polite; she
ought not to say so. Oh! if she were not ill,
I would not excuse her. I recollect also another
trait. Yesterday, you told us that Madame de
B*** was pretty. In the evening I followed
Sophia, and made her walk with me. Your
brother, said she, (for at present it is always
your brother), finds this Marchioness pretty,
and he is, no doubt, in love with her. I replied:
That cannot be, my friend; this Madame de
B*** is married. She took my hand, and said:
Ah! Adelaide, how happy thou art? and there
was something of disdain and pity in her look
and smile. Is that polite? Ah! how happy

thou art!—Well, it is true, I am happy when I am in good health.

But, Adelaide, all that you have told me is no proof that Sophia has ceased to love me. She may be a little angry; but it is common to behave thus towards those they love.—Oh! no doubt, if that was all!—And what else is there, then?—Oh! formerly she talked of you unceasingly; she was delighted to see you: at present, she but rarely mentions you, and always in a very serious tone. Did you not observe it yesterday? She never said a word, not a single word, while you were here. Do not deceive yourself, my dear brother; when we love people, we always speak to them. I assure you that my friend loves you no more.

Here Rosambert joined in the conversation, the subject of which was changed. We spoke of dancing, music, history, and geography. My sister, who had been prattling like a child of six years, now reasoned like a woman of twenty. The Count, each moment more surprised, did not seem aware how the time glided by, although several times warned of it by the Abbé Person. At last, the sound of a bell, which summoned the boarders to the refectory, obliged us to retire.

I confess to you, said the Count, that I can scarcely believe what I have seen. How can they connect ignorance and knowledge; modesty and beauty; the simplicity of childhood and the reason of maturity; in short, permit me to say, such extreme innocence with such precocious faculties and acquirements? I thought this union impossible, my friend. Your sister is the masterpiece of nature and education.—This masterpiece, Rosambert, is the fruit of fourteen years of cares and of pleasure; it was produced by a rare concourse of fortunate events. The Baron de Faublas knew that the education of a daughter was a heavy burthen for a military man: my mother, whom we shall always regret, my amiable and virtuous mother, was found worthy to be charged with it. Chance also has seconded her efforts, she met with servants for her daughter, who obeyed without disputing; a governante, who neither related amorous stories nor read romances; with masters, who were only occupied with their pupil while going through her lessons; a society of attentive persons, who were not guilty of a suspicious gesture, or an equivocal word; and, which is by no means the least essential, a director who, in his confessional, listened, but put no questions. In short, my friend, it is only six months that Adelaide has been at the convent.—Six months! Ah! how many young ladies, whom we call well educated, have acquired great intelligence in a much shorter time; yes, and even received certain lessons, which wonderfully advance young girls.—It is in this respect, Rosambert, that we must still more admire the happiness of Adelaide! Lively, playful, cheerful with her companions, she has selected but one, as delicate, as well bred, as prudent as herself. One, somewhat more enlightened, perhaps, because within a little time, love——I understand you, it is the pretty cousin.—Yes, my friend, Sophia, not less virtuous than Adelaide, though susceptible a little sooner of certain impressions, is become the only friend of my sister. Their two hearts, so pure, are, as we may suppose, attracted and blended together. Adelaide, deprived of her mother, has not thought nor lived but in Sophia. Their friendship, as delicate as lively, saves them from the dangers of which you speak, and to which I can conceive they must be exposed in

such a society, surrounded by so many ardent,
restless and curious young girls, with whom the
nature of the place is calculated to lead them
into intimate connections. The close union of
these two friends has lately been interrupted by
myself: I flatter myself that I am become the
happy object of my pretty cousin's most tender
affections. Adelaide, on whom love (I looked
at the Abbé Person) has not yet exercised his
power, has devoted towards Sophia entire
friendship, and the bitterness of her complaints
proves to us the excess of her affection.—And
you assure yourself, in the meantime, of your
happiness. Indeed, Faublas, I congratulate
you, if Sophia is as amiable and as beautiful as
Adelaide.—More handsome, my friend, still
more handsome! Imagine——Hush! hush!
gently! how warm he gets! Tell me then, my
sentimental friend, since you have so charming
a mistress, why have you choused me out of
mine? Since M. de Faublas loves the conversation room so much, why has Mademoiselle du
Portail slept with the Marchioness? How do
you reconcile this?—That is not difficult, Rosambert.—Nor disagreeable, I conceive.—You
laugh: hear me then, my friend: You know

how things have gone between the Marchioness
and me?—Yes, yes; near the matter.—Nay,
you eternal sneerer, listen to me. Educated
nearly in the same manner as my sister, I was
scarcely less ignorant than her, eight days since.
I have not taken Madame de B***, it is she who
ensnared me. I am excusable.—Go on; come to
the masqued ball: but, at least, you were not
obliged to return to the house. The masqued
ball! hem! what say you?—I say, that they
drew me there; I am scarcely sixteen years, and
my sensations are new to me.—Ah, Sophia!
poor Sophia!—Do not pity her, I adore her!
but I am sure, Rosambert, nothing but the law-
ful rites can insure me possession of her.—That
may be, at least——Well! trusting that Hymen
will unite us, I shall always respect my Sophia.
—That is to be seen hereafter.—In the meantime, my celibacy will seem hard.—I believe it.
—My high spirits will sometimes carry me too
far.—Without doubt.—I shall, perhaps, be
guilty of an occasional infidelity to my pretty
cousin.—That is more than probable.—But as
soon as a happy marriage—ah, yes!—then, my
Sophia, I will love none but thee!—That is not

certain.—I will love her all my life.—That appears to me rash.

Rosambert left me. Jasmin, of whom I enquired if any one had brought home my clothes, said he had not seen anyone. I waited until the evening, in expectation of a messenger, but none came. I was uneasy, because I had left a pocket-book in my pocket, which contained two letters; one had been sent me from the country by an old domestic of my father, in which the good man wished me a happy new year, and the customary compliments on such occasions. I was sorry to lose the other, it was that which the Marchioness had written to me some days before; it was addressed to Mademoiselle du Portail, and I wished to preserve it.

The clothes were brought me in the morning after, but I searched in vain in the pockets, for the pocket-book was not there. At this moment Madame Dutour arrived, and caused me to forget my uneasiness by delivering me a letter from the Marchioness. I opened it with eagerness, and read:—

"My Dear Friend,—Be at the door of my house by seven precisely, this evening. You may follow with confidence, the person, who, after having lifted up your hat with which you will cover your eyes, will call you ' Adonis.' I cannot write more to you, I have been beset ever since the morning, and fatigued with the details of physiognomical science, and it is not that in which I am anxious to become profound. Oh, my friend! you are so well skilled in the art of pleasing, that to know you is to love you—I wish to know nothing more."

This letter was so flattering, and the invitation it contained so seducing, that I could not hesitate in complying with its commands. I assured Dutour that I would not fail to be at the appointed place. Nevertheless, when she was gone, I felt some degree of irresolution. Ought I not, in future, to be entirely occupied with Sophia, and to avoid all occasions of seeing so dangerous a rival? But why shall I impose upon myself this cruel restriction, without necessity? Have I declared my love to Sophia? Has Sophia avowed her's to me? Has she acquired the right of demanding this sacrifice of me? Besides, might not my refusing to indulge the Marchioness be called an infidelity? It is not embarking in a new intrigue! since I have passed a night with the Marchioness—since I have seen her again in that agreeable boudoir—what harm can there be in my paying her one more visit? And then, my pretty cousin will know nothing of it. In short, my word was engaged, and the reader will agree that I could not dispense with going to the rendezvous.

I did not make them wait for me; neither did Justine suffer me to wait at the door; she lifted up my hat: Come charming Adonis! said she. I followed her with gentle steps. Nevertheless, the porter, although half drunk, heard some noise, and demanded who it was.—It is me! it is me! replied Justine.—Yes, replied the other, it is you! but who is that young spark?—Who is it? why, my cousin!—The porter was in good humour, and we passed without any trouble.

Justine conducted me to the bottom of the court, and we slipped up a private staircase. It may easily be conceived that the pretty *soubrette* was embraced several times before we arrived at the first landing-place. She then made a sign for me to be more prudent, and took me through a little door, which conducted me into the Marchioness' boudoir. Go, said Justine, go into the bed-room; you will be safer there.—She went out, and shut the door after her.

I went into the bed-chamber, and my charming mistress came to me. Ah! my dear mamma, I am then here for the second time. She interrupted me; My God! I think I hear the Marquis! and here he is, sure enough, come home for the evening; save yourself! go! I flew in an instant to the boudoir, but I did not think of shutting the bed-room door after me; it remained ajar; and, to heighten my misfortune, Justine had double-locked the other door, which led to the private staircase. The Marchioness, who could not guess that my retreat was cut off, seated herself tranquilly. The Marquis had already entered her apartment, and appeared somewhat disconcerted. I trembled lest he should see me in the boudoir, as there was no means of getting out. What was I to do? I crept under the sofa, and, in a very uncomfortable position, I heard a very singular conversation, which terminated in a manner still more singular.

You are returned in good time, monsieur.—Yes, madam.—I did not expect you so soon.—

I crept under the sofa, and, in a very uncomfortable position, I heard
a very singular conversation.

Page 198.

That is very possible, madam.—You appear
agitated; what is the matter with you?—It is,
madam—it is—I am furious.—Calm yourself,
monsieur; may I know what it is?—It is—there
is no longer any morality in the world—the
women!——The remark, monsieur, is polite,
and the application happy!—Madam, I like not
to be trifled with! and, when I am tricked, I
perceive it very soon!—What do you mean,
monsieur, by these reproaches; these insults! to
whom are they addressed? you will explain yourself, without doubt?—Yes, madam, I will explain myself, and then you will be convinced!—
Convinced of what?—Of what!—in a moment
madam; you do not let me have time to breathe!
You have received into your house, lodged with
you, and had to sleep with you, Mademoiselle
du Portail!—[The Marchioness, with great
firmness:] Well! monsieur.—Well! madam;
and do you know who this Mademoiselle du
Portail is?—I know the same as you, monsieur;
she was introduced by M. de Rosambert; her
father is a respectable gentleman, with whom
you supped the night before last.—That is not
the question, madam; do you know who this
Mademoiselle du Portail is?—I repeat it to you,

monsieur, that I know, as you do, that Mademoiselle du Portail is a young lady of good birth and education, and extremely amiable.—That is not the question, madam.—Well, monsieur, and pray what is the question, then? Have you sworn to put my patience to the test?—In a moment, then, madam, Mademoiselle du Portail is not a girl.—[The Marchioness, in a very lively manner:] Is not a girl!—Is not a girl well born, madam; she is a girl of a certain description; like those girls who—there—you understand me?—I assure you I do not, monsieur.—I have, nevertheless, sufficiently explained myself; she is a girl who—that—in short, you know what I mean.—Oh! not at all, Monsieur, I assure you.—She is, what I would have told you without naming it; madam, she is a wh***; do you understand me now?—Mademoiselle du Portail a wh***! Pardon me, sir, I cannot contain myself, I must laugh.—(And the Marchioness did indeed laugh with all her strength.) You may laugh, madam; but stop! do you know this letter?—Yes, it was what I wrote to Mademoiselle du Portail the day after she slept with me.—Truly, madam, and do you know this?—No, Monsieur.—Look at it, madam, you see the address: " A Monsieur, le Chevalier Fabulas:" and read its contents:—

" My Dear Master,—May I take the liberty of intruding upon you, to wish that the year now commenced may be happy and prosperous for you, etc., etc.

" I have the honour to be, with profound respect,

" My dear Master, etc., etc."

It is a new-year's letter from a domestic to his master, who is a Monsieur de Faublas.—Well, madam, these letters were in the pocket-book which you see here. What then, monsieur?— You cannot guess where I found it?—Tell me; tell me, monsieur.—I found it in a place where ——Well, monsieur, tell me the rest, you delight in being mysterious.—Well, then, madam, I found it in a bad place.—In a bad place?— Yes, madam, where curiosity led me; stop! I am going to explain that to you. A woman has lately circulated some printed letters, by which she informs lovers that she can accommodate them with some charming boudoirs, which she will let at so much an hour; as for myself, I only went to see them out of curiosity, sheer curiosity, as I told you just now.—What day were you there, monsieur?—Yesterday, after dinner, madam; and the boudoirs were, indeed, charming! there is one on the first floor which is very pretty! there are paintings, prints, mirrors, an alcove, a bed, ah, such a bed! imagine to yourself a bed with springs! ah, 'tis very pleasant! one of these days I must show it to you. A husband and his wife go to such a place! replied the Marchioness, that would be very fine!

I heard some noise; the Marquis was embracing his wife, and she was preventing him. Their conversation, which in the commencement rendered me very uneasy, now amused me so much, that it lessened the restraint of my situation. The Marquis continued as follows:

But that nothing may be wanting, there is, in the boudoir on the first floor, a door which communicates with the house of a milliner, who lives adjoining: it is admirably contrived. You might suppose a lady of quality going to her milliner: no such thing; she steps upstairs, and the head of a poor husband is cornuted. In this boudoir I opened a little closet, and there it was

I found the pocket-book. Therefore, it is clear that Mademoiselle du Portail has been there with this M. de Faublas; and that it is very scandalous of her, and it is very bad conduct of M. de Rosambert, who knew it, to introduce her to us, and very imprudent of her father to let her come out accompanied only by a *femme de chambre.* But I was not their dupe! There is in her countenance——You know what a physiognomist——Her countenance is pretty! but there is a something in her features which indicates a blood——She has a warm temperament; I observed it particularly. Do you not recollect the evening that Rosambert said there were circumstances—Hem! circumstances did you not remark that? Ah! they cannot deceive me! and mind you, the same day——Come, come, madam.

The Marchioness, who thought me gone, suffered him to conduct her into her boudoir. The Marquis continued:

She was here, in this boudoir, there; you were reclining yourself on this sofa; and I arrived, madam; she had a most animated and glowing complexion; her eyes sparkled, her looks were peculiar. Oh! I tell you this girl has a tempera-

ment of fire. You know I am a judge; but leave
it to me, I'll set the matter right.—How, monsieur, will you put it right? Yes, madam; I
shall tell Rosambert what I think of his proceedings. Rosambert has, perhaps, been connected with her; Afterwards I will see M. du
Portail, and will inform him of the conduct of
his daughter.—What! monsieur, will you
plunge Rosambert in a disagreeable quarrel?—
Madam, madam, Rosambert knew what she was;
he was jealous as a tiger of me.—Of you, monsieur?—Yes, madam, of me; because the girl
appeared to prefer me. She even made advances to me; and 'tis in that she has trifled with
me, for she had at the same time this M. de
Faublas. I will know who this M. de Faublas
is, and I will see M. du Portail.—What! monsieur, could you go to tell a father?—Yes,
madam, it would be doing him a service; I'll go
and acquaint him with everything.—I hope,
monsieur, you'll do no such thing—I shall do it,
madam.—If you have any consideration for me,
you will leave it to take its chance.—No, no, I
cannot.—I beg it as a favour of you, monsieur.
—No, no, madam.—I see through you now,
monsieur; I discover the motive which interests

you so much in what regards Mademoiselle du
Portail. I know you too well to be the dupe of
this austerity of morals which you put on to-
day; you are angry, not because Mademoiselle
du Portail has been in a suspicious place, but
because she has been there with any other than
yourself—Oh! madam.—And when I invited
home a young lady, whom I thought virtuous,
you had designs upon her.—Madam!—And you
dare come and complain to me of having been
tricked! It is I, it is I alone who have been
the dupe!

She threw herself upon the sofa. Her husband cried out, and then embraced her, saying,
If you knew how I loved you!—If you loved
me, monsieur, you would have had more consideration for me, more respect for yourself,
more tenderness for a child who is, perhaps,
more to be pitied than blamed. What are you
doing, monsieur? Leave me. If you love me,
you will not go to inform an unhappy father of
the errors of his child; you will not go and relate
this adventure to M. de Rosambert, who will
laugh at it, make a jest of you, and spread a
report that I have received in my house a girl
of intrigue! But, monsieur, have done; what

you would do is nothing to the purpose.—
Madam, I love you.—It is not sufficient to say
so; it must be proved.—But for these three or
four days, my love, you would not let me prove
it.—It is not such proofs as these which I demand of you, monsieur. But monsieur; have
done then, I say.—Come on, madam, my love.
—Indeed, monsieur, that is very ridiculous!—
We are alone.—It would be better if there were
other persons here; that would be decent. Have
done then, I say; have we not always time to
do those things! Leave me alone.—What! married people! at your age? in a boudoir! on a
sofa! like lovers! and when I have something
else to request of you.—Well, my angel, I'll say
nothing to Rosambert, nothing to M. du Portail.
—You can promise well.—I'll give you my
word.—Well then! Stop a moment; give me
the pocket-book; leave it with me.—With all my
heart; there it is. (There was a short silence.)
Indeed, monsieur, said the Marchioness, in a
voice almost extinct, you desired it; but it is
very ridiculous.

I heard them stammer, sigh, and die away
both together. One may imagine what I suffered under the sofa during this strange scene.

I could have strangled the actors with my own
hands; and in the excess of my spite I was
tempted to discover myself, to reproach the
Marchioness for this new species of infidelity,
and to repay the Marquis for the bitter mortification he had made me undergo, without knowing it.

Justine came to terminate my irresolution;
she opened all at once, the door of the private
staircase. The Marchioness shrieked out. The
Marquis fled into the bedroom, to put himself in
order. Justine, perceiving a husband instead
of a lover, was struck with astonishment; nor
was the Marchioness less surprised when she
saw me come from under the sofa. I whispered
my thanks to the *femme de chambre*. Many
thanks Justine; you have rendered me as essential service. I was very uncomfortable beneath,
while madam was so much at her ease above.
The Marchioness, alarmed and trembling, dared
neither to reply to me nor to retain me, as her
husband was so near, and probably would enter
as soon as he was decently dressed. Justine
stood on one side, to let me pass. I descended
the private staircase without a light, at the risk

of breaking my neck. I flew across the court
and got out of the house, cursing its owners.

The next morning I was still in bed when
Jasmin announced the arrival of Justine, and
retired discreetly. My dear girl, I dreamt of
you!—Ah, monsieur! let me alone; you must
not do so this time. I will commence by exe-
cuting my commission. Do you know that I
got a fine scolding yesterday? You put us into
a terrible alarm! You had not reached the bottom of the staircase, when the Marquis entered
the boudoir. See this fool, said she to him, who
entered here like a shot from a pistol. As soon
as he had quitted us, my mistress, distracted at
the adventure, told me she could not conceive
why you hid yourself under the sofa. I was
forced to acknowledge that I had, without knowing it, double-locked the door. She flew into
a violent passion with me, and this morning
she sent me with this letter for you.—Very well,
my dear Justine; now your commission is done,
for I shall not open the letter.—You will not
open it, monsieur? No, I am angry with the
Marchioness.—You are wrong.—But I cannot
be angry with thee, Justine.—You are right.—
Well, make haste then.—But, stop; I will, on

condition that you read the letter.—Oh! how happy a mistress is to have a girl like thee! Well; I'll read it.

Justine so cheerfully fulfilled the conditions of the treaty that it would have been perfidious on my part not to have kept my word. I opened the letter.

"My Dear Friend,—I am greatly distressed at our adventure yesterday. That scene, which would only have been strange had you not been a witness of it, has become, by your presence, as disagreeable to me as mortifying to you. What an expression you made use of at parting! You are ungrateful! You know not the pain you gave me! Let me see you again, my dear friend; come to her who loves you! Come at noon to the place you will be told of. There I shall have no trouble in defending myself; there, when my lover shall be well convinced of his injustice, he will find me ready to pardon his hasty remark."

Monsieur, replied Justine, as soon as I had finished the letter, madam expects you by noon at the boudoir, where you met the other day.

You know it well, where we dressed you.—Yes, Justine, and where you cried so much! If thou knew how I suffered for thee! But thou wert not content with playing her queer tricks, but must also say spiteful things to her.—Do not speak to me of that, I am still ashamed of it.— Have done then! Give me your answer for my mistress.—My answer is, Justine, that I will not go to the rendezvous.—You will not go?— No, Justine.—What! will you give this mortifi- cation to my mistress?—Yes, my dear girl.— But you will get me scolded at.—I'll comfort thee for that beforehand.—Are you indeed de- cided, then?—Fully decided, Justine.—Well, in that case there is an end of the letter. (She embraced me.) Write a word for my mistress. —No, my dear, I will not write.—Leave me alone! But I will again, on condition that you write.—Ah Justine! I repeat it, how happy a mistress is to have such a girl as thee. Well, I will write. I wrote as follows:

" I know not, madam, whether the adventure of yesterday gave you much *pain;* but, from the manner in which you fulfilled your employment on the sofa, I have reason to believe you did not think it very painful. When one has a husband who is amiable, gallant, and tenderly beloved, madam, one ought to keep him.

"I am, with the most lively regret, etc., etc."

Oh, my pretty cousin! how much, when I think of you, do I applaud the generous effort I am about to make! Oh, how sweet it was to think that at length I had sacrificed an agreeable assignation on your account, and at the very hour even when the Marchioness thought of seeing me again at the house of her *friend*, I should enjoy the happiness of seeing and admiring you!

Alas! she did not come to the conversation-room!—Why is your friend not with you, my dear sister?—I told you truly, that she was ill! Yesterday, she was crying again all day; in the night, she never closed her eyes, and she is declared to be in a fever this morning.—A fever! Sophia in a fever! Sophia in danger!—Do not speak so loud, brother; I know not that she is in danger, but she suffers a great deal. Her complexion is pale, her eyes are red, her head droops, she breathes slow, her speech short and stammering; I have even thought her delirious

at times. This morning, her face was inflamed
all at once, her eyes became lively and brilliant;
she spoke very quick, and very softly, some
words which I did not understand: but presently, she relapsed into a lethargy: *No, no,* said
she, *that is not possible; I cannot; I ought not
to do it; he will never know it!* I saw the tears
flow from her eyes. She added, in a piteous
tone: *How I am deceived! It will kill me! it
will kill me! the cruel! the ungrateful!* I took
her hand, she pressed mine, and then she said
the same again, and repeated, without ceasing:
Adelaide! Adelaide! oh, how happy thou art!
Her governante entered; Sophia again conjured
me to say nothing. Nevertheless, my dear
brother, it was necessary that I should inform
Madame Munich (which was the name of
Sophia's governante,) for I am alarmed for my
dear friend. What think you?—Have you told
her Adelaide, that I was here?—Yes, but I had
good reason, yesterday, to tell you she loved you
no more, she has told me so herself.—Sophia
has told you?—Yes, she said so, and charged me
to tell you of it. Last night, before supper time,
I told her you brought with you a very amiable
young gentleman. She inquired his name. I

replied that it was the Count de Rosambert. *Rosambert! it was he that introduced your brother to the Marchioness de B****. He is not a good young man! your brother has made a friend of him: he will entirely spoil your brother! He has already begun to render your brother unsteady.—Ah, my dear friend! I have been reproaching him; I have even told him that you did not love him any more. Yes, my dear friend, but he would not believe me; he only laughed at me; and M. de Rosambert laughed also.—These gentlemen laughed, did they! said Sophia, in an angry tone: Your brother laughed, and would not believe you! when will your brother come again, Adelaide?—To-morrow.— Tell him, it is true I felt a friendship for him, but that I feel it no longer; and, to convince him of it, tell him I will not see him again as long as I live. She left me; and, a moment after, she came back, and told me, laughing: Yes, my dear Adelaide, you were right; I love not your brother; I do not love him; do not fail to tell him so to-morrow. She smiled; nevertheless, I assure you, Faublas, that she has been weeping ever since.

During this relation, my heart was alter-

nately elevated with joy, and depressed with sorrow.

I must tell you, continued my sister, a singular notion which has occurred to me, I know not
how, or why. When I saw my dear friend laugh
and cry at the same time, I could not help con-
cluding that she was a little deranged; nevertheless, there is a mystery about her which I cannot
penetrate; surely some one must have done
something to grieve her; I am much afraid that
it is you, my brother. Why can she hate him?
said I to myself. Why will she see him no
more? Can it be him she called ungrateful
and cruel? You may judge, Faublas, that when
I reflect a little, this idea cannot appear reasonable. My brother ungrateful? cruel? that cannot be. And then what harm can he have done
to my dear friend? what evil could he possibly
do to her.

Adelaide! exclaimed I; my dear Adelaide!

Why do you weep? said she, are you angry
with me? I assure you I thought all that in
spite of myself, and I did not tell it you to offend you.—I know it well, my dear sister, I
know it well; it is the malady of your dear
friend that I weep for.—Do you think, brother,

that it will become serious? do you think that
I ought to inform her governante?—No, Adelaide, no; do not inform her. Your fair friend
has a fever, as you have observed; and I know
a remedy which will cure her. I will bring you,
Adelaide, the recipe to-morrow morning, written
upon a piece of paper, and carefully sealed.
You must not show the paper to anyone; you
will give it to Sophia when Madame Munich is
not with her. It is important that Madame
Munich does not see the paper. You understand me well!—Yes, yes, make yourself easy:
ah, what obligations I shall owe you if you cure
my dear friend!—Adelaide, tell my pretty
cousin that I think I know her malady; that I
participate in it, and hope to restore her to
tranquility. Be sure you tell her so, Adelaide.
—Ah, word for word: You know her malady,
you participate in it, and will cure it. I will
tell her even that you have wept. But do not
fail to come to-morrow, to bring the recipe; and,
in the meantime, neglect nothing that can render
her cure certain. Be careful not to act from
your judgment alone, as you know, brother, you
are not a physician: go to-day among the most
celebrated of them, see them, inform them, and

consult them; the disorder is not common, for I have never seen the like, and I tremble less it become more dangerous. Good God! if, in endeavouring to remove the complaint, you should render it incurable! It must be a radical cure, my brother; and expeditious also. Hasten then, Faublas, for Sophia, who is suffering and dying; and for my sake, who am unhappy on her account; and likewise for yourself, my dear brother; for my dear friend, as soon as she is well, will love you, without doubt, as much as she did before.

When I reached home, my mind was entirely occupied with the conversation of Adelaide, and the sufferings of Sophia. Unfortunately, my father had a party to dinner, and I was obliged to sit down at table, and afterwards to play a cursed game of cards, which detained me until midnight. How tormenting it is, when one loves, and believes oneself beloved, and wishes to write to one's mistress—how tormenting it is to be obliged to play! I could not hate my most cruel enemy more than I did the cards.

It may be guessed that I slept little during the night. The next day, I went into a little closet, which joined my bedroom; I had there some books for study, with which my accommodating tutor did not often tire me. The first letter I wrote did not please, and was torn up; a second, which was full of raptures, shared the same fate; and I beg the reader not to say that I ought to have begun again this third, which follows:

"My Pretty Cousin,—The long wished for moment is at last arrived, when I can freely open to you my heart, to solicit from your tenderness a kind of confession; and thus, perhaps, insure our mutual happiness.

"Ah, Sophia! Sophia! if you knew what I experienced the first day that I saw you! how my eyes were confounded! how my heart was agitated! Since then, my love has increased daily, and at this moment a devouring flame circulates throughout my veins. Sophia, I exist but in you!"

I had got thus far, when Jasmin entered abruptly, and announced the Viscomte de Florville. The Viscomte de Florville! I know him not. Tell him I am not at home.—He is already in your bedroom, monsieur.—What! do you let

all the world come there!—He forced the door,
monsieur.—The devil take the Viscomte de Florville!

Fearing that this unknown, so little ceremon-
ious, might come even to my closet, and with an
eye profane glance at the depository of my
secret sentiments, I hastened into my bedroom.
I uttered, involuntarily, an exclamation of joy
and surprise. The pretended Viscomte was
the Marchioness de B***. My first idea was
to push Jasmin out; the second, to bolt the door;
the third, to embrace the charming cavalier;
the fourth——Those who have penetration, have
already guessed.

The Marchioness, already astonished at my
vivacity, as soon as she had recovered her spirits,
said: You are a very singular young man!
There is no one but yourself in the world capable of commencing a reconciliation, where it
should finish!—Well, indeed; mamma takes it
as if there was nothing amiss. Let us see; what
do we dispute about?—To the end that we may
be reconciled again: is it not true, you little
libertine?—Ah! my dear mamma.—I have not
an idea, but you comprehend it immediately.—
Yesterday, though, you did not comprehend me,

ungrateful as you are.——Yesterday I was still sulky.—And for what, if you please? Could I suspect that you were under the sofa? Was it not essential both for you and myself, to get the pocket-book out of the hands of the Marquis? —That is true, mamma; but the vexation!— The vexation! for whom I forget my duty, for whom I forget decorum, and the care of my reputation: and in what a tone did you reply to my most tender letter. (She drew mine out of her pocket.) There, ungrateful boy! Read over your letter again; read with *sang froid* if you can. What cruel irony! what bitter jeering! And, notwithstanding, I pardon you; and come to seek you! I conduct myself with as much weakness and imprudence as a child of twelve years. Faublas! Faublas! the charm must be very great, it must; how have you bewitched me!—My dear mamma!—Well?— scold me well, because we will make it up.— What! you little wag, you merely confess that you were wrong, you do not ask for pardon.— It is done.—Oh, how lovely you are!—Oh! I beg your pardon.

Those who have understanding, and even those who have not, will guess that the Mar-

chioness and myself were reconciled. The most
delightful caresses and tender compliments
passed between us.

My God, Florville, how fascinating you are
in this pretty dishabille! How well this English frock becomes you!—I had it made yesterday on purpose.—It is, if I am not deceived, of
the same cloth and same colour as the charming
Amazonian habit in which love, who was determined to ensnare me, caused you to appear
before my eyes for the first time. Having become the chevalier of Mademoiselle du Portail,
I thought it became me to wear her colours. (I
clasped her in my arms.) And I, in future the
slave of the Viscomte de Florville, shall always
be pleased to wear his bonds. What delightful
reciprocity is this, mamma!—Love, my friend,
is an infant, who amuses himself with these
metamorphoses; he made Mademoiselle du Portail a thoughtless virgin; he makes the Marchioness de B*** an imprudent young man.
Ah! could the Viscomte de Florville appear
to thee as amiable as Mademoiselle du Portail
seems pretty in my eyes—As amiable?—Much
more so.—Oh, no, replied she, admiring herself
with complaisance, and looking at me with

tenderness: Oh, no; you are better, my friend; taller, more easy. There is something in your manner very bold and spirited; you have a martial air.—Yes, madam, and if I believed a great physiognomist, something more vigorous and robust.—Faublas, do pray, leave the Marquis alone. Do we not already play him bad tricks enough? In short, I am not come here to occupy myself with him. Now, my friend, tell me, without flattery, how you find me.— Charming! Whether dressed as man or woman, I defy anyone to be so pretty as you.—That's the language for a lover, always enthusiastical, always exaggerated! What woman will be more happy than myself, if you always view me with the same eyes!—Oh, mamma, as long as I live!

I held her in my arms: she slipped from me, to take up a sword, which she perceived on an armchair. In adjusting the belt she said: I have a fine English horse, which I ride sometimes. The spring is coming on, and I am very fond of riding in the environs of Paris. Will you accompany me sometimes, Faublas? Wilt thou, my friend, ramble, from time to time, in the woods of the Viscomte de Florville?—But they will see us.—No, the Marquis is often obliged to go to court.—Well, mamma, what day?—Let the spring put forth its verdure first.

While speaking, she had drawn my sword, and was fencing before me: Be on your guard, chevalier, said she.—I know not if the Viscomte is redoubtable, but I know well it is not in that; it is not thus that I ought to combat with the Marchioness. Dare she accept another kind of encounter?—(She flew to my arms.)—Ah, Faublas! said she, laughing; ah! if there were no greater murderers!—It is not, mamma, among men that they seek for heroes.

I then placed the Marchioness in a situation which rendered her unable to combat with me, and she took it kindly.

My beautiful mistress staid with me two hours, which we employed very agreeably. If I listened to nothing but the dictates of my own heart, said she at last, I should remain here all day, but the time is now come for me to meet Justine in one place, and my servants in another. We bade adieu; I was conducting the Viscomte de Florville to the door. We had already left my apartment, and were descending the stairs, when I distinguished Rosambert in the vestibule, about to come up. I warned the

Marchioness. Let us go back instantly, said she, I'll hide myself in some corner of your apartment; you'll come back quickly. Having said this, and without giving me time for reflection, she re-entered, and crossing my bed-room, shut herself in the closet.

Rosambert came up. Good day, my friend; how is Adelaide? How does the pretty cousin? —Hush! hush! do not speak of that, my father is there.—Where?—In that closet.—In that closet! your father?—Yes.—And what does he there?—He examines my books.—How! your books?—No; he is not in the closet; for see, he comes here.—There is something of the Marchioness in all this; and why not tell me at once that you were engaged! Adieu, Faublas, until to-morrow.—He passed before my father, and saluted him: You have something to say to your son, monsieur, and I'll leave you.

In the meantime, the Baron regarded me with much severity, and walked up and down with long strides. Impatient to know what this suspicious commencement announced, I asked him respectfully why he had done me the honour to come up to me.—You will know it presently monsieur.

A servant appeared. Tell him to come said the Baron.—Here he is, monsieur.—And my dear tutor entered. The Baron said to him: Have I not, sir, charged you with the conduct and education of my son?—Yes, undoubtedly. —The one is very much neglected, and the other very bad.—It is not my fault, monsieur; your son does not love study.—That is the least evil, interrupted the Baron; but how is it that I am not informed of what passes in my own house? Why have you not warned me of my son's disorderly conduct?—As to what passes here, sir, I can only speak of what I see; and as to what passes elsewhere, I can say nothing. Your son, when he goes out, rarely suffers me to accompany him; and—(a look which I gave M. Person convinced him he had said enough.)—The Baron replied: Monsieur, I have but one word to say to you; if this young man continues to conduct himself so badly, I shall be forced to choose another tutor. I would thank you to leave us.

When the Abbé was gone, the Baron sat down in an arm chair, and motioned me to do the same.—Excuse me, father, I have business.—I know it, monsieur, it is precisely because that

business should not be finished that I come to
speak to you.—Excuse me this time, father, I
must go out.—No, monsieur, you will remain;
sit you down.—I was obliged to sit; I was upon
thorns all the time. The Baron continued: Is
it possible that Faublas can meditate such horrors? Can he wish to abuse innocence and
simplicity, and lay snares for virtue.—Me,
father?—Yes, you! I come from the convent;
I know everything. If my son is still too young
to see that the more easy a conquest is, the less
it is flattering; he must take care not to con-
found an intrigue with a passion, and do not
mistake a love of pleasure for the passion of
love.—Pray, father, speak a little lower.—If
my son, too much intoxicated with what they
call good fortune.—Not so loud, I beg, father—
Too much delighted in the discovery of a new
sense, and the possession of a woman who
is certainly not without attractions; if my
son, in the arms of the Marchioness de B***
—It is too much! I beg, father——Had
forgot his father, his rank, and his duty,
I should have complained of it, but I should
have excused it; I should have given him
the advice of a friend, I should have said to him,

The more handsome the—Father, if you knew —The more, handsome the Marchioness is, the more dangerous she is. Examine with me the conduct of this woman with whom thou art so much taken. At the first glance, your countenance decided her; she takes you for a night.—I conjure you to drop this at present.—To satisfy her wild passion, she exposes both your life and her own. How lively, ardent, and passionate she must be to sacrifice her tranquillity, her honour, and public estimation to a thirst for pleasure!—Oh, father! oh, sir!—I repeat it, my friend, the more handsome the Marchioness is, the more dangerous she is! Thou thinkest, that in her arms, the resources of nature will be inexhaustible.

Mortified at not being able to explain myself, and well convinced that the Baron would not hold his tongue, I determined to wait patiently the end of this remonstrance, which, on another occasion, I might not have found too long. I sat with my left elbow on the arm of my chair, biting my hand out of vexation, and my right foot always in motion, kept beating time upon the floor. My father, in the meantime, continued: Thou wilt become enervated; nature,

at the critical period when youths arrive at the
age of puberty, is working for the development
of the organs, and requires all their strength, in
order to finish her work. I am well aware that
excess of pleasure will produce satiety, but the
disgust, perhaps, will come too late, and thou
wilt have to lament thy health destroyed, thy
memory lost, thy imagination faded, and all
thy faculties impaired. Thou wilt become a
prey to the most bitter mortifications and repuls-
ing infirmities even in the very flower of youth;
and, in the horrors of a premature old age, thou
wilt groan to be obliged to support the burthen
of life. Oh, my friend! have a care of these
evils, which are more common than you are
aware of; enjoy the present, but think of the
future; enjoy thy youth, but preserve some consolation for thy riper years.

Nevertheless, added the Baron, my son, little
affected by my paternal representations, listens
to me with a thousand signs of impatience, and
sits fidgetting on his chair, and interrupts me
continually. More alarmed at his danger than
sensible of my own injuries, I have borne it
tranquilly; I would tell him; the Marchioness
de B***—

It may be conceived what I suffered during a quarter of an hour; I could no longer constrain my impatience: Well, father, cried I, could you not have told me all this another day?—The Baron was naturally violent: he rose with fury. Fearing the effort of his first transport, I fled into the closet, and shut the door after me.

I found the Marchioness in a very painful situation. Her arms resting on my desk, stopping her ears with her hands, and reading and sobbing over a paper placed before her. I approached my lovely mistress.

Oh, madam! how I am distressed on your account! The Marchioness looked at me in a wild manner. Cruel child! what faults hast thou made me commit!—Speak lower.—But what punishment do I receive!—Do pray speak lower.—Thy father; thy unworthy father; he dares.—My dear madame, will you expose your-self?—But thou art a hundred times more cruel than he is. Here, look at this unfortunate writing! Behold these perfidious characters! My tears have effaced them!—(She showed me the letter commenced for Sophia.)

Faublas, cried the Baron, open the door; you are not alone in this closet.—I beg your pardon, monsieur.—I hear someone speak; open the door.—I cannot, father.—I will have it open; do not suffer me to call the servants.—The Marchioness rose briskly: Faublas, tell him that you are with one of your friends, who wishes to go out.—To go out!—Oh, yes! replied she in despair; whatever shame there is in going out, there will not be less in remaining.—I am with one of my friends, father, who wishes to go out —With one of your friends?—Yes, father.— And why did you not tell me sooner that you had someone in the closet? Open it, open it; fear nothing; I am tranquil; your friend can go.

Conduct me, said the Marchioness. She covered her face with her hands: I opened the door, which led to the stairs. My father, astonished at the precautions the unknown took to conceal himself, threw himself in our way, and said to my unfortunate friend: Monsieur, I do not ask you who you are, but let me at least have the pleasure of seeing you.—I conjure you father, not to require it.—What means this mystery then? interrupted the Baron. Who is this young man, who conceals himself with you, and who fears to show his face? I must know immediately.—I will tell you, father, I give you my word of honour, I will tell you.—No, no, the gentleman shall not go out until I know.—The Marchioness threw herself on a chair, keeping her face still covered with her hands: You have, monsieur, a right over your son, but, I believe, not over me.—The Baron, hearing the soft sound of a feminine voice, at length suspected the truth: What, cried he, can it be?—Oh! how sorry I am; how I regret!—You ought, my son, to feel that your father, anxious to restore you to your duty, has dropped some expressions concerning the Marchioness de B***, which are too strong, and which the Baron de Faublas disavows. See your friend down, my son.

As soon as we were on the staircase, the Marchioness gave free course to her tears. How cruelly I am punished for my imprudence, said she. I was endeavouring to console her.—Leave me! leave me! Your barbarous father is less cruel than you.

We reached the vestibule. I ordered them instantly to get a hackney coach; and while waiting for it, I made the Marchioness step into the porter's lodge. We had not been there a moment, when a man, looking into the porter's window, which was half open, asked if the

Baron was at home. The marchioness concealed her face with her hands, and I stood before her to hide her with my body; but all this was not done soon enough. M. du Portail (for it was him) had time to cast a glance at the Marchioness.—The Baron is in my room; if you will take the trouble to go up, I will join you in a moment.—Yes, yes, replied M. du Portail, smiling.

They came to tell us that the coach was at the door. The Marchioness got in immediately; I wished to sit by her for a moment: No, no, monsieur, I will not suffer it.—The grief with which I perceived her heart was oppressed, affected mine. Some tears escaped me, and fell upon her hand, which I held within my own, and which she did not withdraw: Ah! you think that you are near Sophia!—I still wished to get into the coach; she withdrew her hand, and repulsed me. If, monsieur, in spite of the discourses of your father, you have still any esteem for me, I beg you will get down and leave me.— Alas! shall I then see you no more?—She replied: No more: but her tears began to flow in great abundance. My dear mamma, when shall I see you again? In what place will you per-

mit me—Ungrateful wretch! I am too sure
you do not love, but you ought to pity me at
least. Leave me. Go up stairs to the Baron,
who expects you. She told the coachman to
drive her to Madame Le Clerq's, the milliner,
in **** street. I was compelled to leave her.

I found M. du Portail on the staircase, waiting for me: Ah! my good friend, said he, if I
am as good a physiognomist as the Marquis de
B***, this pretty youth who just left you is his
beautiful half. But what is the matter with
you? you have been crying? I knew not where
M. de Person had stuck himself, but we saw him
all at once behind us. He said to me, in a tone
sufficiently loud: I was sure, monsieur, that all
this would terminate badly: you paid no attention to my advice.—Thy advice! Do me the
favour, monsieur, to—Indeed, he is precisely
the schoolmaster of Fontaine: I get into the dirt,
and he scolds me!—But what is this all about?
replied M. du Portail.—Go up; go up into my
room, and you will know all; my father is giving
me a lecture.

On entering, M. du Portail asked my father
what was the matter.—What is the matter? replied my father.—I interrupted him: stop, M.

du Portail; Madame de B*** was in this closet,
my father entered here, he sat down there, and
made some observations to me which were undoubtedly very just, and very paternal, but the
Marchioness heard all, and my father treated
her—ah, you have no idea! I, for fear of exposing an amiable woman, did not explain myself; but my father knows the profound respect
I have for him; I have never swerved from it.
Well, he was witness how I suffered; that I
was racked with impatience; that I could not attend to him; he did not perceive, monsieur, that
there was a something uncommon about me; he
continued his discourse; and would not guess
at anything!—Young man, replied the Baron,
your excuse is in your tears, I pardon the reproaches you make me, on acount of the grief
with which you appear to be oppressed; but the
more you seem to love the Marchioness——My
father——Monsieur, Madame de B*** is no
longer there, why then interrupt me? The more
you seem to love the Marchioness, the more I am
displeased with you. If your heart is pre-oc-
cupied with this passion, it is in cold blood that
you have meditated the ruin of a virtuous girl,
of a respectable child—of Sophia!—Between

Sophia and me, father, there is no other seducer than love.—You do not love the Marchioness, then?—Father!—Are you, or are you not, seriously attached to Madame de B***? You know I must have some care about it, but what concerns me most is, that my son should not be worthy of me.—Ah, Baron! interrupted M. du Portail—I say nothing too strong, my friend: I shall tell you things which will astonish you. I went to the convent this morning; I found Adelaide in tears; my daughter, my dear daughter, whose amiable candour you so well know, informed me her good friend was sick, and that her brother was very slow in bringing the infallible remedy he had promised for Sophia. I pressed her to explain herself to me; she gave me a most exact account of the symptoms and effects of this malady, which you can guess, and which my son knows that he has caused, has been pleased to nourish, and would willingly augment. My son abuses his natural gifts to seduce a too susceptible girl; he obtains an absolute empire over her mind; and prepares, by degrees, her dishonour.—Her dishonour! the dishonour of Sophia!—Yes, young madman; I know the passions.—If you know them, father,

you know that you make my heart bleed.—
Moderate this impetuosity, my son, it only of-
fends me. Yes, I know the passions; yes, this
child, which you respect to-day, to-morrow, perhaps, you will dishonour, if she has the weakness to consent.—(He addressed himself to M.
du Portail.)—The recipe which my son destines
for his pretty cousin will be enclosed in a paper,
carefully sealed, and which Madame Munich
must not see! you understand, my friend?
Thus, all is ready; the correspondence will make
the first impression; Sophia, poor Sophia! already seduced through the eyes, will presently
be so through the heart. She was deceived by a
fine countenance, the common sign of a good
heart, she is going to be still further deceived
by the no less perfidious charms of a borrowed
eloquence; he will, in his studied letters, affect
the language of feeling: Sophia, attacked on all
sides at once, will fall, without defence, into
the snares he will spread for her. And, nevertheless, her seducer is not seventeen! At an age
still so tender, he evinces the most shocking propensities, he employs the odious talents of those
men, who, as cowardly as depraved, shrink not
from carrying discord and desolation into the

bosom of families; who experience a barbarous pleasure in listening to the bewailings of unfortunate beauty; contemplating, with self-applause, the opprobrium and the anxieties of degrading innocence.

This is the result of those natural gifts which I have been pleased to see him possess, and which, perhaps, I was secretly proud of; this is the manner in which the great expectations I had entertained of him have been realised!—I assure you, father, that I adore Sophia.—(The Baron, without listening to me, and still addressing himself to M. du Portail:) And who do you think was to convey these insidious letters? To whom did he intend to confide the execution of his detestable projects? To the most pure and unsuspecting virtue, to my daughter, and his sister, the innocent Adelaide!—Do not condemn me, father, without hearing me. Do you doubt my sentiments regarding Sophia? I am ready to marry her if you will deign to unite us.—And is it thus that you would dispose of Sophia and yourself? Do the relations of Mademoiselle de Pontis know you? Are they known to you? Do you know if the marriage would be agreeable to them? Do you know if it would be agreeable to me? Do you think I would marry you at your age? You have scarcely left childhood, and you aspire to the honour of being the father of a family!—Yes! and I feel that it is as easy for you to consent to my marriage, as it is impossible for me to renounce my love for Sophia.—You will renounce it, nevertheless: I forbid you to go to the convent without me, or without my express permission; and I declare, that if you do not change your conduct I will put you in a place of confinement.—Ah, father! if instead of marrying the young persons who are attached to each other, they are put into prison! I shall not be in the world, and you will be in prison.

The Baron either did not, or pretended not to hear me answer. He went out; I detained M. du Portail, who was going to follow him; I begged him to be a mediator between my father and me; and, above all, to prevail on the Baron to revoke his cruel order which forbade me to visit the convent.

He observed, that the precautions which my father had taken were very reasonable.—Reasonable! that is the way all those talk who are indifferent! Reason is their watchword! When you, monsieur, adored Lodoiska, when the unjust Pulauski deprived you of the happiness of seeing her, you did not find his precautions very reasonable.—But, my young friend, consider the difference.—There is none, monsieur; there is none: in France, as in Poland, a lover, who is worthy of the name, neither sees, feels, or breathes, but in the object of his love; the greatest evil he can imagine, is that of being separated from the idol of his affections. The precautions of my father appear to you reasonable; to me they seem cruel, and I shall do everything in my power to render them abortive. Sophia shall know my love; she shall know it, in spite of my father; she will be glad of it; and in spite of him, in spite of you, and all the world, we will finish by being married. I declare this to you, monsieur, and you can tell the Baron.—I shall do no such thing, my friend; I will not irritate your father, nor would I mortify yourself. At present, your notions are too arbitrary; I will leave you to reflect seriously about it, and I have no doubt you will be more reasonable to-morrow.—Reasonable! yes—reasonable! I expected as much!

I remained alone, and thought of nothing but

the means of eluding the vigilance of the
Baron's precautions, or of rendering them nuga-
tory. Should some austere censor blame my un-
governable disposition, I pity him; and tell him,
if his first or most cherished mistress never
caused him to commit faults, it was because his
love for her was not very strong.

Upon more mature reflection, I found that my
situation, however painful, was not desperate.
Rosambert, having compassion for the troubles
of his friend, would no doubt assist me; Jasmin
was entirely devoted to me, and I thought I
knew enough of my little tutor to be certain
that, by the aid of gold, I could do as I pleased
with him. M. du Portail appeared desirous of
remaining neuter, therefore I had only to combat with my father, who was much occupied
with his pretty opera girl, and went out every
evening, so that he could not be always watch-
ing me. These, then, are the serious reflections
I made, though they were not such as M. du
Portail recommended.

Nevertheless, it would not do for me openly
to oppose the Baron, in the first instance; I
ought, in prudence, to avoid going to the convent for some time; but how was I to get a

letter to Sophia? This letter was so important and so necessary! Who would take it to my pretty cousin? I could think of no expedient to relieve me from this embarrassment. It never occurred to me what a resource I had in the friendship of Adelaide.

An old lady brought me a letter, which I opened immediately; it was signed "De Faublas." 'Twas from my dear sister! I kissed the writing—and read:

"My Dear Brother,—I am greatly afraid that I have recently committed an indiscretion; I informed my father that you had promised me a remedy which would cure my dear friend; he was angry; he said it was poison that you would prepare for Sophia. Poison! Indeed, brother, I did not believe it, although it was the Baron who accused you.

I related everything to my good friend, who was waiting impatiently for the recipe in question. Adelaide, said she, you have done wrong to mention it to the Baron. This remedy of your brother's may not, perhaps, be very good, but we might, at least, have seen what it was. Therefore, my dear brother, make yourself

easy; she   t believe, any more than myself, that y.   l to poison her.

As I see .   dying with the desire to have
this rec pe,   dv ed her to send and request
it. She aga r repeated those words with which
I have alre 'y been so mortified: *Adelaide!
Adelaide! oh, l ow happy you are!*

Neverthel .. I am sure she will be very
happy to hav   is recipe. Send it me immediately, my de.. orother, I will give it to her; and
I will not n en ion it to anyone.

Give the   n who brings this letter three
livres; she tells me she never tattles when they
give her half-a-crown.

Your sister, etc.,
ADELAIDE DE FAUBLAS.

P.S.—Endeavour to come and see me.''

Transported with joy, I went to the old woman. Here are six francs for you, madam, because I will trouble you with an answer, which
I beg you will wait for.

I went into my closet and sat down at my
desk. The letter I had began for Sophia was
before me; it was still wet with tears. Alas! it
was the Marchioness that shed them! What a

conversation she overheard! What a letter has she read! Poor Viscomte de Florville! What mortification my father and myself must have given you! In saying this, I kissed the paper over which the Marchioness had wept so much; and the feeling I then experienced, if less intense than that of love, was, nevertheless, more tender than pity.

I came to myself, and I thought of Sophia. The paper, stained and rendered illegible in several places, was not fit to send. I thought of beginning again the letter which I had written a third time. And why begin it again? At the name, the bare name of my pretty cousin, the tears came into my eyes; I sobbed as I wrote! Would Sophia know that two persons had wept over the same paper? Could even I distinguish between the mingled tears, those of the Marchioness, from what belonged to myself? These reflections determined me not to commence again, but to continue what I had written:

" Sophia, I exist but for thee! Nevertheless, thou complainest, and accusest me of ingratitude and cruelty! Dost thou think, canst thou believe, that there exists in the world a woman that can be compared with thee ?—a woman that one can love who knows Sophia?

Oh, my pretty cousin, with what transport have I received the news of thy tenderness for me! But what grief have I felt on hearing that thy days are clouded with corroding cares, thy growing charms impaired, and thy life endangered! Thy life! Ah, Sophia! if Faublas loses thee, he will follow thee to the tomb!

My sister, who has disclosed to me, without thy consent, the most secret sentiment of thy soul, my sister has announced to me on thy part an eternal separation. She tells me that thou wilt not see me again. If this be true, Sophia, my life, which is become insupportable, will not last me long; and thyself—thyself!——But let us indulge in more pleasant ideas; we shall certainly be more happy hereafter. Let me be permitted to hope that my pretty cousin will shortly be my wife, and that when united we shall not cease to be lovers.

I am, with as much respect as love,
Thy young cousin,
THE CHEVALIER DE FAUBLAS."

This letter being sealed, it was necessary that I should write another.

"My Dear Adelaide.—You have done well to write to me, for I am deprived of the happiness of seeing you. The Baron has forbidden me to go out; he has quarrelled with me, and I must not speak to him of Sophia.

Let my pretty cousin have the enclosed letter as soon as possible; deliver it to her when alone, and, above all, be sure you tell no one of it.

Adieu, my dear sister, etc."

I put these two letters under one envelope, and confided them to the discretion of the old woman.

From that evening, I laboured to form the grand confederation which I had meditated. My father went out. I enquired for the Abbé Person; he also was gone out. It was rather late when he came home, and entered my apartment with an air of triumph: You heard, monsieur, what your father said this morning: he has given me an absolute power over you.— You see, Monsieur Person, that I am delighted at it. I am too happy in having a governor like you, a governor so complaisant, so honest, and, above all so indulgent.—I knew, monsieur, you

would one day do me justice.—A governor full
of politeness and urbanity.—You flatter me,
monsieur.—A governor who feels that a youth
of sixteen cannot be as reasonable as a man of
thirty-five.—Most assuredly.—A governor who
knows the human heart.—That is true.—And
who excuses in his pupil a tender passion which
he is susceptible of himself.—I do not comprehend.—Sit down, Monsieur Person; we must
now discourse together upon a very delicate
subject, which deserves your whole attention.
Among the numerous brilliant qualities which
are conspicuous in you, and of which I could
make a long enumeration, if I did not fear to
wound your modesty; among so many qualities,
I must tell you frankly, that you want one,
which some consider very important, but which
I look upon as useless; I mean the art of drawing—But, monsieur——I do not say this to
mortify you. I am persuaded you do not want
learning; but we see every day persons as unfortunate as clever, who teach very badly what
they know very well. You are in this predica-
ment, Monsieur Person, and on this point, to use
the words of the celebrated Cardinal de Retz, in
speaking of the great Condé, you do not make

the most of your abilities.—Oh, monsieur, the quotation——is not quite correct; I know it well. You are not a conqueror; you have no armies to conduct. But to form the heart of a youth, to study his propensities, in order to oppose or direct them; to smother or to modify his passions, when one cannot eradicate them; to polish his awkward manners, and instruct his uncultivated mind; is that, think you, an easy task?—Most assuredly it is not. I am aware that my profession presents great difficulties.—Well, monsieur, the parents do not know that. They seek a tutor who possesses every talent and every virtue; and they think they have found him. He is a man whom they pay, and it is a god that they require! But let us come to what concerns ourselves: I have also remarked, Monsieur Person, that your attachment to all who bear the name of Faublas has carried you too far.—How?—Yes; this extreme affection which you bear towards the family in general, has not been equally apportioned to each of its members.—I do not understand.—You have a certain predilection for my sister; the Baron will call it love. The difficulty you experience in teaching, he will call incapacity. What I tell you is fact: were I to inform the Baron of these little details, you would not remain here four-and-twenty hours. That would be a great misfortune for me, Monsieur Person, and a still greater for yourself. I am well aware that they would quickly procure me another tutor, but, as we said just now, a perfect man is not to be found. Suppose a new tutor arrives, who is found more capable of instructing me than yourself; at first, he will give me, with great pains, lessons which I shall receive with inquietude, and wish the books at the devil. Nevertheless, my new Mentor will participate in the weakness of humanity; he will have faults or passions, which I shall speedily discover, because I shall be interested in studying them. Prompted by similar motives, he will develop my propensities with the same discernment. In the course of a week we shall be observed like two friends, equally interested in pleasing each other. In the meantime, Monsieur Person, you will not, perhaps, find employ. I know a great many little Abbés, who have less merit than yourself, who obtain pupils, and even keep them; but I also know as many others who vegetate without occupation. You, perhaps,

may be reduced to recommence the rudiments
and the grammar with the spoiled children of a
churchwarden, of a sheriff, or some such beings,
who may be too proud to send their sons to the
university. And be on your guard; for people
of business, who know how to calculate, are always desirous of making their interest and their
vanity agree, they will tell you that the whole
of Restaut is not worth a single page of Bareme;
and if you teach your young citizen but to
speak their own language; if you are unacquainted with the science of figures; the teacher
of arithmetic will be much better paid than
yourself. I would spare you these disagree-
ables, monsieur. I feel that it would be hard
for the governor of a nobleman's son to become
tutor in the family of a cook. I do not pretend
to change your condition, but to render it better:
instead of diminishing your emoluments, I am
about to augment them.—I am very sensible,
sir, I have always been right when I spoke of the
qualities of your heart—Oh! the qualities
of the heart! Yes, my dear governor, I have
a very good heart, very feeling.—You know
that I adore Sophia! My father would prevent me from seeing her.—But, all things

considered, is he wrong in so doing?—How,
monsieur, if he is wrong? You ask me if he
is wrong; but you have not understood what I
said.—Not very well.—I will explain myself
clearly. If you oppose me, I shall inform the
Baron of all that I know concerning you; they
will dismiss you, and give me a new governor.
If you are inclined to serve me——You know,
Monsieur Person, what sum the Baron allows
me for pocket money; I shall divide with you,
and here is some on account. (I presented
him with six Louis d'or.)—Money, monsieur!
do you take me for a valet then?—Do not be
angry; I did not mean to offend you; I thought
——(I put the money back into my purse.)—
I have a great friendship for you, monsieur, but
I am not interested.—You are, then, I perceive,
much attached to Mademoiselle de Pontis.—
More than I can describe to you.—And what
would you that I should do in this affair?—I
only wish that you would take as much pains in
diverting the attention of the Baron as you have
taken in tormenting me.—Your views, monsieur, with regard to Mademoiselle de Pontis,
are, I presume, honorable—legitimate?—I
should be a monster if I had any others! Upon

the word of a gentleman, Sophia shall be my
wife.—In that case, I see no inconvenience.
There is none!—I see none. And yet for a
thing so simple, monsieur proposes to give me
money!—I hope you will excuse me.—I could
not think of taking money; some presents will
suffice. I lived two years with M. L***; he
gave me, from time to time, some trinkets,
jewels, etc.; and his children did the same on
their part. All that was very well. A present
is acceptable.—And now, Monsieur Person, we
understand each other, I shall depend upon you.
—Most assuredly.—Listen then, my dear governor; I have an observation to make. If what
you feel towards Adelaide is love, do not think
that I can approve it. That with which I burn
for Sophia is innocent and pure as herself.
That which you feel for my sister—— Be cautious of it, Monsieur Person! I am well convinced that the virtue of Adelaide will defend
her against the enterprises of a seducer; but the
attempt would, of itself, be an affront; an affront which the blood of the offender would
scarcely expiate.—Make yourself easy, monsieur.—I am so. You may depend upon me,
monsieur.—My dear governor, I shall confide in
you.

The Abbé went out; he came back to tell me that in the afternoon he had been to the convent, by desire of the Baron.—To the convent! for what?—Expressly to forbid Mademoiselle Adelaide to come to the conversation room, when you came by yourself to see her.—You have seen Adelaide?—Yes, monsieur: Did she say nothing to you?—She was much hurt at this prohibition.—Nothing more?—Not a word.— And Sophia? Did you enquire after her health?—Much better since noon.—And at what hour were you at the convent? About five o'clock. Good, very good. (The Abbé retired.)

Much better since noon: that was near about the time she received my letter. Sophia, my dear Sophia! why dost thou not hasten to reply to me! Adelaide! thou shouldst be happy, thy dear friend is already cured! and in the transport of joy, which the news of this speedy cure had given me, I made such leaps, and cut such capers, that the noise brought Jasmin to my room. I had finished a sublime exclamation, when he opened the door: I beg your pardon, Monsieur, but I heard a great confusion, and was alarmed. Go, Jasmin, immediately to the Count de Rosambert, and beg him to call on me to-morrow morning without fail.

Rosambert came as I wished. Of all the events of the preceding day, I only informed him of those which related to Sophia. He reminded me with a smile, that it was not the pretty cousin that was in my closet. I wished to elude this subject; the Count pressed me so closely, and in so lively a manner, that I was obliged to confess all. This Marchioness de B*** is a very astonishing woman, said he. No one knows better than her, how to commence an intrigue agreeably, to carry it on with spirit, to hasten its consummation, which instead of displeasing her, seems necessary to her constitution. No one knows better than her the grand art of retaining a happy lover, and of supplanting a dangerous rival; or when that is impossible, at least to hold the balance uncertain. This woman knows how to vary the pleasures of love in such a manner, that with her, an amour of six months, is still a new amour. An amour of six months at court! You will say it must be decrepid with age; but no, the Marchioness gives it the freshness of youth; though she has quitted me abruptly, I will do her justice; she is not volatile: I think I have even discovered in her some flashes of sensibility. At bottom it is possible that she may have a tender heart. Her genius for intrigue is developed at court in every possible manner. Perhaps if she had been born a simple citizen, instead of a lady of quality, she might have been a steady, sensible woman. I repeat it to you, that she is not what they call volatile. I have had her for six months, I might perhaps have kept her three months longer; but your disguise has deranged everything. To instruct a novice: to correct a puppy, (pointing to himself and laughing;) to dupe an almost jealous husband so agreeably: to surmount all kinds of obstacles:—she could not resist the execution of things so flattering to her turn of mind. Yes! although you have a striking countenance, I would wager that it was the difficulty of the enterprise, more than all, which determined Madame de B***. Besides the Marchioness has taken the pains not to follow a beaten track. To take this week with enthusiasm, a lover, who is received the next with indifference; to form and break engagements with equal facility, is the eternal occupation of our ladies of quality! The person changes, but not the conduct of the intrigue: they say, they do unceasingly the same things:

there is always a declaration to receive, an avowal to make, some letters to write, two or three *tete-a-tete's* to arrange, and a rupture to be consummated. This is their dull monotonous circle. The Marchioness, on the contrary, is not displeased if the same cavalier continues, provided that the intrigue is varied in its conduct. It is not by the number of lovers that she is gratified, but by the singularity of her adventures. A scene does not appear piquant to her, except when it is uncommon, and she will venture anything to bring it about; she prides herself in braving dangers, and combatting with disagreeable events. Thus the idea of her own power sometimes carries her too far. Sometimes it happens that all her address will not shield her from the consequences of her rash enterprises. In her adventures with us, for instance, what mortifying scenes she underwent: In the first;—It was I who tormented her, and in conscience I owed it her. Yesterday she came here to seek a second; and chance perhaps has a third ready for her. But what matters it. The Marchioness, always superior to little mortifications, and accustomed to treat the most disagreeable events with indifference, will derive

even from her misfortunes an advantage over
her enemies, over her rival, over you.—Over her
rival! Ah! Rosambert, Sophia will always be
preferred!—But what say you of my pretty
cousin, who has not answered my letter?—Do
you think that she has slept? Do you not recollect that it is eight days since she has closed her
eyes? Your letter has been sweetly cradled—
but let it enjoy its happiness. Do you know
with what we ought to occupy ourselves?—No.
—We must go and buy some presents for the
dear governor. He told you that a present
would be acceptable.—That is true indeed; but
if I go out, and a letter should come from
Sophia in the meantime?—They can make the
old woman who brings it wait for you.—Well,
let us go quickly then.—You have forgot your
hat.—You are right, replied I, with an air of
distraction, and went to sit down. Rosambert
took me by the arm: what the devil are you
about? what are you dreaming of?—I was
thinking of the poor Viscount de Florville—
How the Marchioness must be affected! Do you
think, Rosambert, that she will write to me.
Must we talk of the Marchioness at present?—
Yes, my friend—do not laugh, but answer me.

—Well then, my dear Faublas, I think she will not write to you.—Do you think so.—It is very probable. The Marchioness has already reflected on your situation and her own. As a well-informed woman, she has, I doubt not, already considered that you could not dispense with coming to her; she will not go to you; she expects you; be sure that she expects you.

I rang for Jasmin. Thou knowest the residence of the Marchioness de B***, and thou knowest Justine: put on the dress of a citizen, go and ask for Justine, tell her you come from me, to enquire after the health of the Marchioness. Rosambert laughed with all his might, and said: Ah! do you think it will be impolite to make her wait too long? But answer me, do you not expect a letter from Sophia?—Without doubt. Jasmin, we are only stepping out for a few minutes; thou wilt not go until we return. Be discreet, for I put great confidence in thee: we are at war; the enemy is yonder, my friend, on the watch!—Oh! monsieur, in all my places, I have always taken the side of the children against their fathers. That's right, my friend; rest assured that I shall recompense thee when I am married to her.—Married to Madame the

Marchioness!—Rosambert laughed: come, come, my friend, said he, you forget yourself.

I bought a very fine ring; but when it was time for us to return, I could not get Rosambert from the shop, he was so much attracted with the beauty of the jewelry.

When I returned, Jasmin gave me a letter. The old woman merely wished to sit down, because they had forbidden her to wait for an answer.

One may judge my grief on reading what follows:

"Monsieur,—If I had not seen my name repeated twenty times in your letter, I should not have thought it addressed to myself. How could I imagine that some words which escaped me without any meaning, and caught up by chance by my dear friend, could be interpreted by her brother in so astonishing a manner. I could not have conceived, that my young cousin, who always called me his friend, would have treated me so injuriously.

Who told you that I loved you Monsieur? Adelaide? She knows nothing of it. Who told you that the words, *cruel—ungrateful—I*

will never see him again,—were addressed to
you? Who told you that I was dying with
mortification, because you did not love me? If
that had been the case, no one but myself could
have known it; and should I have told it, monsieur?

You write with an air of great confidence!
You love someone, and you tell me you love me,
because you think that I love you! You think
then to do me a favour when you demand my
heart and my hand! If I am so unhappy, monsieur, as only to inspire compassion, I shall at
least have prudence enough not to love, or discretion enough to conceal it; and certainly the
lover of another, shall never be mine.

At present, it is to you and for you that I
say those words: ' I will never see you again.'
My family is as good as yours, monsieur, and
you ought to know enough of me, not to push
the resentment, which the outrage you have so
fearlessly done me, deserves."

This fatal letter was not signed. The pain it
gave me can more easily be imagined than described. Sophia loves me no more! Sophia will
see me no more! I fell into a profound reverie,

from which I was only recovered by a torrent of tears. If Rosambert had been with me, he would at least have assisted me with his advice, and have given me some consolation.

I rose abruptly, wiped my eyes, and flew to the jeweller's. The lady who had served us was no longer at the counter, and Rosambert was gone. I appeared so hurt at the disappointment, that a girl in the shop had compassion for me. She said, if I would step to the *Cafe de la Regence,* which she shewed me at a little distance, she would go and tell the Count, who was not far off, and would not fail to be with me in half an hour, or a little more.

I entered this "Regency Coffee-House." I could see only gentlemen profoundly occupied at the game of chess. Alas, they were less reserved, less thoughtful and less gloomy than myself. I sat down immediately near to a table, but the agitation I felt, did not permit me to remain in one place; presently also one of the chess players, raising his voice, lifting up his head and rubbing his hands, said in an exulting tone: To the King. Great gods, cried the other, the queen is forced! the game is lost! —Yes, yes, monsieur, rub your hands! you

think yourself a Turenne! do you know to
whom you are indebted for this fine stroke.
(He looked round at me,) to that gentleman,
yes, to that gentleman. Curse these love-sick
blades!

Astonished at the lively manner in which
they apostrophised me, I observed to the discontented player, that I did not comprehend him.
—You do not understand!—Look here! see
that check-mate!—Well! monsieur, and what is
the matter with that check?—How! what is
the matter! For this hour past, monsieur, you
have been turning about me: and "my dear
Sophia," it was one time, "my pretty cousin,"
another—I could not help hearing this nonsense, and made the blunders of a learner—
when people are in love, monsieur, they do not
come to the *Cafe de la Regence*. (I was going
to reply, but he continued with violence) a
check-mate! I ought to have covered my king;
there was no other means of saving him!—
They profited by the distraction which monsieur occasioned!—A wretched stroke of a novice! A man like me! (He again looked towards me.) Once for all, monsieur, remember
that all the cousins in the world are not worth

the queen which he forced from me! There is no resource!—The devil take the jilt and her affected lover!—Of all the exclamations the last was that which piqued me the most. Carried away by my vivacity, I was rushing hastily to the speaker, and ran against a chess player at an adjoining table; my buttons caught hold of him and he fell, and the pieces rolled on all sides. Here then were two new adversaries for me. One said to me, monsieur should take care what he does sometimes. The other cried out; monsieur, you have balked me of a game— you! you have lost, interrupted his adversary. I had gained, monsieur. That game! I could have played it against Verdoni!—And I against Phillidor!—Well, messieurs, do not break my head, I will pay your loss. Pay it! you are not rich enough.—What do you play for, then?—Honour—Yes, monsieur, honour. I am come post expressly to take up the challenge of monsieur—of monsieur, who thinks he has no equal!—If it had not been for you, I should have given him a lesson!—A lesson! why you may think yourself very happy that this gentleman's blunder has saved you; I had forced the queen eighteen times!—And you did not even the eleventh. In less than ten you were check-mate. It nevertheless, you, monsieur, who are the cause of my discomfiture—learn, monsieur, that in the *Cafe de la Regence,* one ought not to run. (Then another player rose:) Gentlemen, gentlemen, in the *Cafe de la Regence,* they ought not to cry out, they ought not to talk. What a noise you are making.

There were others present, who also joined in the quarrel; and, as I was the author of all the evil, each of them grumbled at me in his turn; I could no longer tell who to reply to, when Rosambert entered; he had much trouble to get me away; we retired to the Palais Royal.

I took Rosambert aside, and showed him Sophia's letter.—And is this what you afflict yourself about? said he, after having read it: Why, you ought to kiss that letter a hundred times!—Ah, Rosambert! this is not a time to joke.—I do not joke, my friend; you are adored!—But you have not read it then?—I have read it, and I repeat to you that you are adored.—We are not comfortable here, Rosambert, come home with me.

On the road, the Count said: Sophia discou-

tinued her visits to the conversation-room from
the epoch of your connection with Madame de
B***. It was from this period also that her
reveries commenced. It was from that time
that she had what your sister calls a fever. She
desires the recipe; she asked for it indirectly;
and more than all this, the remedy has had the
most excellent effect; since yesterday, at noon,
Mademoiselle de Pontis has become better;
we must then conclude, from all this, that in
the afternoon of yesterday something extraordinary took place at the convent. There is no
doubt, my friend, that this letter is the effect of
a trick of the Baron, of the liveliness of your
sister, or the indiscretion of M. Person. The
tone of this letter proves that you are loved;
she has even suffered a tacit avowal to escape
her; she has made you terrible reproaches.
You thought that she loved you. She cannot
bear the idea; but in no part of her letter does
she say that she loves you not.

All that Rosambert had said appeared to me
very reasonable; nevertheless, my heart was
oppressed: the hopes and fears of lovers are
equally foolish.

Are you aware, said the Count, that this

sweet letter of hers is very well framed? Oh! thy pretty cousin will not have written to you ten times before you will find her style entirely formed!—You are rather cruel with your gaiety, Rosambert!

Jasmin arrived at the same time as ourselves. He told me he came from the house of the Marchioness.—Well!—I have spoken with Justine, monsieur; she made me wait a long time, at last she came to tell me that Madame was very sensible of your attention— that she felt very ill on returning home yesterday, and the doctor had found her a little feverish this morning. —There, Rosambert, see how unfortunate I am. They have both a fever at the same time! She whom I adore will see me no more!—And I shall not see to-day the one who amuses me, said the Count, mimicking me: Poor young man! how I pity him!—Be comforted, my dear Faublas; you alone are better capable of curing the ills you have caused than all the doctors of the faculty. But although the malady of thy pretty cousin is something like that of the amiable Marchioness, I foresee, nevertheless, that there will be some difference in the treatment; you will look in the eyes of the pretty damsel

to see if there are not some remains of emotion;
you will take her by the hand, and feel her
pulse, which may be rather high; perhaps it
may be necessary to examine whether her mouth
has lost any of its freshness. But for the fine
lady; oh! the examination will be longer and
more serious! You will be obliged to consider
her more closely and more generally—from the
head to the feet! my friend. I even think the
method of M. Mesmer—yes, chevalier, yes, a
little magnetism!—For God's sake drop your
pleasantry, Rosambert, and talk to me of Sophia.
Let us endeavour, in the first place, to ascertain the value of this cruel letter; and then let
us consider by what means I can obtain an interview and an explanation with my pretty
cousin.—With all my heart, my dear Faublas;
let us commence by calling the Abbé Person.

My father entered as Rosambert rang the
bell. He replied coldly to the salutations of
the Count, and announced to me, in a very abrupt manner, that I must go out with him. The
horses are to, added he; and, (turning to Rosambert) excuse me, sir, but I am pressed for
time. To-morrow morning, early, said the

Count to me as he left us. I followed the Baron
with much dissatisfaction.

He conducted me to M. du Portail's. Lovinski expected me that he might finish the recital of the most secret adventures of his life;
and for fear the Marquis de B***, or anyone
else, should again interrupt us, he ordered himself to be refused to everybody. As soon as we
had dined, he continued thus the narrative of
his misfortunes :—

You must, my dear Faublas, be struck with
horror at my situation. The fire become more
violent, was now communicating with the chamber in which we were shut up, and already the
flames had reached the foot of Lodoiska's tower
—I heard the deep groans of Lodoiska, which
were answered by my furious cries. Boleslas
ran about our prison like a madman; he howled
most frightfully, and endeavoured to break the
door with his hands and feet; and I, leaning out
of the window, shook the bars with all my
might, but could not move them.

Those who had mounted, descended all at
once with precipitation, and we heard the gates
open. Dourlinski himself demanded quarter;

the victors threw themselves into the building, although in flames: attracted by our cries, they came and broke open our door with the blows of an axe. I recognised them to be Tartars, by their costume and their arms. Their chief arrived, and in him I beheld Titsikan.—Ah! said he, it is my brave man!—I threw myself at his feet; Titsikan! Lodoiska! a woman! the most beautiful of women, is in that tower! she will be burnt alive.—The Tartar said a word to his soldiers, they flew to the tower, I flew with them, and Boleslas followed. They stormed the doors: beside an old pillar, we discovered a winding staircase, filled with thick smoke. The Tartars were alarmed at it, and stopped. I was determined to mount.—Alas! what are you going to do? said Boleslas.—To live or die with Lodoiska, cried I.—To live or die with my master! replied my generous servant.

I darted up, and he rushed after me. We ascended about forty steps, at the risk of being suffocated. By the glimmering of the flames we discovered Lodoiska in a corner of her prison. She groaned out feebly with her dying voice: Who comes to me? said she.—It is Lovinski! it is thy lover!—Her joy gave her strength; she rose up, and flew into my arms: we carried her, and descended some steps: a thicker vapour of smoke than we had as yet encountered came up the staircase, and compelled us to remount with precipitation; at that moment, a part of the tower gave way: Boleslas uttered a terrible cry, and Lodoiska fainted. That which would have destroyed us, Faublas, was the means of saving us; the fire, which had previously been confined, now reached the exterior, and spread rapidly on every side, but the smoke was dissipated. Loaded with our precious burthen, Boleslas and myself descended instantly. I do not exaggerate, my friend, when I tell you, that each step tottered under our feet, for the walls were burning! At length we arrived at the door of the tower; Titsikan, trembling for us, had ran there: Well done, brave men, said he on seeing us appear. I laid Lodoiska at his feet, and fell insensible by her side.

I remained in this state nearly an hour. They were alarmed for my life, and Boleslas wept. I recovered myself at the voice of Lodoiska, who, having come to herself, hailed me as her liberator. Everything was changed throughout the castle; the tower had entirely fallen; the Tartars had arrested the progress of the flames, and had pulled down one part of the building in order to save the other; after which they conveyed us into a large hall, where we found Titsikan himself, with some of his soldiers. The rest, who had been occupied in plunder, brought to their chief the gold, silver, jewels, plate, and all the valuable effects which the flames had spared. Close by was Dourlinski, loaded with fetters, who groaned as he looked on the heap of riches which they had pillaged from him. Rage, terror, despair, and everything which can tear the heart of a wicked man, might be read in his wandering eyes. He stamped on the ground with wrath, raised his clenched fists to his forehead, poured forth the most horrid blasphemies, and reproached heaven for its just vengeance.

In the meantime, my fair mistress pressed my hands within her own: Alas! said she, sobbing, thou hast saved my life, and thine own is still in danger; and even should we escape death, slavery will be our lot.—No, no, Lodoiska, be assured Titsikan is not my enemy; Titsikan will terminate our grievances.—With-

out doubt, if I can, interrupted the Tartar; thou
speakest well, brave man! Oh! I see thou art
not dead, and I am very happy; thou sayest and
dost nothing but good things! and there, added
he, pointing to Boleslas, is a friend, by whom
thou art well seconded.—I embraced Boleslas:
yes, Titsikan, yes, I have a friend, and he shall
always bear that name.—The Tartar interrupted me: Tell me, said he, were you not both
in a chamber on the ground floor, and she in a
tower? why was that? I would wager that you
wags were desirous of bearing away this lass
from that booby there, (pointing to Dourlinski:) and you were right; he is a villain, and
she is pretty! Let us know: tell me how it is.

I informed Titsikan of my name and that of
Lodoiska's father, and of everything which had
happened to me up to that period. It is for
Lodoiska, said I afterwards, to tell what she has
suffered from the infamous Dourlinski, since
she has been shut up in his castle.

You know, replied Lodoiska, immediately,
that my father made me leave Warsaw the very
day on which the Diet was opened. He conducted me to the estate of the Palatine de G***,

only twenty leagues from the capital, where he returned to assist at the deliberations.

The day that M. de P*** was proclaimed king, Pulauski came and took me from the residence of the Palatine, and brought me here, that I should be more secure from all researches. He charged Dourlinski to keep me with care, and above all, to be careful that Lovinski did not discover my retreat. He left me, he said, to go and gather together the good citizens, and stimulate them to defend their country, and to punish traitors. Alas; these important cares have made him forget his daughter, for I have not seen him since.

Some days after the departure of my father, I began to perceive that the visits of Dourlinski became longer and more frequent; and in a little time, he hardly left the apartment they had assigned me for a prison. He took from me, under some pretence, the only woman my father had left to serve me; and in order, he said, that no one should know I was with him, he brought me himself what was necessary for my subsistence, and passed the day entirely near me.

You know not, my dear Lovinski, how I suffered from the continual presence of a man who was so odious to me, and whom I suspected of infamous designs. One day he ventured to unfold them to me; I assured him that my hatred would always be the price of his tenderness, and that his unworthy conduct had excited my profound contempt. He answered coldly, that, in time, I should be accustomed to see him, to permit his attentions, and even to desire them. He did not change his general conduct. He came to me in the morning, and did not leave me until the evening. Separated from all that I loved, always under constraint from my tyrant, I had not even the little consolation of delivering myself up to reflections on past happiness. Dourlinski witnessed my uneasiness, and amused himself in augmenting it. Pulauski, he told me, commanded a corps of Poles; Lovinski, having betrayed his country, which he did not love, and a woman that he cared little about, had entered into the Russian service, and it was not doubted but there would shortly be a bloody combat between them. And, finally, that it was very certain nothing could hereafter reconcile my father to Lovinski. Some days after this, he came to announce to me that

Pulauski had attacked the Russian camp in the middle of the night, and that in the affray my lover met his death, by wounds received from my father. The monster made me read these details in a kind of public paper, which, without doubt, he had procured to be printed on purpose; and from the barbarous joy which he affected, I thought the news too true. Implacable tyrant! cried I, thou delightest in my tears and my despair! but cease to persecute, or thou presently shall find that the daughter of Pulauski can, even by herself, revenge her injuries.

One evening, when he had quitted me sooner than usual, I heard him open my door gently about midnight. By the glare of a lamp which I always left burning, I saw my tyrant advance towards my bed. As there was no crime but I deemed him capable of, I had foreseen this, and well assured myself of preventing it. I armed myself with a knife, which I had the precaution to conceal under my pillow: I loaded the wretch with the reproaches he merited, and vowed that if he dared to approach me I would poinard him with my own hands. He stood aghast with surprise and fear. I am tired of receiving nothing but contempt, said he, as he went out; if I did not fear being heard, you should see what a female hand could do against me! But I have other means of overcoming your pride. Shortly you will think yourself too happy if you can obtain my favour by the most humble submissions.—Some minutes after he was gone, his confidant entered with a pistol in his hand. I must do him the justice to say he wept when he announced his master's orders to me. Dress yourself, madam, you must follow me. This was all he could say. He conducted me into that tower, where, had it not been for you, I should have perished this day; it is there that I have languished for more than a month, without fire or light, and almost without clothes; with bread and water for my subsistence, and a straw mattress for my bed: such was the state to which the daughter of a Polish nobleman was reduced! You shudder, brave stranger, and well you may, but I have related only part of my grievances. One thing, at least, rendered my misery less insupportable, I no longer saw my tyrant. While he was quietly waiting for my solicitation of pardon, I passed the days in calling upon my father, and weeping for my lover. Lovinski, with what astonishment was I seized, with what joy was my soul penetrated, the day that I recognised you in the gardens of Dourlinski!

Titsikan listened with attention to the history of our misfortunes, which appeared to affect him greatly, when his advanced guard gave the alarm. He left us abruptly to run to the drawbridge. We heard a great tumult. Lovinski! Lovinski! you base and perfidious couple! cried Dourlinski, who could not contain his joy; so you thought you had escaped me! Tremble! for you will fall again into my power; the news of my misfortune has, no doubt, roused the neighbouring gentlemen, and they are coming to succour me.—They will but bring vengeance on thee, thou wicked wretch! interrupted Boleslas, seizing a bar of iron, with which he was going to knock him down. Titsikan re-entered at this moment. It was only a false alarm, said he; it is a little troop which I detached yesterday to forage the country: it was to join me here; it brings me some prisoners; everything else is tranquil, and nothing appears as yet in the neighbourhood.

While Titsikan spoke to me, they brought before him the unfortunate persons whose hard

fate had delivered them up to the Tartars.
Five of them at first came before us. They
say that this one had given them a great deal
of trouble, and that is why they have thus bound
him, said Titsikan, pointing to a sixth. Oh,
God! it is my father! cried Lodoiska, running
to him. I threw myself at the feet of Pulauski.
Thou art Pulauski, art thou? continued the Tartar; well, the rencontre is not unlucky. Stay,
my friend, it is not more than a quarter of an
hour since I have known thee; I know that
thou art fierce and obstinate; but never mind, I
esteem thee, thou hast courage and head-piece;
thy daughter is handsome, and does not want
wit: Lovinski is brave; more brave, I think,
than myself. Pulauski, rendered motionless
with astonishment, scarcely listened to the Tartar; and struck with the strange spectacle which
was presented before his eyes, conceived the
most frightful suspicions. He repulsed me
with horror. Unhappy wretch! thou hast betrayed thy country, a woman who loved thee,
and a man who would have been pleased to call
thee a kinsman; there was nothing wanting to
you but an alliance with robbers. Titsikan interrupted him. With robbers, if you will have

it so; but robbers are, occasionally, good for
something: without me, your daughter, from to-
morrow, would no longer have been a maid. Be
not afraid, added he, turning to me; I know he
is fierce, and I will not offend him.

We had placed Pulauski in an arm-chair; his
daughter and myself were bathing his bound
hands with our tears, but he continued to re-
pulse me and load me with reproaches. What
the devil is the matter with him? replied Titsikan. I tell thee myself that Lovinski is a brave
man, and I wish to marry him and your daughter. Dourlinski is a scoundrel whom I mean to
hang. I repeat it to thee, that thou alone art
more obstinate than all three of us. Listen to
me, then, and let us conclude, for I must go.
Thou belongest to me by the most incontestible
right—that of the sword. Well, if thou givest
me thy word to be sincerely reconciled to Lovinski, and to give him thy daughter, I will set
thee at liberty.—He who can brave death,
knows how to endure slavery; my daughter shall
never be the wife of a traitor.—Wouldst thou
prefer that she were the mistress of a Tartar?
If thou dost not promise me to marry her
within eight days to this brave man, I marry

her this night myself. When I shall be tired of thee and her, I will sell you to the Turks; thy daughter is handsome enough for the seraglio of a bashaw; and as for thee, thou canst be cook to some janisary.—My life is in thy hands; do as thou pleasest with it. If Pulauski falls by the blows of a Tartar, he will be pitied; they will say that he merited a better fate; but I cannot consent. No; I had rather die!—Ah! I do not wish you to die! I wish that Lovinski may espouse Lodoiska. But is it for my prisoner to lay down the law for me? What a dog of a man! It is nothing but obstinacy! He reasons badly.

I saw the anger kindle in the eyes of the Tartar, and I reminded him that he had promised me not to be passionate. Certainly: but this man would tire the patience of one of the prophet's favourites! I am nothing but a robber, aye! Pulauski, I repeat it to you, I wish that Lovinski may marry your daughter. By my sword, he has well earned her: if it had not been for him, she would have been burnt this evening. How?—Ah! yes: look at these ruins: there was a tower, this tower was in flames, no one dared to enter; he and Boleslas ascended;

they have saved thy daughter.—My daughter
has been in that tower?—Yes, she was there;
this scoundrel had placed her there, and wished
to violate her. Come on, tell him the whole,
and make haste, that he may decide; I have
business elsewhere; I do not wish the quartuaires* to surprise me here: in fact, I have
something else to do, for I laugh at them.

Whilst Titsikan was superintending some
carriages, which were loaded with the considerable booty he had made, Lodoiska informed her
father of the treachery of Dourlinski, and
mingled so adroitly the recital of our tenderness
with the history of her misfortunes, that nature
and gratitude appealed at the same time to the
heart of Pulauski. Most sensibly affected with
the sufferings of his daughter, conscious of the
important service I had rendered him, he embraced Lodoiska; and looking at me without
animosity, seemed to wait with patience for me
to finish, by deciding him in my favour.—Oh,
Pulauski! said I; oh, thou whom heaven hath
left to console me for the loss of the best of

* Quartuaires is the name given to the dragoons es-
tablished to watch the safety of the frontiers of Podolia
and Volhymnia against the Tartars.

fathers! Oh! thou for whom I feel a friendship
equal to my respect, why hast thou condemned
thy children without hearing them? Why hast
thou suspected a man who adores thy daughter,
of the most horrible treason? When my voice
placed on the throne the man who now fills it,
I swear, Pulauski, by her whom I love, that I
thought I was doing good for my country. The
evils which my youth did not foresee, thy experience foresaw; but because I have failed in
prudence, dost thou accuse me of perfidy?
Canst thou reproach me for having esteemed
my friend? Canst thou consider it a crime in
me still to esteem him? For three months I
have seen, like thee, the misery of my country;
like thee I have bemoaned it; but I am sure
that the king is ignorant of it; I will go and
inform him at Warsaw—Pulauski interrupted
me: It is not there that thou must go. Thou
sayst that M. du P*** is ignorant of the sufferings of his country, I am willing to believe
it; but whether he knows them or not it is of
little consequence now. Insolent strangers can-
toned in our provinces will endeavour to establish themselves there, even in spite of the king
whom they elected. It is not a weak or bad in-

tentioned monarch who will drive the Russians from my country. Let us expect nothing but from ourselves Lovinski; let us avenge our country or die for her. I have assembled in the Palatinate of Lublin a band of gentlemen, who wait but the return of their general to march against the Russians. Follow me, come into my camp—on this condition I am free, and my daughter is thine.—Pulauski, I am ready, I swear to follow thy fortune and to partake of thy dangers. And think not that 'tis Lodoiska alone for whom I make these oaths! I love my country as much as I adore thy daughter: I swear by her, and before thee, that the enemies of the state have always been and will never cease to be mine: I swear that I will shed even the last drop of my blood, to drive from Poland the strangers who govern it under the name of its king. Embrace me, Lovinski, I acknowledge thee, I acknowledge my kinsman. Come on, my children, all our griefs are at an end.

Pulauski told me to unite my hands with those of Lodoiska. We were embracing our father as Titsikan re-entered. Good! Good! cried he, that is right; that is what I wished. Come, father, I will have thee unbound. By my sword! continued the Tartar, while the soldiers cut the cords with which Pulauski had been tied, I am here doing a fine action, when I think of it! But it will cost me a great deal of money.—Great Gods of Poland! that beautiful girl would have paid me a large ransom! Titsikan, that will not matter, interrupted Pulauski. Ah! no, no, replied the Tartar; it was but a simple reflection, and one of those ideas of which a robber is not the master!—My brave fellows, I want nothing from you—and what is more, you shall not go on foot, for I have got horses at your service. And for this lady, if you will have it, I will give you a litter, in which they have carried me for ten or twelve days. That youth there thrashed me so well, that I could not sit on my horse. The litter is very homely, being made of the branches of trees; I have but that, or a little covered carriage, to offer you; you will therefore make your choice. In the mean time Dourlinski had not dared to speak a single word, but held down his head in consternation; unworthy friend! said Pulauski to him, could you abuse my confidence to such an extent, and are you not afraid of exposing yourself to my resentment! what

demon has blinded you? Love, replied Dourlinski, an insane love. Thou knowest not to
what excess the passions may carry a man who
is born violent and jealous! Let this frightful
example teach thee, at least, that a daughter as
charming and as beautiful as thine, is a rare
treasure, the care of which you should not trust
to anyone. Pulauski, I have merited thy
hatred, yet you owe me notwithstanding some
pity. I acknowledge myself highly culpable;
but you see me cruelly punished. I lose, in a
single day, my rank, my riches, my honour and
my liberty; nay, I lose more than all that, I
lose thy daughter! Oh! Lodoiska, whom I have
so much outraged, will you condescend to forget
my persecutions, your dangers and your misfortunes; will you condescend to grant me a
generous pardon? Ah! if there is not a crime
which a true repentance cannot expiate, Lodoiska, I am no longer criminal. I wish I could at
the price of my own blood, redeem the tears
which you have shed. Shall Dourlinski, in the
horrible slavery to which he will be reduced,
carry the consoling remembrance of having
heard you say, he was odious to you? Too
amiable girl, and up to the present time, too

unfortunate, how great soever my wrongs towards you, I can repair them by a single word. Come here, I have a secret of importance to reveal to you.

Lodoiska approached without fear. At that moment I saw a poinard glitter in the hands of Dourlinski. I threw myself upon him—It was too late, I could only parry the second blow; my mistress, struck beneath her left breast, had already fallen at the feet of Titsikan. The furious Pulauski wished to revenge his child; no, no, cried Titsikan, you will give this monster too soft a death. Well! said the infamous assassin as he contemplated his victim with a malicious joy: Lovinski, thou appearest so anxious to be united to Lodoiska, why not follow her? Go, my happy rival, and join thy mistress in the tomb. They are preparing my punishment, which will appear to me mild, because I leave thee delivered up to torments, longer and more cruel than mine. Dourlinski could not say more, the Tartars dragged him away and threw him among the flaming ruins of his castle.

What a night, my dear Faublas, what various cares, what conflicting sensations agitated

me in their turn! How often I experienced in
succession, fear and hope, grief and joy! After
so many anxieties and dangers, Lodoiska was
restored to me by her father, I was intoxicated
with the delightful thoughts of possessing her.
Then a barbarian assassinates her before my
eyes!—This moment was the most cruel of my
life!—But be assured, my friend, that my happiness so rapidly eclipsed was not long in reap-
pearing. Among the soldiers of Titsikan, there
was one who knew something of surgery; we
went for him; he examined the wound, and as-
serted that it was but very slight: the wretch
Dourlinski, confined by his chains, and blinded
by his despair, had given but a bad aimed blow.

As soon as Titsikan ascertained that there
was nothing to fear for the life of Lodoiska, he
bade us adieu. I leave you, said he, the five
domestics which Pulauski brought, some provision for several days, six good horses, two
close carriages, and all Dourlinski's people, well
chained. Their villainous master is dead. The
day begins to break, and I must go. Do not
leave here until to-morrow; to-morrow I shall
go to visit other cantons. Adieu, my brave fellows; you will tell your countrymen, that Titsi-

kan is not always a mischievous devil; and that he gives sometimes with one hand what he takes with the other. Adieu. He gave the signal for departure; the Tartars raised the drawbridge and galloped away.

They were not gone two hours, when several neighbouring gentlemen, supported by some Quartuaires, came to invest the castle of Dourlinski. Pulanski himself went to receive them. He gave them an account of all that had passed; and some of them brought over by his arguments, determined to follow us into the Palatinate of Lublin. They only asked two days to make the necessary preparations for their departure. They did indeed join us on the next day to the amount of sixty. Lodoiska having assured us that she felt herself in a condition to sustain the fatigues of the journey, was placed in a convenient carriage, which we had time to procure. After having set the servants of Dourlinski at liberty, we left them the two carriages which Titsikan's singular generosity had left as a part of the booty, which they divided amongst them.

We arrived without any accident at Polowisk, in the Palatinate of Lublin, which Pulanski had named as the general rendezvous. The news of his return being spread abroad, a crowd of the discontented came in the space of a month, to enlarge our army, which was then about ten thousand men. Lodoiska entirely cured of her wound, and perfectly recovered from her fatigues, had acquired her usual appearance, and all her charms shone forth with their former brilliance. Pulanski called me to his tent. He said to me: three thousand Russians have appeared on the heights within three quarters of a league hence, take this evening, four thousand chosen men, and drive the enemy from the advantageous post which they occupy: remember that on the success of the first combat almost always depends the success of the campaign; and remember that thou must revenge thy country. To-morrow, my friend, when I hear of thy victory, to-morrow thou espousest Lodoiska.

I marched about ten o'clock in the evening: at midnight we surprised our enemy in their camp. Never was a defeat more complete: we killed seven hundred of their men, we made nine hundred prisoners, we took all their cannon, military chest, and camp equipage.

At break of day, Pulauski came to join me with the rest of the troops. He brought Lodoiska with him. We were married in the tent of Pulauski. The whole camp rung with shouts of joy. Valour and beauty were celebrated in their verses; it was the *fete* of Love and of Mars; they have said, that every soldier had my soul, and partook of my happiness.

After devoting to love, the first days of so cherished a union, I thought of recompensing the heroic fidelity of Boleslas. My father-in-law made him a present of one of his Chateaux, situated some leagues from the capital. Lodoiska and myself added to that, a considerable sum of money, to secure him a tranquil independence. He would not leave us; we ordered him to go and take possession of his castle, and live peaceably and honourably in the retreat which he had merited. The day he left us, I took him aside: thou wilt go to our monarch at Warsaw: thou wilt inform him that Hymen has united me to the daughter of Pulauski: thou wilt tell him, that I am armed to drive from his realm the foreigners who devastate it: thou wilt tell him, above all, Lovinski is the enemy of the Russians, but not the enemy of his king.

I will not fatigue you, my dear Faublas, with the recital of our operations, during eight years of a bloody war. Sometimes beaten, but more frequently the victor, as great in his defeats, as redoubtable after victories, and always superior to events, Pulauski excited the attention of Europe, and astonished it by his long resistance. Obliged to abandon one province, he went to fight fresh battles in another; and it was thus, that overrunning all the Palatinates he signalized in each of them, by some glorious exploits, the hatred he bore to the enemy of Poland.

The wife of a warrior, and daughter of a hero, accustomed to the tumult of camps, Lodoiska followed us everywhere. Of five children that she bore me, one daughter only was left me, aged eighteen months. One day, after an obstinate battle, the Russians being victorious, rushed into my tent for plunder. Pulauski and myself, followed by some gentlemen, flew to the defence of Lodoiska, and saved her, but my daughter was carried away. The child, by a wise precaution which her mother had not neglected in those unsettled times, bears, marked under the arm-pit, the arms of our family, but I have hitherto sought her in vain. Alas! Dorliska, my dear Dorliska groans in slavery, or exists no more.

This loss made me grieve excessively. Pulauski appeared almost insensible, either because already occupied with grand projects which he was not slow in communicating to me, or that the evils of his country alone had a right to touch his stoic heart. He gathered together the rest of his army, made an advantageous encampment, which he employed several days in fortifying, and maintained himself three months against all the efforts of the Russians. He was obliged, nevertheless, to think of abandoning it, for our provisions began to fail. Pulauski came to my tent, ordered those present to retire, and as soon as we were alone, Lovinski, said he, I have reason to complain of thee. Formerly, thou supported with me the burthen of command, and I could rest upon my kinsman a portion of my painful cares. For these three months past thou hast done nothing but weep; thou groanest like a woman! Thou abandonest me in the critical moment when thy aid is most necessary! Thou seest that I am pressed in all parts. I fear not for myself, it is not my life which renders me uneasy; but if

we perish, the state has no more defenders.
Rouse thyself, Lovinski! Thou hast partaken
so nobly of my labours, do not now remain a
useless looker on. We have bathed ourselves in
the blood of Russians; our fellow citizens are
avenged, but they are not saved; presently perhaps we may not be in a condition to defend
them. I am astonished, Pulauski, at what thou
sayest; from whence came those gloomy presentiments!—I do not alarm myself without
reason; consider our actual position: I am
forced to awaken in their hearts the love of
country; I have found almost everywhere degraded men, born for slavery, or weak men
sensible of their misfortunes, but contented
with making useless complaints. A small number of true citizens are arranged under my ban-
ners; but eight campaigns have almost destroyed them. I am weakened by my victories,
but our enemies appear more numerous after
their defeats.—I repeat it to thee, Pulauski: I
am astonished! In circumstances equally pressing, I have seen thee sustain thyself with courage.—Dost thou think it abandons me? Valour
does not consist in being blind to danger, but in
braving it when we meet it. Our enemies are

preparing to defeat me; nevertheless, if thou art willing, Lovinski, the day which they have marked for their triumph shall, perhaps, be that of their loss, and the salvation of our fellow citizens.—If I am willing! Dost thou doubt it? Speak; what wouldst thou say? What must I do? Strike a bolder stroke than I have even meditated. Forty chosen men are assembled at Czenstochow with Kaluvski, whose bravery is well known. They must have an adroit, firm, and intrepid chief: it is thee I have chosen.—Pulauski, I am ready.—I will not dissemble from you the danger of the enterprise; the uncertainty of its success; and that if thou dost not succeed, thy loss is infallible.—I tell thee I am ready; explain thyself. —Thou canst not be ignorant that I have now scarcely four thousand men. I can still, without doubt, harass the enemy a great deal; but ought I to hope, with such a small force, to drive them from our provinces? All our gentlemen would flock to my standard, if the king was in my camp.—What sayest thou, Pulauski? Dost thou think the king will ever consent to come here?—No, but we must bring him.—By force? Yes: I know that an early friendship binds thee to M. de P***; but since thou sustainest with Pulauski the cause of liberty, thou knowest also that everything ought to be sacrificed to the good of thy country, that an interest as sacred——I know my duties, and I will fulfil them: but what dost thou propose to me? The king never leaves Warsaw.—Well! it is at Warsaw we must go and seek him; it is from the bosom of the capital we must snatch him.— What hast thou prepared for this grand enterprise?—Thou seest this Russian army, three times as strong as mine, encamped for these three months before me. Its general, remaining tranquil in its entrenchments, expects that, compelled by famine, I shall surrender at discretion. At the back of my camp are some dangerous morasses; as soon as it is night we will cross them. I have disposed everything in such a manner, that the enemy, being deceived, will discover our retreat when too late. I hope to steal more than one march upon them. If fortune favours me, I can gain a day upon them. I will advance directly upon Warsaw, by the high road that leads to the capital, and through the little corps of Russians who hover in its environs. I reckon on beating them separately, or should they unite to stop me, I will at least occupy them sufficiently to prevent them incommoding thee. Thou, in the meantime, Lovinski, wilt push on. Thy forty men, disguised, armed only with sabres, pistols, and daggers, concealed under their clothes, will enter Warsaw by different roads. Thou wilt wait for the king coming out of his palaces; thou wilt seize him and bring him to my camp. The enterprise is rash and unheard of, I agree; the entrance is difficult, the stay dangerous, and the return of extreme peril. If thou sinkest under it, if they arrest thee, thou wilt perish, Lovinski; but thou wilt perish a martyr to liberty; Pulauski, jealous of a death so glorious, will mourn to be obliged to survive thee, and some Russians yet will follow thee to the tomb. If, on the contrary, Almighty God, the protector of Poland, inspires me with this bold project in order to terminate its troubles; if his goodness gives a success equal to thy courage, think what prosperity will be the fruit of thy noble temerity! M. de P#### will see in my camp none but soldiers, and citizens, inimical to foreigners, and faithful to their king. Under my patriotic tents he will breathe, as I may say, the air of liberty, the love of his country: the enemies of the state will become his; our brave nobility, roused from its langour, will fight under the banner of their king, for the common cause; the Russians will be cut in pieces, or will repass the frontiers; and then, my friend, thou wilt have saved thy country.

Pulauski had my word. As soon as it was night, we happily accomplished our retreat; the morass was crossed in silence. My friend, said my father-in-law to me, it is time for us to part: I am well aware that my daughter has more courage than another woman; but she is a tender wife and an unhappy mother; her tears will weaken thee; thou wilt lose in her embraces that spirit, that fierceness of soul, which becomes more necessary for you at present than ever. I recommend you to leave without taking farewell. Pulauski advised me in vain; I could not determine to do it. When Lodoiska knew that I set out alone, and found us decided not to tell where I was going, she shed a torrent of tears, and endeavoured to detain me. I began to waver. Come on, cried my father-in-law, thou must be gone; father, wife, children, and everything else must be sacrificed when our country is at stake.

I left immediately. I made such haste, that I arrived about the middle of the following day at Czenstochow. I found there forty gentlemen determined to act. Messieurs, said I, we are required to seize a king in his capital. Men capable of attempting so daring an enterprise, are alone capable of accomplishing it: success or death awaits us. After this short harangue, we prepared for our journey. Kaluvski had in readiness twelve waggons loaded with hay and straw, each drawn by four good horses; we disguised ourselves as countrymen, and concealed our clothes, our sabres, our pistols, and the saddles of our horses, in the hay with which our waggons were filled. We agreed upon several signs, and on a word for rallying. Twelve of our comrades, commanded by Kaluvski, were to go into Warsaw with the twelve waggons, which they would drive themselves. I divided the rest of my little troop into several brigades. To avoid all suspicion, each was to march at some distance, and to enter the capital by different gates.

We set out; on Saturday, November 2, 1771, we arrived at Warsaw, and took up our lodgings among the Dominicans.

The next day, Sunday, a day ever memorable in the annals of Poland, Stavinski, covered with rags, placed himself near the college, and begged alms from thence, even unto the door of the royal palace, and noticed everything that passed. Several of our comrades prowled about the city; and even in the six narrow streets which terminate at the great palace, where I walked with Kaluvski. We continued in ambuscade the whole of the morning and part of the after-noon. At six in the evening, the king came out of his palace; we followed him, and saw him enter that of his uncle P***, the arch-chancellor of Lithuania.

All the conspirators were informed; they stripped off their disguises, saddled their horses, and prepared their arms. In the extensive es-tablishment of the Dominicans our motions were not noticed. We came out, one after the other, under the shelter of night. Being too well known in Warsaw to appear without dis-guise, I retained my rustic habits; I mounted an excellent charger, but it was covered with a common horse-cloth, and shabbily harnessed. Our comrades took the various posts I had as-signed them in the suburbs, in order that all the avenues to the arch-chancellor's palace might be guarded.

Between nine and ten o'clock the king came out, and we observed that his suite was but small. The carriage was preceded by two men who carried flambeaux, followed by some officers of artillery, two knights, and an esquire. I knew not the lord who was in the carriage with the king. He had two pages at each door, two Hungarian soldiers, and two valets on foot behind. The carriage moved slowly; our comrades assembled at a little distance; twelve of the most resolute detached themselves; I headed them, and we advanced at a gentle pace. As Warsaw was garrisoned by Russians, we affected to speak the language of these foreigners; that our troop might be taken for one of their patroles, we came up to the carriage about a hundred and fifty paces from the palace of the arch-chancellor, between those of the Bishop of Cracow and the late commander-in-chief of the Polish army. All at once, we placed ourselves before the horses of the carriage, and divided the retinue in such a manner, that those who preceded it found themselves separated from those who surrounded it.

I gave the signal. Kaluvski came up with the rest of the conspirators: I presented a pistol to the postillion, who stopped. They fired on the coachman, and attacked the two pages. The two Hungarians defended themselves; one of then fell, pierced through by balls; the other was knocked down by a blow of a sabre on the head. The esquire's horse sunk with his wounds; one of the pages was dismounted and his horse taken; the balls were whistling on all sides. The attack was so hot, the firing so violent, that I trembled for the life of the king. He, however, having preserved the greatest tranquility during the danger, descended from his carriage, and sought to regain the palace of his uncle. Kaluvski arrested him, and seized him by the hair; seven or eight of the conspirators surrounded and disarmed him; they kept him running between their horses, who galloped on his right and his left to the end of the street. At this moment, I must confess that I thought Pulauski had unworthily deceived me, that the death of the king had been resolved on, and this scheme formed for his assassination. In an instant I was decided how to act, and flew to join those who had advanced before me: I cried out to them to stop, and that I would kill him who disobeyed me. God, the protector of kings, watched over the safety of M. de P***. Kaluvski and his comrade recognised my voice, and halted. We put the king on a horse, and followed our course, at full speed up to the moat which surrounds the city, which the monarch was obliged to leap with us.

After this a panic of terror ran through my troop. At fifty paces from the ditch there were but seven of us near the king. The night was dark, and the rain came down in torrents; we were obliged every minute to descend from our horses to feel our way over a miry morass. The king's horse fell twice, and broke a leg in the second fall. By these accidents, the king lost his pelisse and one of his boots. If you wish me to follow you, said he, give me a horse and a boot. We remounted him, and with a view to gain the road in which Pulanski had promised to meet me, we made for the village of Burakow. The king with great tranquility, said, Do not go this way, there are Russians. I believed it, and changed the route. In proportion as we advanced in the Wood of Beliany, our number diminished. Presently, I could only perceive

Kaluvski and Stravinski; and shortly well heard the call of a Russian sentinel. We stopped in great alarm. Kill the king, said Kaluvski. I was struck with horror at such a proposition, and expressed it in an unguarded manner. Well then, said this ferocious man, you must take upon yourself the charge of conducting him! He plunged into the wood, and Stravinski followed him, leaving me alone with the king.

Lovinski, said he, it is you, I can no longer doubt it. It is you; I recognised your voice. I answered not a word. He continued with mildness: It is you! Who would have thought this ten years back? We found ourselves then near the Convent of Beliany, about one league distant from Warsaw. Lovinski, said the king, let me enter this convent, and save yourself.— You must follow me, was all my answer.—It is in vain, said the monarch, that you are disguised; it is in vain that you now try to alter your voice: I have recognised you; I am sure that you are Lovinski. Ah! who would have thought this ten years ago? Ten years since you would have risked your own life to preserve that of your friend.

He was silent. We advanced for a while
without speaking. At length he said, I am overcome with fatigue: if you would take me alive,
let me have a moment's rest. I helped him to
dismount. He sat down upon the grass, and
making me sit down beside him, he took one of
my hands within his own: Lovinski, you whom
I have loved so much, you who know better than
anyone the purity of my intentions, how is it
that you are armed against me? Oh, how ungrateful! Do I not find you with my most cruel
enemies? Do you see me again but to sacrifice
me? He then, in a most affecting manner, re-
counted the pleasures of our youth, the tender
friendship we had sworn, and the confidence
which he had ever since reposed in me. He
spoke of the honours he could have loaded me
with during his reign, if I had been desirous of
meriting them. He reproached me, above all,
for the unworthy enterprise of which I appeared to be the chief, but of which he well
knew I was only the principal instrument. He
threw all the horror of the design on Pulauski,
but nevertheless, he said, the author of such an
outrage was not alone to be blamed, and that
I was not without crime in undertaking its ex-

ecution. That my compliance with such views,
already so punishable in a subject, was still
more inexcusable in a friend. He concluded
by begging me to set him at liberty. Fly, said
he to me, and if they come to me for informa-
tion, I shall direct them a contrary road to that
which you shall take.

The king entreated me in so agreeable a
manner, his natural eloquence, enforced by the
danger, carried persuasion to my heart, and
awakened in it the most tender sentiments. I
was shaken: I began to waver; but Pulauski
triumphed. I thought I heard the fierce republican reproach me for my weakness. My dear
Faublas, the love of country may, perhaps,
have its fanaticism and its superstition, but if
I was culpable, I am so still. I am still more
than ever persuaded, that in forcing the monarch to remount his horse, I did both a brave
and a good action. So, cried he, in a melancholy tone, you reject the prayer which a friend
has addressed to you! You refuse the pardon
which your king offers you! Well, let us go;
I deliver myself to my evil destiny, or you
abandon yourself to yours.

We recommenced our march; but the re-

proaches of the monarch, his entreaties, and
even his menaces, and the internal struggles
which I experienced, had so far affected me,
that I could no longer see my road. Wandering
in the country, I took no certain road. After
proceeding half an hour, we found ourselves at
Marimont.* I had gone astray, and we had to
retrace our steps. A quarter of a league from
there we fell among a party of Russians. The
king made himself known to their commander;
after which he added, I have lost my way this
evening, while hunting; this good countryman
whom you see, wished, before he guided me
home, to give me a frugal repast in his cottage;
but as I thought I had seen some of the soldiers
of Pulauski roving about in the neighbourhood,
I wished to return as quick as possible to Warsaw, and you will do me a pleasure to accompany me there. As for thee, my friend, I am
sorry thou hast taken so useless a trouble, for
I would rather return to my capital with these
gentlemen, than go any further with thee.
Nevertheless, it would be singular if I was to

* Marimont is a country residence belonging to the
court of Saxony, and is nearer to Warsaw by half a
league than Beliany.

leave thee without some recompense. What wouldst thou? Speak; I will grant thee the favour thou demandest.

You may easily conceive, Faublas, how much I was embarrassed. I still doubted the intentions of the king, and endeavoured to penetrate the real meaning of an equivocal discourse, which was either full of the most bitter irony, or remarkable for its magnanimity. M. de P*** left me some time in this painful uncertainty.—I see thou art much embarrassed, replied he at last, with an air of goodness which touched me to the heart; thou dost not know what to choose! Come, my friend, embrace me; there is more honour than profit in the embrace of a king, added he, laughing: Nevertheless, we must agree that at the present day few monarchs are so generous as myself.

Having said this, he went out, leaving me confounded at so much greatness of soul.

In the meantime, the danger which the king was so generously going to save me from, began at every moment to threaten me. It was more than probable that a great number of couriers, dispatched from Warsaw, had spread in every quarter the astonishing news of the king being

carried away. A warm pursuit had no doubt
already commenced after the ravishers; my
remarkable equipage might betray me in my
flight; and if I fell again into the hands of the
Russians, who might be better informed, all the
efforts of the king could not save me. Supposing that Pulauski had obtained all the success
he could wish, he would still be at some distance; ten leagues, at least, remained for me
to get over, and my horse had given in. I endeavoured to spur him on; he had not run fifty
paces before he dropped down under me. A
well-mounted cavalier who passed on the road at
this moment, saw the animal fall, and thinking
he could amuse himself at the expense of a poor
peasant, said to me: My friend, I can inform
thee that thy good horse is no longer worth
anything.—Piqued at the buffoonery, I immediately resolved to punish the joker, and at the
same time insure my flight. I very abruptly
presented a pistol at him, and compelled him
to deliver up his horse; and I will even confess
that, pressed by circumstances, I plundered
him of a good cloak, as large as it was light,
under which I concealed my rustic habit, which
might have led to my discovery. I threw my

purse, full of gold, at the feet of the dismounted traveller, and left him as swiftly as my new horse could carry me.

He was fresh and vigorous; I rode twelve leagues without stopping; at length I thought I heard the noise of cannon, by which I conjectured that my father-in-law was not far off, and was combatting the Russians. I was not deceived; I arrived on the field of battle at the moment when one of our regiments gave way. I reconnoitred them, and having rallied them behind a neighbouring hill, I came to attack the enemy in the flank, while Pulauski opposed them in front with the rest of his troop. We charged so *à propos,* and with so much vigour, that the Russians were put to the rout, after suffering a great slaughter among their men. Pulauski deigned to attribute to me the honour of the victory.—Ah, said he, embracing me, after having heard the details of our expedition, if thy forty men had equalled thee in courage, the king would now be in my camp; but it was not the will of heaven; I am thankful that thou at least art saved to us; I return thee thanks for the important service thou hast rendered me, for without thee, Kaluvski would have assassinated the monarch, and my name would have been covered with eternal infamy. I could, added he, have advanced two miles further, but I preferred fixing my camp in this respectable position. Yesterday, on the road, I surprised and cut in pieces a party of Russians; I beat, this morning, two of their detachments; another considerable corps having gathered the remains of the former, has taken advantage of the night to attack me. My soldiers, fatigued with a long march, and three successive combats, began to fail, when victory entered my camp with thee. Let us entrench ourselves here: let us here wait the Russian army, and let us fight while we have breath.

In the meantime, the camp re-echoed with shouts of joy: our victorious soldiers mingled my praises with those of Pulauski. At the sound of my name, which a thousand voices repeated, Lodoiska ran to the tent of her father. She proved to me the excess of her tenderness by the excess of her joy. I was obliged to recommence the recital of the dangers I had undergone. She could not withhold shedding tears, on hearing of our monarch's rare generosity. How great he is! cried she with transport: How worthy is he to be king who has pardoned thee! What tears has he spared to a wife whom thou hadst forsaken, to a lover whom thou didst not fear to sacrifice! How cruel it was! Wert thou not exposed to sufficient dangers every day?—Pulauski, interrupting his daughter with much severity, said: Thou weak and indiscreet woman! is it before me that thou darest to hold such discourse?—Alas! must I be unceasingly trembling for the life of a father and a husband?—It was thus my Lodoiska addressed to me her affecting complaints, and sighed for a happier future, while fortune prepared for us a more frightful reverse.

Our Cossacks came from all quarters to inform us that the Russian army approached. Pulauski reckoned that he should be attacked at break of day: he was not, but in the middle of the following night, we were informed that the Russians were preparing to force our entrenchments. Pulauski, always ready, had already defended them. He did, during this fatal night, all that could be expected from his experience and his valour. We repulsed the assailants five times, but they always returned to the charge with fresh troops, and their last attack was so concerted, that they penetrated into our camp by three places at the same time. Zaremba was killed by my side: a crowd of nobles perished in this bloody action, for the enemies gave no quarter. Furious at seeing all my friends perish, I wished to throw myself among the Russian battalions: Madman! said Pulauski, what blind fury carries thee away? My army is entirely destroyed, but my courage remains. Why should we die uselessly here? Come, I will conduct you into those climates where we can excite new enemies against the Russians. Let us live, since we can still serve our country: let us save ourselves, let us save Lodoiska.—Lodoiska! I was going to abandon her! We ran to her tent—we were in time— we carried her away, and plunged into the neighbouring wood, and early in the morning we ventured out of it, to present ourselves at the door of a castle, with which we thought we were acquainted. It was, indeed, that of a gentleman named Micislas, who had served sometime in our army. He recognised us, and offered us an asylum, which he advised us to accept but for a few hours. He told a very astonishing piece of news, which was circulated the night before, and appeared to be confirmed, that some one had dared to seize even the king in Warsaw, and carry him away; that the Russians had pursued the ravishers, brought the king back into his capital, and it was thought a price would be set upon the head of Pulauski, who was suspected to be the author of the conspiracy. Believe me, added he, whether you have had a hand in this bold plot, or not, I would have you fly: leave here your uniforms, which will betray you, I will give you some clothes which are less remarkable; and as to Lodoiska, I will undertake to conduct her myself to the place you may choose for your retreat.

Lodoiska interrupted Micislas: The place of my retreat will be that of their flight! I will accompany them everywhere!—Pulauski represented to his daughter that she could not sustain the fatigues of a long route, and that moreover we should be perpetually exposed to danger.— The more danger there is, replied she, the more I ought to partake it with you. You have repeat to me a hundred times that the daughter of Pulauski ought not to be a common woman! For the last eight years, I have lived in the midst of alarms. I have seen nothing but scenes of carnage and horror: death surrounded me everywhere, and menaced me every instant: you would not permit me to brave it by your sides: does not the life of Lodoiska depend on that of her father? Lovinski! the shock you have given me will hurry me to the tomb! And since I am no longer worthy——

I interrupted Lodoiska, and joined her father in detailing the reasons which determined us to leave her in Poland. She listened to me with impatience: Ungrateful that you are! will you go without me?—Yes, replied Pulauski, you will remain with the sisters of Lovinski, and I forbid him——His daughter, quite distracted, would not let him finish: I know thy rights, and I respect them—they have always been sacred to me; but thou hast not the right to take a wife away from her husband! Ah! pardon me, I offend thee, I forget myself—but pity my sufferings—excuse my despair—Father! Lovinski! listen both of you; I wish to accompany you everywhere—Everywhere?—Yes, I will follow you—cruel as you are, I will follow you in spite of you! Lovinski! if thy wife has lost all the right she had over thy heart, remem-

ber at least thy lover: recollect that frightful
night when I was about to perish in the flames!
—that terrible moment when you mounted the
burning tower, crying, " To live or die with
Lodoiska! " Well! what thou felt then, I feel
at this moment. I know no greater evil than
that of being separated from thee!—I said, in
my turn, To live and die with my father and
my wife!—Wretch that I am! what is to become of me when thou quittest me? When I
have to weep for you both, where can I find
comfort in my affliction? Can my children
console me? Alas! in two years, death has
snatched four from me, and the Russians, implacable as death, have torn from me the last!
I have none in the world but you, and you
would abandon me! Oh, my father! Oh, my
husband! let not two names so dear find you
insensible!—have pity on Lodoiska!

Her grief stopped her utterance. Micislas
wept, and my heart was torn in pieces.—Thou
dost wish it, my child, well! I consent, said Pulauski, but may heaven not punish me for my
compliance! Lodoiska embraced us both with
as much joy as if our troubles were at an end.

I left with Micislas two letters, which he undertook to forward; one was addressed to my sisters, the other to Boleslas.

I bade them farewell, and entreated them to neglect nothing in order to find my dear Dorliska. It was necessary to disguise my wife, so she put on the dress of a man: we exchanged ours, and employed all possible means to alter our appearance. Thus disguised, armed with pistols and sabres, provided with a considerable sum of money in gold, some jewels, and all the diamonds of Lodoiska, we took our leave of Micislas, and hastened to regain the wood.

Pulauski communicated to us the design he had formed of taking refuge in Turkey. He hoped to obtain some appointment in the armies of the Grand Seignior, who, for two years, had carried on an unsuccessful war against the Russians. Lodoiska did not seem dismayed at the long journey we had to make. As she could neither be recognised nor sought after, she undertook the charge of going before us, and conducting our provisions. As soon as day appeared, we retired into the woods; concealed in the trunks of trees, or tufts of thorns, we waited the return of night to continue our march. It was thus that, during several days, we escaped the searches of the Russians, who were eagerly pursuing us.

One evening, as Lodoiska, always disguised as a peasant, was coming from a neighbouring hamlet, where she had been to buy some provisions, two Russian marauders attacked her at the entrance of the forest in which we were hid. After having robbed her, they prepared to strip her of her clothes. At the cries which she made, we came out of our retreat; the two robbers fled as soon as they saw us, but we feared lest they might recount their adventure to the party they belonged to, and that this singular rencontre might excite their suspicions, and cause them to drag us from our asylum. We resolved to change our route, and that they might not suspect the one we had taken, it was determined that, instead of going direct for the frontiers of Turkey, we should proceed, by a circuitous route, for Polesia, afterwards for the Crimea, from whence we could pass to Constantinople.

After some very troublesome marches, we entered into Polesia. Pulauski wept on quitting his native land. I have, at least, said he, done everything in my power to serve it, and I only leave it with a view of continuing my exertions in its cause.

So many trials and fatigues had exhausted the strength of Lodoiska, when we arrived at Novogorod, where we rested, on her account. Our design was to let her repose there for some days, but the country people, who were inquisitive and communicative, as is usual, happened to tell us that troops were scouring the neighbourhood, in search of one Pulauski, who had conspired against the King of Poland. Necessarily alarmed, we remained but a few hours in this town, where we bought horses. We passed the Desna, above Czernicove, and following the banks of the Sula, we crossed to Perevoloczna, where we learned that Pulauski had been recognised at Novogorod, had only left Nezin a few hours before they came after him, and that he was still closely pursued. We, therefore, found it necessary to fly, and change our route once more. We penetrated the immense forests which covered the country between the Sula and the Sem.

We arrived at a cavern in which we wished to establish ourselves. Our entrance into this asylum, as frightful as it was solitary, was disputed by a bear. We killed it and ate its young ones. Pulauski was wounded; Lodoiska exhausted, supported herself with difficulty, and the cold was become severe. Pursued by the Russians in all places that were inhabited, and threatened by ferocious animals in this vast desert, without any arms but our swords, and shortly reduced to eat our horses, what was to become of us? The danger of my father-in-law and my wife was so pressing, that I thought of no other. I resolved to procure them, at whatever price, the assistance their situation required, as it was still more deplorable than my own, and left them, promising to come back speedily. I took with me some of Lodoiska's diamonds, and followed the banks of the Warsklo. You will observe, my dear Faublas, that a traveller, wandering in these extensive countries, and reduced to proceed without either guide or compass, is obliged to follow the rivers, because it is on their banks that he generally meets with habitations. I wished to reach, as soon as possible, some mercantile city; I followed then the course of the Warsklo, and walked day and night, I found myself at Pultawa at the end of the fourth day. I there passed for a merchant of Beilgorod. I knew that they sought for Pul-auski, that the Empress of Russia had sent his description into all quarters, with orders to take him, dead or alive, wherever he might be found. I hastened to sell my diamonds, and to buy powder, arms, all kinds of provision, various tools, some necessary furniture, and everything which I thought we should stand in need of to alleviate our misery. I packed the whole into one waggon, drawn by four horses, of which I was the only conductor. My return was as difficult as fatiguing, and eight days passed before I arrived at the forest.

It was there that my painful and dangerous journey terminated: I went to relieve my father-in-law and my wife: I went to see again what was most dear to me in the world, and never-theless, my dear Faublas, I could not deliver myself up to joy. Your philosophers think nothing of presentiments; but I can assure you, my friend, that I experienced an involuntary uneasiness; my soul was dismayed: I felt a kind of warning that the most unhappy moment of my life was approaching.

I had, at starting, placed some flints here and there, by which to recognise my road, but I

could not find them; I had notched with my
sabre the bark of several trees, but I could not
discover them. I entered the forest, and called
out with all my strength; from time to time
I discharged my musket, but no one replied
to me. I dared not go too far, for fear of
losing myself: I dared not go far from my waggon, the contents of which were so necessary to
Pulauski, his daughter, and myself.

The night, which overtook me, obliged me to
cease my researches. I passed that as the
preceding ones, wrapped up in my cloak, under my waggon, with some of my heaviest com-
modities piled round me to protect me
from beasts of prey. I could not sleep; I felt
the cold very much, and the snow fell in abundance; at break of day the ground was covered
with it. This greatly discouraged me; my
flints, which would have directed my road,
were all buried, and it appeared impossible for
me to find Pulauski and my wife.

Could the horse which I had left them at
my departure have supported them till then?
Might not hunger, dreadful hunger, have compelled them to leave their retreat? were they
still in these frightful deserts? If they were

not, where could I find them? where drag out my miserable existence? But could I think that Pulauski had abandoned his kinsman, that Lodoiska had consented to be separated from her husband? No, certainly not. They were then in this dreadful solitude, and if I abandoned them, they would die of hunger and of cold. This despairing reflection determined me: I no longer considered that in going a distance from my waggon I should run a risk of not finding it again; to take some provisions for my father-in-law and my wife, was the object which pressed most upon me.

I took my musket and some powder; I loaded a horse with provisions, and went much further into the forest than I had gone the night before. I continued to cry out, and to discharge my gun. The most solemn silence reigned around me.

I found myself in a part of the forest that was so very thick, that my horse could no longer pass; I tied him to a tree, and my despair, absorbing all other considerations, I advanced with my gun and a part of my provisions. I wandered for two hours longer, and my misery kept accumulating, when, at last, I perceived the steps of a human being imprinted on the snow.

Hope inspired me with fresh vigour. I followed the traces, and presently I saw Pulanski, almost naked, emaciated by hunger, and scarcely recognisable by my own eyes. He was endeavouring to draw himself towards me, and to answer my calls. The moment I reached him, he seized with avidity the aliments which I offered him, and eagerly devoured them. I asked where was Lodoiska. Alas! said he, thou shalt go and see her. The tone in which he pronounced these words made me tremble. I arrived at the cavern, in some respect prepared for the spectacle which awaited me. Lodoiska, wrapped up in her clothes, and covered with those of her father, was stretched on a bed of leaves, which were half rotten. She made an effort to raise her head, which she could scarcely hold up, and refusing the food which I offered her: I am not hungry, said she, the death of my children, the loss of Dorliska, the length and difficulty of our marches, and thy dangers continually increasing, have killed me. I have not been proof against fatigue and grief. I am dying, my dear Lovinski. I heard thy

voice, and my soul was arrested in its progress.
I see thee again! Lodoiska ought to die in the
arms of the husband she adores! Support my
father! Let him live! Live both of you!
Cherish yourselves, and forget me! Search
everywhere for my dear—She could not pronounce the name of her daughter—she expired.

Her father dug her a grave a few steps from
the cavern, and I saw the earth receive all that
I loved. What a moment! Pulauski watched
over my despair: he compelled me to survive
Lodoiska.

Lovinski would have continued, but his grief
interrupted him. He begged to be excused for
a moment, and went into his private closet; he
returned presently with a miniature in his
hand: Behold, said he, the portrait of my little
Dorliska, see how handsome she was even at
that age! In her features, which are scarcely
developed, I recognise all the features of her
mother—Ah! if at least.—I interrupted Lovinski: That charming countenance, cried I, resembles my pretty cousin!—That is just the
speech of a lover, replied he—the object which
he adores is always in his imagination, and he
thinks he sees her everywhere. Ah! my friend!

if only Dorliska was restored to me! But, I ought not to expect it.

His eyes were again filled with tears, which he endeavoured to restrain. He resumed, in a faltering tone, the history of his misfortunes.

Pulauski, whose courage never abandoned him, and whose strength was reinforced, obliged me to assist him in looking after our subsistence. By following my own footsteps on the snow, we arrived at the place where I had left the waggon, which we immediately unloaded, and afterwards burnt, that our enemies might have no index to our retreat. By the aid of our horses, for whom we found a passage by making several turnings, we conveyed to our cavern the provisions and other things, which would have enabled us, if we were willing, to continue a long time in this solitude. We killed our horses, as we could not support them, and lived upon their flesh, which, though the rigour of the season preserved for several days, became corrupted at last, and the chase procuring us but a slender support, we were obliged to begin upon our provisions, which were entirely consumed at the end of three months.

We still had some pieces of gold, and the

greater part of Lodoiska's diamonds. Was I to make a second journey to Pultawa, or were we to risk the quitting of our retreat? We had already suffered so cruelly in this solitude, that we determined on the latter.

We left the forest, we passed the Sem, near to Rylks. We bought a boat, disguised ourselves as fishermen, and went down the Sem. Our boat was visited at Czernicove. Misfortune had so changed Pulauski, that it was impossible to recognise him. We entered the Dnieper, we passed Kiove to Krylow. There we were obliged to receive into our boat, and to carry to the other side, some Russian soldiers, who were going to join a little army employed against Pugatchew. We learnt at Zoporiskaia the taking of Bender and of Oczacow, the conquest of the Crimea, and the defeat and death of the Visir Oglon. Pulauski in despair would have crossed the vast countries which separated him from Pugatchew, and have joined himself to that enemy of the Russians, but our fatigues compelled us to remain at Zoporiskaia. The peace which was concluded shortly after, between the Porte and Russia, enabled us to enter Turkey.

We crossed, (on foot, and always disguised) Budsiac, parts of Moldavia, and Walachia; and, after the most excessive fatigues, we arrived at Adrianople. We were arrested and accused before the Cadi, of having offered for sale, on our journey, some diamonds which we had apparently stolen. The humble garments in which we were clothed excited this suspicion. Pulauski discovered himself to the Cadi, who sent us, under a strong escort, to Constantinople.

We were admitted to an audience of the Grand Seignior. He gave us a lodging, and ordered his treasurer to provide a suitable revenue for us. I then wrote to my sisters, and to Boleslas. We learned, by their answers, that all the property of Pulauski was confiscated; that he was degraded, and condemned to lose his head.

My father-in-law was dismayed; he was indignant that they had accused him of being a regicide. He wrote in his justification. Always occupied by the love of his country, and stimulated by his mortal hatred to its enemies, he did not cease, during the four years we remained in Turkey, to make every exertion in

order to embroil the Porte in a new war with
the Russians. In 1774, he received, with transports of rage, the news of the triple invasion,*
which plundered the republic of a third of her
possessions.

It was in the spring of 1776 that the insur-
gents determined to take up arms in defence of
their violated rights: My country has lost its
liberty, said Pulauski, let us at least fight for
the liberty of a new country!

We passed into Spain, and embarked in a
vessel about to sail for the Havannah, from
whence we transported ourselves to Philadel-
phia. The Congress employed us in the army
of General Washington. Pulauski, a prey to
melancholy, exposed his life like a man to
whom it had become insupportable: he was always to be found on the most dangerous post.
Towards the end of the fourth campaign, he
was wounded by my side. They carried him to
his tent.—I feel that my end approaches, said
he; it is true, then, that I shall never see my
country! What a cruel caprice of destiny!

* Dismemberment of Poland by the Empress of Russia, the Emperor, and the King of Prussia.

Pulauski falls a martyr for American liberty, and the Poles are slaves!

My death would be horrible, Lovinski, if I did not cherish a ray of hope. Ah! can I be mistaken? No, I do not deceive myself, continued he in a stronger voice. A god of consolation has lifted the veil of a happy futurity to me before I close my eyes; I perceive one of the first nations in the world awaking out of a long sleep, and demanding its honour, its ancient privileges, and the sacred and imprescriptible rights of humanity from its oppressors. I see, in an immense capital, long degraded and dishonoured by every species of servitude, a crowd of soldiers prove themselves citizens, and thousands of citizens become soldiers. Under their redoubtable strokes the Bastile crumbles into dust; the signal is given from one extremity of the empire to the other; the reign of tyranny is finished; a neighbouring people, sometimes enemies, but always generous, always capable of great actions, applaud these unexpected efforts, crowned with such prompt success. Ah! may a reciprocal esteem commence and strengthen between the two nations an unalterable friendship. May that horrible science of fraud and treachery which courts call *policy* present no obstacle to this fraternal union! Noble rivals in talent, and in philosophy! French, and English, cease at last, cease forever those bloody discords, the fury of which has too often extended itself over both hemispheres! Let the empires of the universe be no longer divided, but by the force of your example, and the ascendancy of your genius, instead of terrifying and enslaving mankind, dispute the glory of enlightening their ignorance, and of breaking their chains.

Approach, added Pulauski, and observe, at some paces from us, in the midst of the slaughter, among so many famous warriors, one celebrated by them all for his heroic courage, his truly republican virtues and his premature talents. He is the heir of a house long illustrious, but he has no need of the glory of ancestors to aggrandise his name: it is the young La Fayette, already honoured by France and dreaded by tyrants; nevertheless, he has scarcely commenced his immortal labours. Envy his lot, Lovinski, and endeavour to imitate his virtues; tread, as near as thou canst, in the steps of this great man. The worthy pupil of Washington

will presently be the Washington of his country.
It is nearly at the same time, my friend, it is
at this memorable epoch of the regeneration of
the people, that eternal justice will also bring
back the days of vengeance and liberty for our
fellow citizens; then, Lovinski, in whatever
place thou mayst be, let thy hatred awake!
Thou hast fought so gloriously for Poland! Let
the remembrance of our injuries and our exploits stimulate thy courage! Let thy sword,
so often wet with the enemy's blood, be again
turned upon the oppressors! Let them tremble
in again recognising thee! Let them tremble
at the remembrance of Pulauski! They have
plundered us of our property, they have assassinated thy wife, they have torn away thy daughter, they have tarnished my name! The barbar-
ians have divided our provinces amongst themselves! Lovinski, this is what thou must never
forget. When our persecutors are those of our
country, vengeance becomes indispensable and
sacred. Thou owest the Russians an eternal
hatred, thou owest to thy country the last drop
of thy blood.

Having said this, he expired.* Death, in

* Pulauski was killed at the siege of Savannah, in 1795.

striking him, snatched from me my last consolation.

I fought for the United States up to the
happy period which secured their independence. M. de C***, who had long served in
America, in the corps commanded by the Marquis de la Fayette, gave me a letter of recommendation to the Baron de Faublas. He took
a lively interest in my fate, and we soon became
bound in the closest friendship. I only quitted
his neighbourhood in the country to establish
myself at Paris, where I knew he would not be
long in following me. In the meantime, my
sisters had collected some small relics of my
fortune, formerly immense. They, informed
of my arrival here, and of the name I have
taken, write to me, that in a few months they
will come and console, by their presence, the
unfortunate du Portail.

END OF VOL. I.